CLAWING FOR SURVIVAL

CLAWING FOR SURVIVAL

THE DRAGONCLAW SWORD™ BOOK ONE

KEVIN MCLAUGHLIN

MICHAEL ANDERLE

DISRUPTIVE IMAGINATION

Version 1.00 June 2021
eBook ISBN: 978-1-64971-708-5
Print ISBN: 978-1-64971-709-2

THE CLAWING FOR SURVIVAL TEAM

Thanks to the JIT Readers

Dave Hicks
Wendy L Bonell
Zacc Pelter
Deb Mader
Daryl McDaniel
Veronica Stephan-Miller
Dorothy Lloyd
Debi Sateren

If we've missed anyone, please let us know!

Editor
The Skyhunter Editing Team

CHAPTER ONE

Vala Gagnon knew she should be thankful to be where she was.

By rights, she should not be there at all.

This was a dwarf college in dwarf country, and although she was a dwarf, it was still a human-style university. The subjects mirrored those taught at universities in the United States very closely. Among other things, the professors there taught things her family's shaman had deemed as magic and therefore not at all acceptable for a proper dwarf like the youngest daughter of the Gagnon family to practice.

She knew she should be thankful but still felt restless. Engineering was interesting in a certain kind of way. With it, one could make previously inert objects—like automobiles—spring to life. One could communicate with people on the other side of the Earth. With the vast caches of information that had accumulated on the Internet, one could learn almost anything. She knew her older sisters had not been allowed to practice engineering at all and that her even being there represented a dramatic shift in her father's religious beliefs.

Yet she had little interest in the circuit board in front of her. What she desperately wanted to do was be an artist. There was something...well, magical about the way a few strokes of a pencil on paper or a splash of pigment on the side of a building could transform it into something more. With a little art, one could travel to worlds that would not exist and could never exist in this world.

So, while she should have been thankful to study a body of knowledge that had been denied to her older sisters and all the members of the Gagnon family who had gone before her, Vala doodled on her circuit diagram.

This particular sketch depicted the programmable pressure cooker on the desk in front of her—truly one of the world's modern marvels, the professor had said when he'd gleefully introduced the assignment.

Vala had added hands at the end of two wires that extended and took vegetables from the table beneath it to fill its central chamber. A little cartoon face added the dose of humor she wanted. She was debating whether to put a knife in one of the pressure cooker's wires or if that would ruin the charming nature of this particular doodle when the professor clapped and called for attention.

"All right, class. It has been forty-five minutes. That's time enough to replace the damaged component, plug your appliance in, and start it. I know a few of you are not quite finished so I'll start with volunteers. If you're not done, you need to be."

Like most dwarves, Professor Swolp was short, stout, and bearded. Also like most dwarves—but unlike her and her family because of her father's devotion to their religion—he wore brightly colored clothes and had garish piercings adorned with gems and stones.

Canada had been given to the dwarves after the mages created them, imbued them with resistance to magic, and tried to turn them against the dragons. They had opted to not be used as a weapon and in return, the dragons granted them an enormous body of land in which to reside. Since then, they had been content to live there, although most liked to brighten up the color palette of the frigid north.

Vala was not allowed such garish colors, though. She wore a beige, rough-spun dress that was neither designed to hide nor accent her stout figure. It was simply made to keep the cold out. Over that, she wore a gray shawl and a heavy black belt.

She currently wore a brightly colored necklace made of glass worn smooth by a river but she would, of course, take it off before she returned home. Her father would not like it any more than he would like that she had let her frizzy hair escape the tight bun she'd worn when she left her parents' house to head to class.

Although he also would not like her to waste her tuition money by failing this practical exam.

The young dwarf was fairly certain she had not finished fixing the pressure cooker. She had opened it and discovered that a fuse had been snipped. When she'd replaced it, the LED display on the front of the pressure cooker remained dark.

A furtive glance confirmed that those students with the same kind of device seemed to be doing better. Their machines counted down or alerted the users to the level of pressure the contents were under. She was worried she had missed something else. Professor Swolp had said there might be two or even three things wrong with each of the broken appliances, but she had been thoroughly distracted by her doodling.

Now, the professor was at the next table over. There was nothing to be done now but hope that the screen lit up when she plugged it in.

Vala connected the power cable to the receptacle, pressed the relevant button on the pressure cooker, and was immediately zapped by enough electricity to blacken one of her fingernails and make her already frizzy hair stand on end.

"Son of a moose!" she bellowed before she shoved it off the table. "To the depths with you, cursed appliance!" she yelled and wished she could make the glorified cooking pot skitter away from her.

To her shock, it did.

Something rose from deep within her—somewhere near where the son of a moose curse came from, she assumed—and went into the pressure cooker.

It responded immediately. Wires extended from its broken casing, scratched at the tiled floor, and began to drag it away from her.

"Uh...Professor?" one of the other students asked and his voice rose in pitch over the four syllables.

"I'll be right there, Dogo," Professor Swolp replied absent-mindedly.

"I don't know if that will be necessary, sir," Dogo replied as the toaster on the table in front of him used its springs to hop across the counter.

"Oh, dear marmots and minks," Vala mumbled as she looked across the classroom. Twenty-two appliances in front of twenty-two engineering students had all—somehow—come to life.

Blenders spun away from those tasked with replacing their blades. Coffeemakers ejected their pots, which shattered on the floor. The student working on a remote control watched as the car streaked off her worktable and performed a double backflip before it landed and raced out the door of the class.

"There is no need to panic, class—no need to panic!" Professor Swolp said over the din of electric motors, heating elements, and beeping touchpads. "Evacuate the room. Leave your projects where they are—or where they are going, I suppose. Do not touch that blender. No, I don't care that your skin can withstand dragon's fire. I will not have you lose a finger in my classroom!"

Despite the chaos of the moving appliances, the class proceeded to evacuate in a fairly orderly manner. By the time Vala stepped into the hallway, the moment was over.

The appliances stopped grinding, heating, and beeping and the room settled into calm again.

"Professor, I hope that won't count against our final grade," Dogo whined.

"No, no. Not at all. Although for those of you I did not get to, we will have a retest."

"What happened, Professor?" Vala asked, quite concerned that he would offer the same answer she had in mind.

"Magic happened. Someone using magic nearby went a little overboard or lost control of their spell, that's all. There are disadvantages to allowing mages to escape to Canada, you know. Even though their magic can't directly impact dwarves, the...uh, side-effects of their experiments are sometimes chaotic."

Professor Swolp paused for a moment and seemed to feel the need to backtrack. "Not that I have anything against mages, of course. I don't think we dwarves would be nearly as successful without mages in our communities but sometimes, they muck about with things and cause an upswell in magic like the one we experienced.

"Why, I remember once—this was long before any of your time and long before the Steel Dragon's Revolution—a group of mages came to town to hide from dragons. We sheltered them, of course, but they were discovered because they had changed all the smoke in town to different colors. It wasn't hard for the dragons trying to bring them home to find them, what with hot-pink or lime-green smoke pouring from the chimneys of the homes where they were hiding."

He chuckled at the memory before something darker about those times came to mind. His expression settled into a scowl and he shook his head as if to brush the memory away.

"What happened to those mages, professor?" Vala asked.

"Ask your history professor," he replied. "We'll finish this next time. If you did not get tested today, you will be tested next week.

For homework, I want a written description of a human machine and how it works. No drawings, Vala. This is not that class."

"Right, sir." She nodded.

"All right. I'll see you all next week." He dismissed them.

She wanted to ask him more questions about what it had been like before the Steel Dragon's Revolution that gave dwarves rights outside of Canada and treated mages like citizens instead of the property of dragons. What had happened had scared her, though, and she held back.

He had said it had been an upswell of magic and she did not doubt that. What she now wondered was whether the mage who had caused all the appliances to freak out was her.

After all, they had stopped as soon as she had left the room. Admittedly, all the other students had left too, but she had looked into the room when she had stepped over the threshold. The appliances had all gone dead at that precise moment.

Also, there was the fact that everything had done essentially what she had willed them to do—get away from her.

This last point seemed particularly emphasized by the remote-control car she found around the corner of the hallway. It seemed to be waiting at the top of a stairway but soon as she moved close, it sprang to life again and threw itself down the stairs and against the doors at the bottom.

"To the depths indeed," the girl muttered as she stepped into the chilly night and hurried home.

CHAPTER TWO

When Galen Stormwing had hidden in the desert, stuck in a half-dragon, half-human body, he had missed the grand hall of the Stormwing castle. He had finally returned and now stood before his parents who were seated on their ornate dragon-sized thrones. The rest of his dragon relatives lined the sides of the hall, watching him and judging him, and there was nothing he wanted more than to leave.

"Tell us again why we should not banish you for treason?" Torren Stormwing—formerly Torren Thunder before his marriage to Galen's mother—asked. The youngster licked his scaly lips, a human gesture that looked odd in his dragon body. This was bad. His father had always been the nicer one.

"Banishment would be kind given what he did to poor Eustace," Gabriela Stormwing—his mother and matriarch of the entire family—said icily.

He could not help but glance at his cousin Eustace, who stood below one of the many windows along the walls of the grand hall of Stormwing castle. Outside, a storm raged as it always did when the family was meeting.

Some thought it was geography that made Seattle so rainy

and there was truth to that, but the family had a part in it as well. Even though the wind howled, not a drop of water entered through the open windows to wet any of the tapestries that hung between them.

Almost every dragon in this room could control the weather. Even Galen's father had some control over the weather, although he was not technically of the Stormwing line— although there were those who said he was not as distantly related as he had claimed when he had asked for Gabriela's hand in marriage.

It would not do for the family to let water enter their grand hall and Eustace protected his window effortlessly. Any injuries the boy had inflicted on him during their fight over Detroit had long since healed. Like Galen, he was a dragon. He had healing abilities that rendered anything but death a mere flesh wound. Well, almost anything.

He had torn his cousin's wings and landed hard on top of him. The appendages had healed but not well enough to allow him to fly. In the Stormwing family, being crippled was almost as bad as being born powerless like Galen had been.

"Mother—"

"You will address me as Lady Stormwing in this hallowed hall."

The young dragon swallowed. He knew that all those present could read his aura and discern his emotional state effortlessly, which meant that he had to remain confident. "If I had not battled Eustace, the Stormwing family would have been declared an enemy of the Steel Guard. Our castle might have been stripped from us and given to mages."

This earned a titter of disapproval from the other family members. The idea of losing this castle and it ending up in the hands of mages was appalling to them. The only thing worse than that would be if it wound up in the hands of dwarves or even worse, regular humans.

"He makes a fair point," Torren said to quiet the discussion in the grand hall.

"Is it, though?" Gabriela asked rhetorically. Her husband knew better than to answer.

"Galen's quick action revealed the goddess to the enemy. Had you not intervened, she might not have been imprisoned at all. Do you disagree?"

She had asked him a direct question, which meant he could answer. "I couldn't risk this family on Eustace," he said. "If his powers faltered and Tiamat failed, we would have been branded an enemy of the Steel Guard. I attempted to hedge our bets."

"An admirable goal," his father said thoughtfully. "That is, after all, what we tried to do when we got you—a powerless dragon—enrolled in the Lumos School."

"An advantage you squandered," Lady Stormwing was quick to point out. "We spent considerable wealth and favors to gain you a place in the stupid school in the hopes of getting another powered dragon for our clan."

"We did not expect you to be as successful as you were," Torren added.

"Nor did we expect you to lose control of your ability, damage the school, and earn expulsion," his mother snapped.

"You are too hard on the boy, Gabriela," Torren said in a rare direct rebuke. "It was Galen's power that brought Lord Boneclaw back from the dead. You cannot deny that the feat was impressive."

"It might have been," she admitted, "had he not let Boneclaw be killed a second time."

"The students at Lumos School are powerful, Mothe—Lady Stormwing. It was a student who defeated Boneclaw, not me."

He was always incredibly careful to not point out how powerful his friend Kylara Diamantine was. Not that he was particularly worried that anyone in his family could hurt her, but they could almost certainly hurt Tanya, her best friend and his...

9

girlfriend? That was possibly somewhat optimistic. Still, he was careful to not ever talk about Tanya in front of anyone from his immediate family or even anyone in the clan. If they read his feelings for her—which they most surely would—they might use her against him.

It would have been wonderful to have the backup of his friends during this meeting, but he was determined to do this himself. His family was his problem and his friends had already done so much for him. The last thing they needed was for him to pile additional troubles on their already burdened shoulders. No, this was his fight and he steeled his mind to deal with it as best he could.

If only standing up to his parents wasn't so damned terrifying.

"Yes, yes." Gabriela waved a claw dismissively. Even this simple gesture from the matriarch of the Stormwing clan was enough to cause lightning to strike with enough force to rattle the castle. "You have made it quite clear that you were the weakest student at that foolish school. What you have made less clear is where you were after Boneclaw was defeated and before the rise of Tiamat."

"The rumors are astonishing, you understand," Torren interjected. "They say you were a half-human, half-dragon mongrel who ate the filthy beasts of the desert to survive. If you could tell us where you were, it would go a long way toward dispelling these...embarrassing rumors."

"I...did not want to bring shame to the family," Galen said. He knew it was not much of an answer but at least it was true. He could not lie, not there and not while everyone from his clan could sense his aura. Even if he could fool his mother, he would not fool this entire room.

"And yet you return to us now. Why?" she demanded.

"I had thought that after what had happened in Detroit with Tiamat and the Steel Guard, I might have earned my place in Stormsiege."

"You're a traitor to this family and our cause!" Eustace shouted from his position below the window. In his rage, he lost control and water got into the grand hall.

"You mistake your importance," Lady Stormwing said to Eustace, who regained his composure and forced his window to block the rain from entering again. "As does young Galen. The Steel Guard would not risk moving against us. We are too powerful and Stormsiege is too strong a castle. You did nothing to prove yourself to us by interfering in that battle."

Galen considered the possibility that he could drop to his knees and beg for his place. He knew his mother lived for others submitting to her will and that her weakness was watching the wills of others bend to her own. But he would not give her this victory.

"Mother, you're right. I've messed up and in almost every way possible. Instead of building alliances, I broke them. I gained a new power, but I threw it away. I endangered the Lumos School and the students there. My actions caused Boneclaw to return. I know I can no longer return to the school and I can't go to the Steel Guard either. I had hoped that my actions against Tiamat might be worth something to this clan, but I can see now that I was wrong—yet again. I had hoped that I would be welcome here again but obviously, I'm not."

He paused and looked at his mother and father in turn. "But that's fine. I learned to survive on my own. I can do so again."

Galen turned his back to his parents, transformed into his human form, and marched down the grand hall. While he knew he should feel terror, he felt palpable relief instead. He knew part of that was simply because he had taken his human form. Ever since he'd regained his ability to transform between dragon and human shapes instead of remaining as a monster locked between the two, it had been more difficult to maintain his dragon shape than his human one.

But the greater part of his relief came from finally standing up to his mother and deciding to strike out on his own. And why not? If he could survive as a monster in the desert, he could survive as a young man who could take the form of a dragon.

Or so he thought until thunder cracked outside, wind rushed through every single one of the grand hall's windows, and the heavy doors at the end of the room were blown shut.

When he turned, his mother grinned viciously at him. She was undoubtedly responsible for the intrusion of the weather as she was the strongest member of the Stormwing clan. Although it would not fall on her to clean the mess.

"Not so fast," she growled.

CHAPTER THREE

"Let me go," Galen said and his voice became more pleading. "I can disappear again. I did it before. I won't bother this family if you don't want me to." He knew that everyone in the room could sense how he truly felt about leaving via his aura.

He had come not because he enjoyed the company of his family but because he had nowhere else to go. Despite his considerable misgivings, he had hoped that he might still have a place among those he had grown up with, even though they had always treated him as an inferior dragon for not having storm powers. Still, he could forgive them all that—he'd released much of the resentment already—if they would allow him to stay.

Unfortunately, his mom had made it clear that he had no place there. Yet she would not allow him to leave either, which might be a cause for greater concern.

Galen turned to her where she stood on the far side of the grand hall. Even from this distance, she was an imposing figure. Her scales were the color of bruised clouds and the spikes on her head and elbows were reminiscent of the jagged streaks of lightning.

"Whether you are an embarrassment to this clan or not, you are still a Stormwing," she said. "As long as you bear the family name, your actions will carry weight for all of us."

"Yes, Lady Stormwing," he replied, not at all sure where this was going.

"You will not speak to our clan leader in that manner!" Petrov Stormwing—one of his many uncles and brother to his mother—snapped from beneath one of the windows of the grand hall. He was a real piece of work. While he did not have the same level of control over the weather as his sister, he made up for it with blind loyalty to the clan and a streak of viciousness toward those who did not share her vision of what the Stormwing clan should be.

"Sure," Galen said and took his dragon form once more. It was hard to transform but he made himself do it. Mist ejected from every pore of his skin and shrouded his body as it changed. His arms and legs extended, grew claws, and became covered in scales. Wings sprouted from his back and his spine extended into a tail. He grew to his full size and the mist retreated into his blue scales, almost the same color as his mothers' but missing their heavy storm-cloud shading.

It was extremely unpleasant because he felt so tired in this body. He had already been in his dragon for hours today and needed to rest in his human form—something that had never been an issue until his dragon powers were taken from him. Although he had regained them, they hadn't been restored at the same level they'd once been. Even so, he would not show that fatigue now—not in front of the clan, not in front of Petrov, and certainly not in front of his mother.

With grim determination, he pushed his feelings aside—not because he wanted to but because he could not show weakness, fear, betrayal, or heartbreak, not now and not there. He raised his head high despite wanting to do nothing more than rest it on the slick floor of the grand hall.

"Lady Stormwing, you have made it clear you do not wish me to stay here, but you also do not wish me to go out into the world. What then, would you have me do?" It took considerable effort, but he thought he managed to make it seem like he did not particularly care. Indifference was the only emotion his mother respected.

"If I could do you the kindness of stripping your name from you, I would," his mother said and her aura made it seem like she truly believed that casting him out would be a kindness. "But I can't, not while you have scales that so closely resemble mine. I would let you wander about but I am quite certain that you will— what was the human phrase you used?—Ah, yes. Mess up again. I think it would be easier to simply clean up the mess you have come to represent."

Galen swallowed. He knew exactly what cleaning a mess up meant to her. Although he was young by dragon standards— centuries younger than most of the dragons in the hall—he had still seen his mother clean up a mess of a dragon once. His bones still hung in the dungeon.

Fear surged in him and battled the ever-present feelings of guilt and shame. The fear was likely from her, yet he knew it was valid. She would kill him herself if she thought it was in the best interest of the clan. Despite his feelings of self-doubt and rejection, he didn't want to die either. He had survived in the desert and when trapped between Boneclaw and a mage who could summon the elements. Surely he could survive his own family. He had to.

"I can do better, Lady Stormwing. I swear I can." He tried to keep his voice steady as he bowed his head almost to the floor. "I apologize for my actions and the shame I have reflected on the clan." As much as he wanted to simply rest his head on the floor, he would not. Despite the effort his dragon form now demanded of him, he raised his head high again. "How can I do better? How can I demonstrate that I am worthy of once more living in Stormsiege?"

Every dragon snout turned to Gabriela Stormwing. The rain outside abated slightly while those gathered waited for her decree. The young dragon knew as well as everyone else in the hall did that he might already be dead. If he had said the wrong thing—or if his mother was in a particularly foul mood—she would exact her punishment for him there and now where everyone could see just how powerful she was.

"You have had many chances," she pointed out as lightning cracked outside to punctuate this simple statement. It began to rain harder again. "Now you want another one."

It was not a question as to whether he wanted another chance. It was a statement. From Gabriela Stormwing, this was supposed to be seen as kindness and generosity.

"Yes, please, Mother," Galen said and hoped that reminding her that he was her son would not send her into a rage. When he had been very small—before it had been clear that he would never manifest the ability to control the weather—his mother had not been so cruel to him. Now, he wondered if he would be murdered for daring to speak despite being asked a direct question.

He decided that if this gambit to appeal to the matriarch's motherly instinct worked, he would agree to anything. His mind was already made up to say whatever it took to get out of there and he would vanish again once he had escaped. He had hidden in the desert without the ability to fly or sense the emotions of animals or humans and could hide again. If he were given the chance, he could hide somewhere they would never find him.

Unfortunately, his gambit failed.

"I think it would be simpler to end your life. Petrov, the method is your choice."

His uncle moved forward, a malicious grin on his face, but

before he could seize the youngster, Torren cleared his throat. "Petrov, a moment, if you please."

The dragon stopped in his tracks. Gabriela had said the method was his, not that he should kill him immediately, which meant he could listen to what Torren had to say and indeed, would be expected to. If he were to kill Galen against the patriarch's wishes, it might cost him some level of prestige in the clan. Of course, if his sister had said, "Kill him now," his life would be ended, Petrov's honor would remain unblemished, and Torren would accept it as part of the game he had played when he had married into a clan above his station.

"Times are different than they once were, Gabriela, my dear," her husband said in a kindly tone that was still pitched loudly enough to carry over the wind that howled outside. "Not long ago, the Stormwing clan had a legion of mages, but no longer. We cannot throw away one of our own as easily as we once could."

"What can he accomplish when he struggles to remain a dragon? He is broken, an embarrassment," she snapped.

"Perhaps he will prove to be exactly that, but surely we can afford him the opportunity," Torren argued.

"You are soft because the boy is of your loins, nothing more," Gabriela retorted. "Let us end him and make another if you so wish."

Galen swallowed. It was surreal and wildly uncomfortable to have his parents talking about killing him and replacing him with another hatchling as if he were not even there. If anything, it clarified further how much of a mistake it had been to come. His mother was a monster. What else but a monster could discuss killing their child and creating another in the same breath?

"He may prove to be an embarrassment," Torren admitted, "but he still defeated Eustace in combat despite Eustace being blessed with the powers of a true Stormwing."

The young dragon could not help but glance at his cousin, who fumed at the insinuation of his weakness. He managed to control his temper enough to not allow any more water in, though. Not that it mattered since the floor was still wet from the matriarch's show of force.

"And how many times would you let him dishonor this clan before you see reason?" she demanded. "Because I will not have this argument again. It is a waste of my time."

Torren turned to his son but said nothing. Galen could feel the pressure in the room building despite the storm raging outside. Everyone now waited to hear what the patriarch would suggest. Was his loyalty to the clan or his embarrassment of a son?

He would have liked to pretend that he had a special relationship with his dad. After all, neither had the powers of a Stormwing and both were outsiders, relatively powerless compared to some members of the clan. But he would not lie to himself. His father had made it quite clear that he should have been able to summon lightning at the very least. He had hoped to sire Stormwings, not a wimpy vanilla dragon like the one who stood before him.

"What about three days?" Torren said thoughtfully. "Seventy-two hours, as the humans count time. Do you think you have time for that, my thundercloud?"

"Three days for what?" Gabriela asked although she was intrigued.

"Quite frankly, I am not entirely certain," he responded and warmed to his idea now that his wife had given it some degree of approval. "I had hoped the boy would earn a power at the Lumos School, but I did not expect that he would find a way to summon the dead nor a hero like Boneclaw."

His wife nodded thoughtfully but said nothing.

Torren stood from his throne and sauntered down the grand hall toward his son. He looked completely at ease in his dragon form, while Galen struggled merely to keep his head high enough to meet his father's gaze.

"Nor did I expect him to play a role in the Steel Guard's battle against the followers of Tiamat. Much as I would have liked to see the Mother of All Dragons victorious, the boy is correct in that if he were not there, the Steel Bitch would have used Eustace's actions to strip us of our titles."

"She would never take this castle from us." Petrov hissed in indignation.

"Oh, hush, brother," Gabriela admonished sharply. "The Steel Dragon has already taken our mages and much of the farmland we once took livestock from as we wished. And although I too would have liked to see Tiamat ascend, she has failed and we must admit that if she had been victorious, she might also have attempted to take Stormsiege from us. I would hear my husband speak."

"I propose we give the boy three days to demonstrate that he is worthy of being a member of this clan. What say you?" Torren asked.

She smiled and looked at her son.

"Yes, of course," Galen said quickly, "But what exactly would you have me do?"

"I do not know," his father said. "I didn't anticipate many of the things that have happened over the last few years and I do not wish to give you a task only to watch you fail. I wish you to prove yourself a Stormwing by making your mark on the world. The method is yours, as is the reasoning, but I am sure you will think of something. When you have accomplished it—if you can in three days—return to us and you will once more be welcome in Stormsiege."

"And if you fail at the task you give yourself or if your actions amount to nothing, we will make quite certain that you will never embarrass this clan again." Gabriela's cruel laughter echoed through the hall as the wind shook the castle and threw the doors open.

Galen was immediately soaked almost to freezing by the rain, but he embraced it over the stifling emotional pressure that had built up inside the grand hall.

He stepped out into the unfriendly weather, lucky to be alive, and wondered what he could possibly do to live longer than three days.

CHAPTER FOUR

Vala walked home and although she tried to enjoy the stroll, she was too lost in her worries for that to be even remotely possible.

She felt as if her entire world had changed. On the way to class, she had thought her town small and almost rural. It was boring and far from the cutting edge of technology. Now, she saw it as an almost oppressively technologically rich place.

Would the streetlights that had yet to click on suddenly start hopping around? On the way to class, she had thought the street seemed downright empty, but she now looked at the few cars with open suspicion. What if one of them activated and tried to run her over?

Of course, she was a dwarf and thus far more robust than a human. She could likely survive being hit by a car, but what damage would it do to her community? When a semi-truck turned down Main Street, she chose to go another direction.

"There is no reason for a mouse to taunt a cat," she muttered.

The strangest part about all this was that she did not think of herself as someone who particularly liked technology. She liked doodling—animals, plants, and people most of all. When she did draw machines and objects, she almost always gave them big silly eyes and dopy grins. There seemed to be no reasonable explanation for why this had happened to her.

Vala reached her house almost without realizing it. She opened the door as a gust of wind picked up, extinguished the candles her family used to light their home, and cast the room into darkness.

"Do you mind?" her dad snapped.

"You can simply turn the lights on and this wouldn't happen!" she retorted. Candles were her parents' compromise over technology in their new home. Her father had watched with distress as new pieces of tech gradually insinuated themselves. First, it was a phone and a long list of other items, but when her mom came home with a TV set, though, that had been the final straw.

He had almost blown a gasket at that point, which was when candles became the only acceptable illumination in their house.

She hated it, although her feelings on the matter were irrelevant.

Even though she could barely see him in the gloom, she knew he was smiling placidly like he always did when she dared to question their beliefs. But how could she not when he acted more backward than anyone else she knew?

"I understand that you wanted to go to school but if this is the kind of behavior they're indoctrinating you with, I won't have it," he said finally. He'd never wanted her to attend and especially not for engineering. If it weren't for her mother, she'd have followed the same path as her sisters.

Vala drew a deep breath and tried to calm herself. "The only reason I'm even learning about electrical engineering is because you—"

"Don't conflate me with your mother," he interjected waspishly.

"Dad, we moved into this town because you and Mom agreed—"

"Vala!" her mom said as she exited the basement and cut the old, familiar argument short. "How was school?"

"They're brainwashing her, Marma. They truly are." Her dad answered for her and she rolled her eyes. "I knew we never should have moved here. We had a good life in the forest. A simple life. None of this...this magic."

"It's not magic!" she shouted and immediately saw how wrong she was.

The lights blinked faster until the room was practically strobing. The television turned on, began to flip through channels, and lingered on each one barely long enough to hear someone say a few words.

The vacuum cleaner—another of her mother's attempts to live a modern life—activated and began to race around the room. Vala had been in her electrical engineering class long enough to smell that the motor was burning itself out.

"We've been cursed!" her dad yelled. "We have to escape!" He ran to the front door but tripped over the vacuum's cord and knocked it out of the wall. Being denied its source of electricity did not stop the runaway appliance, however. It wheeled and raced toward him as if it intended to swallow him.

Vala's mom knocked it over with the long wooden handle of a broom. "You never did work as well as the old ways, did ya?" she asked the fallen machine and her eyes gleamed.

"Mom, what's happening?"

"That's like asking a river otter how a beaver dam works. Now, help me with your dad."

The girl ran to him and pulled him to his feet.

"We've been cursed," he muttered again. "For leaving the forest for all this modern mayhem. I knew it was all magic. I told you it was all magic."

"This has nothing to do with that," his wife said and hurried him out the front door.

They almost escaped but the washing machine blocked their

path. It had somehow managed to move from their garage and now rocked from side to side near the front door. Its front-loading door opened and closed to barf water and soap at them.

"It burns!" her dad screamed, wiped soap from his eyes, and fell heavily.

"Stop it!" Vala yelled.

Thankfully, the appliance obeyed although it spat liquid once and sprayed her father who still lay prone in front of it before it became utterly motionless.

The young dwarf looked around and saw that the interior of the house had also fallen into stillness.

"Well, that was quite an adventure, wasn't it?" her mom asked.

"An adventure, Marma? Seriously?" Her husband sputtered.

"Come now, Viktor, We're all right. It's merely a little soap."

"And what if it had eaten me? I could have drowned inside it."

"I don't think so, Dad."

"And besides, it stopped," Marma pointed out.

"About that..." Vala would wonder later if she should have said anything at all. She knew some people would have hidden what had happened from their parents. It wasn't like hers were likely to understand any of it. Her father was a retired lumberjack, a man who thought the pinnacle of technology was an ax or maybe, at a stretch, a lathe. Her mother was a naturalist and something of a poet. Neither knew anything about technology or magic. They had only moved to this town because she and her sisters had begged them to—although as soon as they'd moved, her sisters had met partners and moved in with them.

But she was not the kind of person to whom lying came easily. Inevitably, she related the truth although she knew she would regret it later. "This happened at school today too. I was doing a test on a pressure cooker and all the machines...uh, came to life."

"Oh dear, Vala, you must be more distressed than a robin who was robbed of its worms."

"This is wrong, Vala. I should never have allowed you to go to that school. This is terribly wrong."

"Oh, Viktor, calm yourself. This has nothing to do with her school."

"Of course it does," he snapped. "Someone must have seen her going there and put a curse on her. To think, a Gagnon learning about electricity." He scowled at the sheer audacity of it.

"I very much doubt someone cursed Vala by making her animate appliances when she gets frustrated."

"I never said it happened when I got frustrated."

"Calm yourself, sweetie. You said it happened during a test and it happened again when you and your father were…getting into it." That was her mom's preferred euphemism for when her husband and daughter argued. "Besides, there are streetlights nearby." She cast a suspicious glance at these.

"The fact remains that something is happening," Viktor pointed out indignantly.

"Very well said, dear. I agree." Marma winked at her daughter. "Something is indeed happening."

"But I don't want any of this to happen," Vala said. "I want—" *To be an artist. To leave this town, to be accepted by my dad, and to wear bright colors.* "To go to school."

"We want what you want, dear," her mom said firmly.

"We want this to stop," her father said. "If she's cursed, I know who can help. Shaman Mytrov."

"He cannot solve everything, dear."

"Oh, he most certainly can. He understands the intersection between magic and dwarves better than anyone. If anyone can solve this, it's him!"

"You might be right, dear," his wife said placatingly. "But what if something is…unusual about Vala?"

"Like what?" she asked and frowned at her mother.

"All the more reason to go to Shaman Mytrov," Viktor said.

"And what do you think he would say? Dwarves are not

supposed to be able to do magic. It's something even I know. What would he say about your daughter if he caught her doing this?"

"I didn't do anything," she said weakly.

"He would... I'm sure he would..." But her dad knew that Shaman Mytrov had never been a huge fan of Marma or his marriage to her. Viktor had made it clear on more than one occasion that the shaman blamed her for him moving his family into the "city" as he called the small town where they now resided.

"What if, instead of going to Shaman Mytrov, we talk to Trevor instead?"

"Trevor?" he whined. "But he's a—"

"Mage. Yes. I know. Think about it, dear. Shaman Mytrov might be able to help but why worry him if Trevor can handle this with a flick of his wrist?"

"Do you honestly think it's magic?" Vala asked.

Both her parents looked at her. With as much as they argued, she sometimes thought she would find their agreement to be something pleasant. When it was directed at her, however, it was anything but.

"I think talking to Trevor would be wise," her mom said cautiously.

"I agree. And if the mage can't help, we go to the shaman."

They were united, it seemed, and their daughter agreed with them for once. Together, they set off into the slowly darkening evening toward the house of the man she secretly hoped could be blamed for all this.

CHAPTER FIVE

Galen flew east out of Seattle and across the mountains. When he had left the meeting, he had felt like he was free and had a chance, but the sense of exultation had faded as he'd flown farther afield. The problem was not that he didn't know what to do but that he did not know which path to take.

He debated which of his two options would be the best—either to try to earn his family's respect or simply run.

The first sounded difficult while the second sounded impossible. Dragons lived for a long time—millennia if they could avoid fighting other dragons. Of course, that would be impossible if he ran afoul of the Stormwing clan. Their influence was strongest in North America, but with the ascension of the Steel Dragon, they had attempted to create strongholds on other continents beyond the Steel Guard's prying eyes. He could move somewhere completely and utterly desolate—somewhere like Antarctica—but that didn't exactly sound like a long-term solution to him.

No, running did not sound easy and besides, if he failed to impress his family in three days, he would have to run. He knew that trying to survive on his own would be difficult but he would still fight to do so. History had convinced him to not submit meekly to execution. He had uncles who had done that, thinking Gabriela might respect their loyalty and spare their lives at the last moment.

It had never happened. Those who were condemned to death by the Stormwing clan died. Period.

The better strategy, he decided, was to try to find a way to impress his family.

Galen was not sure exactly how to go about that, but he felt he could do worse than travel east. That direction would take him to Detroit, where the Steel Guard was stationed. It would be a gamble to try to help them, but he resolutely believed that Kristen Hall had changed the world for the better and that his family would have to adapt.

He had not always liked the fact that she had changed the world but—after a stint of being relatively powerless himself—he had come to see why a better world was one in which power was more evenly distributed. Power was not guaranteed and having it did not mean one would have it forever.

It was better to know that if you ran afoul of a dragon, you no longer had to worry about them killing you without repercussions. Although dragons could still kill people, of course. If the Stormwings hunted him and found him, he very much doubted that the Steel Guard could protect him. The most he could hope for was that they would at least prosecute his family. It wasn't much but it was progress.

Maybe he could help them? If he could prove his worth to the Steel Guard, perhaps his mother would see the value of his position.

That seemed like the kind of relationship that would take years to develop, however, especially given his past with Boneclaw. He did not think the Steel Dragon would vouch for him in three days' time.

A gust of wind from the north caught him and he banked reflexively to the south—and why not?

The only people who would vouch for him were at the Lumos School. Maybe they could help him. It seemed unlikely and too much to ask given that they had already given him his body back, but he had no better ideas and couldn't resist the idea of seeing Tanya.

So he turned south and landed near a diner on the side of the road to fuel up and rest in his human form for a while before he headed south again.

This new direction certainly felt better. Not because he thought Tanya would be able to help him to solve his problem— he knew it was his to solve or fail at—but because seeing her sounded so much more appealing than seeing the Steel Dragon.

Now that he had given up on the idea of going to Detroit, it seemed like a flimsy plan. The Steel Dragon had defeated Boneclaw and he had brought him back. In every major battle Kristen had fought—at least according to his mom—a Stormwing had fought against her.

Galen's arrival at the Steel Guard headquarters would be treated with suspicion if he was lucky and downright violence if he was not. What reason could he even give them to prevent them from locking him in a prison cell and shackling him with a magic-dampening cuff? Would he tell them he was trying to do something "impressive"—something that he could not define— for Lady Stormwing? They would think he was a terrorist trying to infiltrate their organization, and with good reason.

No, he thought as he scarfed his second burger and downed the entire contents of his forty-four-ounce soda. He would not go to Detroit.

Tanya might not be able to help him, but it would be nice to see her and maybe she could offer him some advice.

Although there were other reasons to see her as well. He could admit this to himself, at least. The two of them had shared some wonderful moments before he had left and he would not lie to himself and pretend he didn't want to spend more time with her.

It would be tricky, though. He did not want to tell her he would be executed by his parents in three days and risk the possibility that she would treat him differently. There was a temptation to do exactly that, of course, as he was certain she would spoil him rotten. Maybe telling her would be best. If nothing else, it would be good to have a sympathetic ear. It was always possible that she and her friends could offer him solid counsel too.

As he soared on, the landscape beneath him changed from mountains to plains to desert scrub to more mountains. All things considered, he thought he had made very good time. His family knew how air currents worked and although he could not sense them in the same way the rest of the Stormwing clan could, he could see signs of them and knew how to use them to make his flight faster and easier.

Still, it took hours to reach the Lumos School but finally, Galen saw it. Nestled between two mountain ridges, it was invisible from the road but from the sky, it was beautiful.

Three buildings housed most of the campus and framed a central green space to form a U. Nearby were the dorms for boy dragons, girl dragons—each with separate quarters for those who liked to sleep in their human forms and the others who preferred their dragon form—and the mage dorms. It seemed so odd to see the small human-sized dorms and feel such a longing to be there. He had always scoffed at them before but he doubted that he would ever sleep in his dragon body again.

Behind the U and nestled farther back in the canyon were the dueling grounds and some of the wooded areas. It was a beautiful setting and interesting to him because it was so different from the climate and ecosystem of the Pacific Northwest. Although, after his time surviving in the desert on his own, he could see how lush the Lumos School grounds were.

Compared to the Seattle area, it looked all brown and desiccated, but he could now see exactly how healthy this little valley was.

Perhaps he had paid a little bit too much attention to the landscape, though. He had thought he had taken a wide circle around the campus grounds so he could enter through the front gate, but it seemed he had not gone wide enough.

Someone was coming to meet him.

"Ahoy!" Galen said and tried to exude friendliness with his aura.

Strangely, he felt no aura at all from whoever ascended to meet him. He wondered if that meant it was Kylara Diamantine. She had a pendant that hid her aura and he did not know of any other dragon with a similar ability.

He noticed another figure now approached on an intercept course as well.

"Did I get too close? I thought I stayed outside the boundary—"

"Intruder!" the figure yelled.

Galen could now see that it was not a dragon at all but some kind of beast. It had the head and wings of an eagle but the body of a lion. A griffin, then, although this one was made of granite, not flesh.

That was when he realized he had activated the school's upgraded defenses.

"I'm sorry. I'll back up," he told the stone griffin but it was not interested in talking.

It flew toward him. One pump of its wings propelled it far faster than any dragon's could, but that made sense. It was a creation of magic while he only harnessed power for his flight.

The beast collided with him and sank its claws into his chest.

"Do not resist," the other statue ordered. This one was in the shape of a winged serpent, although it spoke in the same monotonously loud and robotically threatening voice.

"I'm not resisting!" He grunted as the griffin flexed its claws and dug them deeper into his side.

While he had made no effort to resist, this was a little too much. He struck his attacker across the face and chipped flecks of stone away with the force of his claw, but the statue did not seem to notice at all.

Galen blasted it with fire but this accomplished even less. The stone did not even grow hot from his blast of flame. He dove and went into a barrel roll. The motion was enough to dislodge his attacker but it took a chunk of meat with it. He gasped in pain and tried not to look at the wound.

As he spun out of his barrel roll, the other statue rocketed into him. It wound coil after coil of its serpentine body around him and promptly ceased all attempts to fly.

He tried to free himself but he had been airborne for hours. It took effort merely to stay in his dragon body and this was too much. Instead, he struggled to stay in his dragon form although he almost slipped when his first assailant caught up to him and gored his shoulder.

The griffin had as little interest in flying as the winged serpent. It grasped him tightly and together, the three of them pounded into an outcrop of boulders. His captors used his head to break their fall.

CHAPTER SIX

Given Galen's current shortcomings with his dragon form, he should probably have been knocked unconscious when his head thunked into a granite boulder with enough force to crack it. Then again, his parents had always called him hardheaded.

Instead of being knocked out or forced out of his dragon form, the two animated statues that pinned him to the ground invigorated him.

"If you want to fight, let's do it," he said and struggled out of the hold of the winged snake.

As soon as he was free, the griffin pounced and he sprawled heavily. He righted himself, whipped his tail with enough force to crack another boulder, and noticed that his two assailants had called for backup. Although he hesitated for only a moment, that was enough for the winged snake to spring at him again.

He kicked and scratched but it was an odd opponent to tangle with because it felt no pain. This meant that his claws—despite the fact that they gouged chunks of stone away —did not make the snake retreat. It continued to pile its coils on top of him to trap him as it reiterated its message. "Do not resist!"

The voice was extremely annoying so Galen obeyed. He might have been able to escape the winged snake and the griffin but there was no way he would be able to stand against them as well as a stone centaur, a gargoyle, and a statue of what appeared to be Hercules.

"All right, all right. You got me," he said.

The snake did not release him but it did stop constricting. The other four statues approached and stood in a circle around the young dragon.

"So, do you guys like this gig or what?" he asked.

None of his captors acknowledged him. A minute later, a team of security mages raced out from the center of campus. They stopped a good twenty feet away from the ring of statues that had him pinned.

"Do not resist!" one of the new arrivals yelled.

"Oh, not this again," Galen muttered.

"You have entered restricted airspace. Identify yourself!" the same mage shouted. He didn't recognize him or the geometric patterns he had tattooed all over his face. He could have been a Steel Guard sent to augment the security team and certainly had the vibe of an overzealous cop.

"My name is Galen Stormwing. I used to be a student here."

"Stormwing, huh? It's a good thing the statues got you."

"No, it's not like that."

"Then why are you still in your dragon form?" the mage demanded.

"Because I don't want to be crushed by this giant black turd," he replied.

The guard grunted. From this guy, that seemed like a full-throated agreement. "We will call the Quetzalcoatl off and you will change into your human form. Then, I will approach and cuff you. Any deviations from this plan will result in all five of these statues testing your healing ability to its fullest potential. Acknowledge."

"Yeah."

"What?"

"Yes, sir. Come on, man. Let me up."

The mage gestured and the snake crawled off. Exhaustion from his long flight and battle with these constructs washed over him and it was with relief that he took his human form. That feeling vanished, however, when one of the mage's comrades stepped forward and with a little more roughness than was necessary and snapped silver cuffs on the intruder's wrists.

Immediately, he felt his powers leave him. Although his human form did not show the wounds that had been inflicted on his dragon body, the muscles of his chest ached where the griffin had clawed him. Without healing powers, he felt the wound acutely. Gone too were the emotions of the mages. Where before, he had been able to sense their distrust, apprehension, and willingness to fight, he now saw only the toughness they tried to project on their faces.

"I said I was a former student here. Is this how you treat your alumni?" Galen demanded.

"Almost every dragon of consequence on this continent for the last four hundred years graduated this school. Many of them are not exactly all right with mages training the current generation of young dragons."

"Times have changed, bro," he snapped.

"How about this, then. It's how we treat Stormwings."

He grumbled but he had nothing more cogent to say to them than that. His mom was a monster, his dad was hardly any better, and the rest of the family went along with their tyranny like sycophants. The mage was right to be cautious.

Although now that he was cuffed, the guard seemed to relax, at least slightly. He ordered the statues to return to their places and sent all his teammates but one to sweep the area.

"You truly are Galen?" the other mage asked. She had tattoos on her hands but not her neck or face and seemed both a little in awe and a little horrified. Galen wished he could sense which it was. Without knowing, he couldn't help but feel shame at her horror instead of pride at her awe.

"Yeah," he admitted. "I'm the jerk who brought Boneclaw back."

"But you also discovered the chest that was used to imprison Tiamat, correct? I recently completed my Master Mage's thesis on the implications of that device. Your discovery has revolutionized what we thought magic could do."

"That's enough, Morris," the older mage snapped.

"Yes, sir," she responded and hung her head.

"This way, kid. The headmaster is on her way."

Galen nodded and followed Morris and her boss into the wooded area of the campus. He felt like such an idiot. Earlier, he had thought about meeting Tanya in these very woods. Now, he was being escorted through them like a prisoner, all because he had failed to remember that the school had been forced to set up such powerful defenses because of his actions.

It was a bitter reminder but not as bitter as the look on the headmaster's face. She stood in front of a thorny mesquite tree in her dragon form and stared at him while some of the stones in the woods levitated off the soil.

Lady Amythist made it look effortless, but he understood the show of power. *I can do this without breaking a sweat,* the headmaster was saying. *Try something, I dare you.*

Perhaps to show that she was not scared of him, she transformed into her human form. She folded her arms and her wrinkled face creased with displeasure. For such a tiny, withered old woman, she commanded the utmost respect. He swallowed and decided that his decision to fly there like this had possibly been a huge mistake.

"You can release him now," Amythist said.

The mage pushed Galen forward, although he did not touch the magic-dampening cuffs on his wrists. He was no stronger than a regular human right now—a regular human with an extremely bruised chest. He, the headmaster, and the mages all knew he was no threat.

"Ma'am," he said, bowing respectfully.

"Galen Stormwing. What on Earth am I supposed to do with you?" she asked.

"I—"

"You're no longer a student here and our security protocols are strict."

"I only wanted—"

"Regardless of what you wanted, you should not have attempted to sneak in. I have every right to turn you over to the Steel Guard."

"But I didn't do anything—"

"You damaged our security statues while trying to break in. We have direct evidence of that," Morris said. It seemed she was suddenly not that big a fan of his discovery. But it made some sense. She seemed interested in magical artifacts and he had damaged some.

"What do you have to say for yourself?" Lady Amythist tutted and fixed him with a gimlet stare.

"Well...." He paused and half-expect to be cut off again.

"Well water, yes, yes. Now speak! Why did you try to sneak in?"

"I honestly didn't try to sneak in," Galen said. "I tried to go to the front gate but the security footprint is larger than I remember."

"Thanks to your actions."

"Enough, Perez," Lady Amythist said to her head mage. "But that's a fair enough point, I suppose. You were one of those who would know the old boundaries of this school better than most. Very well. Let's say you truly were heading to the front gate and were merely caught cutting a corner you should not have. Why?"

"I...was trying to see Tanya," he admitted.

The old dragon smirked although she wiped the expression off her face as quickly as it had appeared. "And you merely want to talk to her?"

"Yes, headmaster."

"Ma'am, this has to be the thinnest cover story I have ever heard," Perez said.

"Which is why I'm inclined to believe it," Lady Amythist said. "Tanya's classes are over for the day. I don't see why it would hurt for you to see her. I will check with her first, of course. You understand that if she does not wish to see you, we will not grant you any further access to our grounds?"

"Yes, ma'am. Of course." Galen could agree to that. He thought Tanya would want to see him. That was why he was there, after all, but if she didn't…well, there would be no reason to stay.

"Lady Amythist, it would not be wise to let him have the run of our school simply because he has a crush on one of our students."

"I agree wholeheartedly, Perez, which is why I would like you to accompany him for the duration of his visit."

The mage looked annoyed at the order but he managed to respond with, "Yes, ma'am," although his tone was a little rough with displeasure.

"Galen, do I have your word that if we remove your cuffs, we will not regret doing so?"

"You have my word," he agreed quickly. "I only want to talk to her, I swear. I don't want to cause any trouble."

"Very good," Lady Amythist said. "Remove the cuffs, Perez. One way or the other, I want young Galen to be able to sense Tanya's aura when they speak. I'd like him to be able to feel what she wishes him to."

Galen agreed to the terms, of course. He understood what Lady Amythist meant. If Tanya did not want to see him and only agreed to speak to him out of a sense of politeness, he would be able to sense it if he had access to his aura.

Perez removed the cuffs and sent Morris to check with the girl to ensure that she did indeed want to speak to her unexpected visitor. The young dragon glanced at the sun that had already moved toward the horizon and felt time ticking inexorably past.

CHAPTER SEVEN

Vala's mom pushed the door of the mage's shop open and the tinkle of a bell hanging on the inside of the door alerted the proprietor to their presence.

"Hello, Trevor?" Marma said into the workspace. It was a small shop, not much more than a ten-by-ten room that pushed up against a big glass counter. On the walls were various magic items he had enchanted. These included spoons that stirred soup pots without being held, brooms that could sweep a room by themselves—although admittedly, they did not work as well as most vacuum cleaners—and a few other assorted time-saving devices.

Behind the glass counter, the items were a little more interesting. One was a music box that Vala had pined over when they'd first moved there. Trevor said it could replicate any song it heard. A knife that grew sharper every time it was used and a self-climbing rope were the only other two items she could identify. Most of those behind the counter—like the music box—had been there for a long time so she at least recognized them, even if she had no idea what their purpose was.

Dwarves—even dwarves outside her family's religion—were

not magic-using folk. Over the decades, most had come to recognize the utility of a spoon that kept one's stew from burning, but the idea of a knife that would take the job of a smith away was not exactly something people wished to pay a high price for.

"Oh, hello, Vala, a pleasure! Did you come to hear one of the latest on the old music box? It does a delightful rendition of the new hip hop song about a woman's wet—oh. Mr. and Mrs. Gagnon. Welcome. I did not expect you."

"It's all right, Mr. Miller. Dad's not here to protest," Vala said quickly. "He'll be as calm as a grizzly in the dead of winter."

"An apt comparison. But Vala, come now, you know I prefer to be called Trevor. What can I do for you all this evening? Mrs. Gagnon, did you finally convince your husband to purchase one of my self-cleaning pots? I have a cast-iron Dutch oven I can cut you a great deal on. Some would say it's lightly used but I would describe it as pre-seasoned. If you'll give me only a moment to—"

"We're not here for trinkets, mage," her dad replied belligerently, which—unfortunately for her embarrassment—was a fairly polite word for her father to use to address Trevor.

"Oh? Forgive me, but I did not expect you to wish for a spell."

"We're here because of the one you cast on our daughter," Viktor retorted.

"Viktor!"

"Dad!"

Trevor—wisely—said nothing.

"Mr. Miller, pardon my husband. We're here because—"

"Electrical devices keep turning on all around me," Vala blurted.

"Have you been mucking around with existence? You'd best tell us if you have," her father said to the mage with open disapproval.

"I have left existence well enough alone today, thank you, Mr. Gagnon."

Viktor grumbled an incoherent reply but thankfully, he shut up before he killed his daughter with embarrassment.

"Have you ever heard of something like this?" Marma asked.

"No...not precisely, but there is a great deal of magic I have not heard of."

"Is there anything you can do to help?" Vala asked.

"And how would you have me help?" Trevor asked in reply.

"Well, presumably you could—I don't know—turn it off or something," her mother said.

"And tell us the name of the mage who put the curse on our daughter," Viktor added forcefully.

The proprietor nodded. "I'll see what I can do. I make no promises, though. Even the simplest of curses might be far beyond my power level."

"So you can't help?" Vala asked.

"I didn't say that." His eyes twinkled like they did any time he showed her one of his new items. "If there is a curse in place, I should at least be able to detect it. Come. To my lair!" With a flourish of his robe, he lifted a panel of the counter and led them deeper into his shop.

"I don't mean to be rude but I thought your lair would be more... uh, impressive." Vala gestured to the bare walls, stained concrete floor in need of sweeping, and fluorescent lights. It looked like the back of any shop—the kind of place where someone might fix cell phones.

"What did you expect? I can only afford this because I live up top." The mage fussed over a broom and coaxed it into sweeping the back room for them.

Marma smiled at it while Viktor frowned.

Their daughter wondered how it worked and wanted to draw it.

"Vala, if you would be so kind as to step into the middle of my lair." He raised an eyebrow to dare anyone to disagree with him.

"Sure." She stepped into the center of the room and Trevor drew a circle around her with chalk.

He added a few flourishes to the simple circle—a tangential line that morphed into a spiral here and a series of hexagons that bordered the circle there. His doodles complete—and immensely interesting to the artist hopeful—he straightened and walked around her.

"Hmm… No curses. Of that I'm certain. I suppose she could have a spell cast on her that causes these effects…" He raised his hands and moved his fingers in patterns that to her seemed reminiscent of the geometric patterns on the floors. Tiny motes—like chalk dust—shot from his hand and covered her. For a moment, she looked like she had been baking and had been a little exuberant with the flour before the flecks of magic glowed and puffed into nothingness.

"No spells either. Nothing at all that is magical in nature has been done to her."

Viktor breathed a sigh of relief, which she found almost endearing. Her dad had beliefs she could not make herself share but at the end of the day, he still cared about his youngest daughter.

"So, it was a coincidence then?" Marma asked.

"Well, I wouldn't go quite that far," Trevor said and his eyes twinkled like he had an entire box of trinkets to show the girl.

"What do you mean?" Vala asked.

Her parents seemed to have both simultaneously become quite incapable of speech.

"Well, no magic has been done to you, but I sense magic all the same. Vala, you feel very much like a human mage," he exclaimed and made no effort to hide his excitement.

"I feel like a mage?" she asked, not at all sure what that was supposed to feel like.

"You do. This is remarkable. We'll have to do a few more tests, of course, and we should consult a mage more skilled than a simple artificer like myself. But if this is true, you could be the first dwarf in history to be able to wield magic. This is amazing, interesting, and even astonishing. Oh, Vala, it's what you used to talk about when you first got here. Well, you were the same height then but you get my meaning!"

"Are you certain?" Marma asked after the color returned to her face.

"Of course, he's not certain!" Viktor shouted. "How could he be certain of something that's impossible! Dwarves don't use magic. Period. You know, when you moved to this town, I thought you were different. Now I see you are merely trying to make a buck off us."

"Mr. Gagnon, I lived in this town before you did," Trevor said calmly.

"That is not the point. You…you…charlatan! Come on, Vala. We will get a second opinion!"

"That is a good idea, Mr. Gagnon, as I am quite certain there is something magical about your daughter. She said so herself."

"That is quite enough out of you. The mayor will hear about this."

"We don't have a mayor here, Mr. Gagnon."

"Regardless!" Viktor continued to mumble his displeasure as he pulled Vala out of the mage's lair and out the front of the shop.

"You didn't have to act like a cat in a mouse's house," she said.

"You and your mother with these…wisdoms." He snorted derisively. "We will go to the shaman like we should have from the start. He'll sort this all out, we'll have a little ale, and everything will be fine in the morning."

"I don't want to go to the shaman—"

"Vala, this is not up for debate," her father said. "Besides, who knows what Mytrov will say?"

She did not know exactly what that was supposed to mean,

but she didn't care. All she knew was that she did not want to visit the shaman, although she had little choice in the matter. She wasn't about to disobey her parents and she was already beyond any help Trevor might have been able to give her.

Regretful that he hadn't provided the answers they wanted, she looked through the glass front of his shop to where he held his phone to his ear and chatted animatedly to whoever he had called. He was no doubt telling a distant friend about how poorly the Gagnon family had behaved.

On the fourth ring, Trevor knew Amy Williams would not pick the phone up. That did not particularly bother him, though. Ms. Williams was a hero and the most powerful mage in the world. He was a mage who had never been able to determine how a music box worked. She was therefore allowed to let him go to voicemail.

Still, when it picked up, he knew she'd call him. He was disappointed that he was not able to examine Vala's condition in more detail and even more so that he would not be able to help her. Well, that was not quite true. By calling Amy, he would be helping, but not as directly as he would have if she had come to him without her parents.

"This is Amy. Yes. That Amy. Leave a message and I'll get back to you if it's important."

The sound of a skateboard clacking on the ground marked the end of her voicemail and it beeped to indicate that he could speak.

"Amy. It's Trevor. Long time no talk. You will not believe what I just sensed coming off a dwarf."

CHAPTER EIGHT

Morris waved to Galen and Perez from a door of one of the buildings in the U and gestured for them to approach her. The young dragon looked for Tanya as they marched across the green area but he saw no sign of her. He had a feeling he would be put in a secure location before she would be allowed to see him.

It made sense, he reminded himself and tried to not let it bother him. He had betrayed this school and endangered the students and the faculty. The headmaster was entitled to a little paranoia.

Perez entered the U and moved toward Morris who stood in the open doorway.

"Right this way, kid," his mage escort said and gestured for Galen to go first. He obeyed, walked toward Morris, and let the mage stand behind him. Now that he was there, he did not intend to do anything stupid, but if he did, he had no doubt that this guy could slap cuffs on him before he could so much as transform.

The young dragon stepped through a doorway that held a flimsy wooden door and a window of frosted glass. The room expanded into a far larger space than his brain said should be possible. The walls were made of concrete, although there was nothing rough about them. They shimmered with blue energy that danced at the corners of his eyes.

What light there was in the room came from skylights that were set deeply into the ceiling. He swallowed and tried to downplay the sense that this was more of a prison cell than a classroom. Even the back of the door looked unbreakable. Instead of flimsy wood and frosted glass, it was heavy metal with bars on the side that would slide into the frame and secure it to the wall.

In the center of the room were two tall stone pillars like those at the dueling fields. The back of the room held bookshelves that stood against a few walls made of plywood that looked incongruous in the heavily constructed space.

"You know, a few throw pillows would bring this room together," he quipped.

"Are you trying to be the world's first dragon stand-up comic or something?" Perez asked.

Galen nodded, grimaced, and decided to shut up.

A few minutes later, Morris returned with Tanya.

"Galen!" his friend said and quickened her pace as she approached him.

Her aura felt wonderful. Surprise was the most prevalent emotion but she was not upset or angry to see him. If anything, she was pleased. His heart soared in response.

"Tanya, hi!" he managed to say before she wrapped him in a hug.

"What are you doing here?"

"You mean in this prison cell? Not hoping for a conjugal visit, if that's what you mean."

She slapped his arm playfully but her aura did not indicate that she was offended.

"This isn't a prison cell. Kylara and I convinced the headmaster to build it. After everything that happened at the Chrome Castle, we thought the students could use more practice fighting indoors. It's a whole different challenge. There are walls to drive opponents through, cover, and for dragons like me, it severely limits our powers. This whole room is made to be trashed except for the walls. But look at me, blabbering on. What about you? The rumor was you were not enrolled this year."

"I'm not," he admitted and glanced at Morris and Perez who had retreated enough to give the two young dragons at least the semblance of privacy. He had no doubt that the distance at which they stood was calculated to let him feel comfortable that they would not overhear but was still close enough that they could intervene if he tried anything.

Galen thought he could maybe draw Tanya deeper into the prison-like classroom but decided against it. He did not want the mage to trust him any less if that were even possible. Besides, everyone knew the Stormwing clan were jerks, especially to mages. If Perez heard that they were all about to kill him, it might make the head of security like him more.

"So?" Tanya asked into the short silence.

He'd debated exactly what he ought to tell her since he'd decided to visit her. Now that she was there in front of him, he was still unsure. How would she react if he told her what had happened at the Stormwing castle? He didn't want her pity. Of all the possible reactions she could have, that one might break him.

But Galen did want her help and advice so he took a deep breath and told her about the seventy-two hours his parents had given him to prove himself worthy of keeping his life. He wasn't sure what he had expected—advice, probably, which might have been a ludicrous thought. What he did not expect was the colorful string of expletives she used to describe his mother. Her aura cooled after a moment and she was finally capable of using words that did not have only four letters.

"The nerve of her! She should be thankful that you helped Kristen. And then she expects you to prove yourself and doesn't even say how? What does she expect—you to raze a city to the ground?"

He laughed. "Honestly? If I was able to summon a hurricane and demolish somewhere with more than a hundred thousand people, I'm sure that would be enough for her."

"That is disgusting." Tanya wrinkled her nose.

"So, you've never been expected to earn your parents respect?"

"No! No, of course not. They were so proud when I was accepted into the Lumos School. I was the first dragon from the Fastwing line to ever get in here—we're all vanillas, of course, or we all were—and now that I can control plants...well, my parents are delighted. If I make my mom's grapevines bear fruit, she acts like I solved world hunger."

"Dang. Here I was hoping you had been forced to battle to the death against one of your cousins or something."

Tanya laughed and he let the sound wash over him and warm his heart. "No! Honestly, Galen, I've never even heard of a family like what you've described. The truth is that we were always excluded from the top of dragon society because we didn't have any powers. I guess controlling the weather itself puts you squarely in the middle of the hierarchy of super-powerful dragons."

"The only power I've ever seen them more interested in than controlling storms was when I could control the bones of the dead."

"Ew. What is wrong with them?" Her aura filled with revulsion. "It sounds like growing up there was an absolute nightmare."

"It was, I guess."

"You guess?"

"I don't know. It was weird. I knew they were mean but I always thought it was my fault because I didn't have any storm powers. I grew up in this hierarchy of power so it was normal to me. That's why…well, that's why I was such a jerk. If I perceived a dragon as being weaker than me, they were therefore also inferior."

Admitting that aloud felt both terrible and like a burden had been lifted. He had to confront his biases and not only because he was now even lower on the power spectrum but because he now saw the way he had been raised was wrong.

"Do you want to prove yourself to them?" Tanya asked. Her aura was cautiously neutral. She had feelings about this but she tried to not let them show. It was a common dragon courtesy.

"I don't know. No? Yes? My first instinct was that I could bring them into the fold of the Steel Guard more and show them that working together with mages and vanilla dragons is the way forward. But my mom didn't like that idea. Do you think it could work?"

Tanya paused and he had the sense that she was wrestling with her aura.

"You don't need to hide your feelings from me, Tanya. I want to know what you think."

"Honestly?"

"Honestly."

"Well, frankly, I think you ought to tell them to jump in a lake except they can control the weather so it probably wouldn't do much. Come on. They've given you three days to somehow prove yourself? That's ridiculous! What kind of measure will they even use? There's no way you can ever know what they will judge you by. So yeah, if you could do some big honorable thing and prove yourself to them, that might be great, but it sounds as likely that your mom would be angry if you saved a school bus full of children or whatever."

"I know for a fact that saving a bus full of humans wouldn't count for anything."

She snorted. "Even if you do something they would like, it

sounds more like their reaction will be based on their mood rather than on facts. Unless you want to destroy a city, I guess."

"I don't!" he said quickly.

"I know, Galen. That was a joke."

"Right, yeah. Sorry. Well then, what do you think I should do?"

"You could come back here. Re-enroll?"

He shook his head. "No. It wouldn't be fair to the other students. Simply seeing me would freak many of them out and besides, I'm sure someone has filled my slot. I wouldn't want to kick a first-year out because I'm scared of my family. Plus...well, I don't think it would come to this, but if my family tried to attack the school to get me out..." He couldn't bring himself to finish.

"They wouldn't!"

"Not at first, no, but if they told Lady Amythist about the agreement I made, it would complicate everything. She might protect me but I couldn't let anyone risk their life for me. Not even Perez over there."

The mage must have been listening because he grunted when his name was mentioned.

"So then you have to run," Tanya said.

"You think?"

She nodded. "I do. The whole obligation scenario used to apply to mages before the Steel Dragon's Revolution. They would run to Canada and find safety there. The dwarves are still neutral and still independent. If you go north of the border, the deal you struck with your parents wouldn't hold there."

"You think?" Galen repeated. It was an idea that had occurred to him earlier but he still wasn't sure.

Tanya shrugged. "Well...dwarves hate pushy dragons and are impervious to magic or dragon fire. I don't see them simply surrendering because of a little rain."

He nodded. "Yeah...yeah, that could work."

"But your aura says you don't want to," she said.

"Well...I mean...you're not in Canada."

Her face lit up. "No, I'm not, but I do have this friend who can open gates through the pixie realm and enjoys sneaking out. I'm sure I'll see you again, Galen."

He nodded and decided he could live with that. The frozen tundra of the far north didn't sound that bad if he had his feelings for Tanya to warm his heart—and more importantly, her feelings for him.

"I guess this is goodbye then?" he said.

"For now," she agreed and hugged him.

Galen could count the number of times he had been hugged on his claws. Despite his inexperience with the gesture, this was easily the nicest one he'd ever experienced. She hugged him tightly, and the feel of her silk dresses and the smell of her skin—slightly earthy with a hint of grass, probably from her power over plants—was intoxicating. He returned her embrace and made no attempt to hide his feelings from her.

"All right, Perez. Let's get out of here," he said when they drew apart and Tanya had said her farewells.

"That sounds great to me, kid."

Galen had accepted the need to run but vowed that it wouldn't be forever. He had somewhere to go rather than simply somewhere to get away from. It wouldn't necessarily be easy but he could do this. Perez and Morris led him to the front gate and he stepped beyond the protection of the Lumos School, transformed, and flew north.

CHAPTER NINE

The young dragon pushed northward at a steady pace. He knew he had to make good time if he wanted to be deep enough into Canada to avoid notice when the three days were up.

There was still one stop he had to make while he was in the desert, however.

Galen flew north of the Lumos School and scanned the landscape below for a particular outcropping of rock. He knew from living out there when he had been trapped as a half-dragon, half-human that although the desert landscape could seem eternal, it could change in the blink of an eye. All it would take was a desert storm on high ground to start a mudslide and his careful landmark would be erased and the hidden cache of treasure it marked lost.

Floods of that caliber did not come every year, however. He scrutinized the land below him and finally located the place where he had left it.

Once he'd checked to make sure he was alone, he descended and changed to his human form. After talking to Tanya, he felt invigorated and stronger than he had when he'd left Stormsiege. He wondered if his emotional state affected his powers. There was a time when he would have laughed the notion away as crybaby nonsense, but he was no longer so sure.

Part of his power profile was the ability to read emotions. When he had been stuck between forms, that power had been denied him and he had been weaker for it. Maybe, if he could get a better hold on his emotional state, he could hold his dragon form longer. It certainly sounded better than constant self-doubt.

As much as he disliked the notion of retrieving what he had left there, he also knew that having it on him would give him confidence. It always had before.

He approached the stony outcrop and paced around it until he found the large rock he had put there. To a casual observer, it would look like it was part of the outcropping but was a recent addition. It rested on none of the other stones, nor did any of them rest on it. He had positioned it there when he hadn't known what to do with the claw.

After another hasty glance at his surroundings, he shoved the stone aside—a feat that would have been impossible to a human even if they somehow knew what was beneath it—and revealed his hidden treasure.

This was the claw of the Prairie King, taken from his body that had been interred in his castle in the middle of the American Midwest. Galen had summoned the skeleton to life with the power he had found in the pixie realm. Eventually, the Prairie King had been put to rest again but he had retained the claw.

It was both unusual and special as it was made of an extremely strong black material that was insanely sharp. He knew it was sharp enough to get past Kylara's almost impenetrable diamond scales and long enough to reach the heart of any dragon. It was a formidable weapon and almost unbreakable besides. Although he had tried to destroy it multiple times, he could do nothing to it.

He did not know exactly what he hoped to do with it, but he knew it would serve him well. And although he did not like to think about the horrors he had inflicted on the world with his revenant skeletons, it was not something he could pretend had never happened either. He would take this claw and it would serve him rather than him serving its power as he had to admit had happened before. It was a macabre trophy, perhaps, but his life was anything but simple these days.

In his hands, it felt like a sword—thicker at the base than the sharp tip and with one sharp edge. He made a few practice swings against a nearby patch of cactus. Despite the old, gnarled, woody growth, he felt almost nothing as he sliced through it.

It was a formidable object, a legendary artifact and the kind of thing his mother would doubtlessly love to put on display in Stormsiege. He wondered if giving it to her would earn him a place at her table.

Galen shrugged and decided it did not matter. He would not give his mother a relic of his shame to try to win honor in her eyes. Even if it worked, it would be wrong.

No, he would keep the claw of the Prairie King, and so help his family if they tried to take it from him.

Unsure of how to carry it in his dragon form, he clasped it tightly, transformed, and tried to absorb it into the other form as if it were nothing but clothing.

To his shock, it didn't simply get absorbed but replaced one of his claws. His right index finger was now jet black, ample proof that his dragon form had incorporated it into his body. Startled, he wondered if he could make it appear somewhere other than his hand. Boneclaw had used it as a barb on the end of his tail so it wasn't impossible.

Now was not the time to test it, however. He needed to reach Canada before his time was up.

As Galen flew farther north, he realized how right he felt about this decision. He did not want his family's approval. They were monsters who had always treated him like nothing more than a dog. Why did he want to be a part of that? The life ahead of him would be hard compared to living in the luxury of Storm-siege but it would be easy in that he could pursue things besides his mother's approval.

He was ticking through the list of what he might be able to do —he had always been a decent swimmer and dragons didn't mind the cold all that much, so maybe he could become a fisherman on Hudson Bay—when the Canadian border came into view. The dwarves kept the border itself logged clear of forest growth.

When he crossed from one clump of forest across the strip of grass between them to the other side, he would no longer be in dragon territory. His family could still follow him—stopping dragons was not as easy as giving them a map—but they would never receive the succor they might have south of the border where people lived in fear of them.

The young dragon was about to cross the border when lightning cracked in the sky in front of him.

Galen could not control the weather but he knew enough about it to recognize that the blast of lightning was unnatural. It was the work of a Stormwing.

"Who's there?" he shouted to the sky and Petrov Stormwing emerged from a puff of cloud.

"Hello, little Galen," he said. "Heading to Canada?"

"I was thinking about it."

The two dragons circled each other in the air and gave one another a wide berth. Galen did not like this at all. His uncle could not control the weather with the same level of control as his mother, but he had other talents that she knew how to put to use.

"You're not trying to escape your agreement with my sister, are you?" Petrov never called her his sister in front of her yet he would also not entertain him calling her his mother.

"Of course not, Uncle."

"Land, boy."

He considered this and could not see a reason to argue. While he had the claw, he did not want to reveal that he had something like that to his family. Keeping it secret would give him the element of surprise if he ever had to use it. Besides, maybe Petrov had an idea for how he could earn his place at Stormsiege. Even after deciding that he didn't want that, he still thought about it.

When he landed, the other dragon did as well. Although he wanted to change to his human form to rest, he didn't dare. If he did, he would not only reveal that he was tired but the claw would be visible. It was better to hope that this didn't last too long.

"It looked like you were going to go to Canada," his uncle said.

"Did it?"

"It did." The older dragon grinned. "And I can't help but wonder if you were trying to disappear and break your word."

"Of course not, Uncle."

"That's good to hear, boy. Have I ever told you about my powers?"

"Uncle, I don't have much time—"

"I can't control the weather like my sister can. No one can. She's the strongest Stormwing in generations. But unlike you, I do have my talents. I can sense the air, you see. I can sense pressures, air currents, moisture, and things that have passed. Do you know how many molecules a dragon leaves behind as they fly?"

"No, Uncle."

"Of course you don't because you no longer have any powers at all, not since you gave up your one chance to make something of yourself. My powers let me sense these...trails. You did well hiding out there in the desert, but you're less careful now, aren't you?"

"I'm merely trying to find a way to prove myself—"

"Good. That's good, boy. Because I was sent to make sure you don't try to drop off the map again. You need to realize that the only reason your little sabbatical worked the first time is because my sister didn't think it was worth wasting my time to bring you home. Your deal changes that."

"Mother knew I was out there that whole time?" Galen asked. He had suspected that it might be possible but knowing they had been aware that he was out there, alone and barely surviving, hurt.

"There is little that escapes the eyes of Lady Stormwing."

"I understand," he said.

"I don't think you do, boy. Let me make it clear to a dropout like you. If you fail to do something noteworthy, my job is to bring you home where you can be executed in front of the clan. If you resist, I will kill you and bring your head back in your place. You have three days to do something to redeem yourself. No—it's considerably less than that now. You already spent almost a whole day at the Lumos School before you came here. Do you have any idea what you're doing?"

"I didn't think you cared, Uncle."

Petrov laughed at that. "You always had a sharp tongue, didn't you, boy? It'll be a shame to rip it out of your throat if you fail a final time."

"Then give me a clue. What does moth—Lady Stormwing expect me to do? If I can find a way to ally with the Steel Guard, would that be enough?"

"You wish to weaken our clan further?" His uncle spat and thunder cracked in the distance. "Your mother has no interest in groveling at the feet of dragons who value mages and dwarves as equals. No. You will bring us something of power. A mage—broken and ready to rebuild as one of our servants—might do if they're strong enough."

His aura betrayed him. He couldn't help but feel shock and revulsion at such an idea.

Petrov noticed this and he threw his head back and laughed. "So you're not interested in the old ways, eh? Who knows, maybe you'll think of something. If not…well, you can't hide from me, Galen. Not as long as you draw breath."

With those words, the older dragon took to the air and flew west toward Stormsiege.

Galen waited for his silhouette to vanish over the horizon before he transformed to his human form and let himself collapse.

This was going so much worse than he had hoped. He knew enough about his uncle to know that he couldn't run, not for any length of time anyway. If he could somehow cross the arctic circle to another continent, he might last a week or maybe a month, but he would not be able to outrun Petrov forever.

Eventually, he would have to fight him and as much as he hated to admit it, the older dragon would win. He was centuries older than him and had brought back many a dragon for punishment. Without a doubt, he would fetch him as easily as a dog retrieved a ball.

It was ironic, he thought despondently. He had finally decided to not please his family and now, he had no choice but to do exactly that.

CHAPTER TEN

The walk to their church was an uncomfortable one for Vala. It had started fine enough, but when her father mentioned that Shaman Mytrov would hopefully be able to perform a cleansing ritual, her mom freaked out.

"What do you mean *cleansing?*" Marma demanded.

"I'm only saying that this...this...well, whatever this is, can hopefully be purged."

"Purged? She's not infected, Viktor!" his wife retorted waspishly.

The young dwarf did not know what to do. She loved her parents and she knew they both loved her, but when they started these arguments, it felt safest to simply stay out of it. Even though—in this case—she was smack dab in the middle as the cause of it.

"Why do you think we are taking Vala there? You want to be better, don't you, Vala?"

"I—"

"I thought we were taking her to the shaman to see what he thinks, but that's not the case at all, is it?" Marma had stopped walking with them. With her hands on her hips and feet planted wide, she looked as stubborn as a boulder.

"I want to know what the shaman thinks," Vala said but it seemed like her parents did not even hear her.

"Of course I want his opinion!" Viktor bellowed as loudly as any moose.

"Do you want his opinion, or do you want him to fix our daughter?"

"I want him to fix her, of course."

"But she's not broken!"

Viktor looked at Vala and his eyes filled with tears. "I never said you were broken, sweetheart. I only want things to go back to normal."

"I know you didn't say I was broken, Dad," she said.

"Oh, and I did?" Marma demanded.

"Marma, *calm down!*" he roared.

"I will not calm down, Viktor! You keep acting like you're ready to evolve but you're not. Your heart is still in our cabin in the woods. Times are changing and Vala is part of that."

"Oh, like I'm the one stuck in the woods. You still fill feeders for the animals, even though that squirrel you lured to our yard ruined the wiring to your precious porchlight."

"So, you did know what happened to the light."

"Your squirrel happened. It fried itself. I didn't tell you because I didn't think you could handle it."

Marma turned beet-red at that. "Fine," she said, her voice now quiet and cool instead of hot with rage. Vala knew this was when her mom was well and truly furious. "Vala. I am going home. If you want to go with your bone-headed, backward-thinking father, fine. If you would like to come with me, that is fine too."

"Let's see what Mytrov says, Vala," her father said although he left it at that. He knew better than to press his wife when she was in this state.

The girl looked from one parent to the other and back again. She wanted to go with her mom. It sounded so much easier to simply go home, maybe have a cup of ale, and go to sleep. She would wake in the morning and all this would feel like a bad dream.

But she was no longer a kid. She knew that what had happened today on campus was a reality. Not only that, but the strange magic had come again while she was at home. What if she had a nightmare and her mom's curling iron somehow attacked her in her sleep?

"I'd like to know if Shaman Mytrov thinks the same thing is happening to me as Mr. Miller," Vala said, not at all certain that "is happening" was the right way to think about this. Trevor had made it sound like this magic had come from her, not from some external source.

Vala knew very little about human mages, but she knew that their powers normally manifested shortly after they transitioned into adulthood. Most of the runaways to Canada were in their late teens or twenties, sometimes older but never younger. If she was a mage—as impossible as that sounded—it made sense that the magic powers would have only manifested now.

"Fine," Marma said, her voice still that placid calm. "I'll have a pot of stew going when you two get home, all right?"

"Come with us, Marma," Viktor said.

"I will not speak to that dwarf who thinks there is more beauty in wood, leather, or bone than in living trees or animals, thank you very much." And with that, she spun on her heel and stormed away.

He cleared his throat. "Your mother…"

"I know her well enough, Dad. You don't have to apologize for her."

Her dad nodded. "Come on. Let's go see Shaman Mytrov and find out if he knows a thing or two more about a dwarf than a mage in a trinket shop claims to."

The walk was not far, which meant the silence between them

felt companionable rather than awkward. After a short time, they turned down the dirt road that led to their destination.

Although Vala was not afraid of the church, she had never liked it all that much. Part of it was simply the architecture of the building. Even calling it a building seemed generous compared to where she went to school.

The Seventh Branch of the Church of Dwarfish Origins was a humble structure. The walls of its single floor were made of rough-cut stone. Its roof was made of waxed timber and shingles. The light that came out from the cracks around its wooden front door was all from torches or candles. There was no electricity in the church and there never would be.

She knew from previous sermons that no electricity had been used in the church's construction, nor had any electricity been used in the construction of the tools that made the church. It meant the chisels that had cut the stone were all made on forges fueled by nothing but coal and the muscles of dwarven black-smiths. The same applied to the axes that felled the lumber for the roof and shaped the shingles.

It wasn't that she had anything against building things in the old way but she was an artist and saw no artistry in the church. The stones were heavy and thick but not particularly flush. The roof was beautiful, but if the timbers had been varnished in different colors, they would have made the shingles stand out.

She had spent considerable time wondering what a few strings of electric lights would do. If they were positioned in such a way as to accentuate the simple architecture and the beauty of the handcrafted materials, the church could be transformed from a humble workman's building that was perpetually too dark to a spectacular ode to the beauty of dwarf craftsmanship. But Shaman Mytrov would never agree to have wires run through the building.

Compared to the Church of Dwarfish Origins' stance on magic, however, its views of electricity were downright progressive. Viktor had been chided for allowing his wife to convince him to move into a house with electrical wiring in the walls. That was nothing, however, compared to how Shaman Mytrov would have reacted had he known how often Viktor's daughter visited the mage shop in town.

Still, it was obvious to Vala that going to window-shop at Trevor's was quite different than a dwarf activating electronic equipment without meaning to.

"Are you ready, Vala?" her dad asked.

"Do you honestly think Mytrov can tell us what's going on?" she asked.

"I certainly hope so," he replied.

She nodded and tried to push her nervousness aside.

He drew a breath and knocked on the door.

A moment later, it swung inward and Shaman Mytrov stepped into view. Even though she had known exactly what to expect, seeing the shaman was always somewhat mind-boggling.

Like all dwarves, he was short and stout and like all dwarf men, he had a thick beard that covered most of his chest. Unlike most dwarves, he did not wear brightly colored clothes as a contrast to the bleak Canadian winters. There were artificial ingredients in some of those dyes and some of the yarn that the more adventurous dwarves used to knit were—*gasp*—artificial. Shaman Mytrov believed in materials that were less processed.

He wore a vest made of deer leather and a brown shirt beneath made of rough-spun wool that looked horribly itchy. Instead of pants, he wore a woolen kilt although it lacked the brightly colored plaid that made the Scottish variant of this particular garment so popular. These were teamed with thick brown socks—also wool, no doubt—and shoes made of yet more leather.

Over this ensemble, he wore a cloak that Vala knew her mom would describe as an abomination. It was made from a wolf pelt, complete with a hood made of the skin of the wolf's head that rested upon the shaman's head. Immediately behind the ears of the wolf skin, elk horns had been affixed. The tip of each antler point was either black with charcoal or red with clay. In the flickering torchlight of the church, it was hard to tell which of the points was which color.

"Viktor, what brings you here? It's not a prayer day," Shaman Mytrov said amicably enough, although the streaks of black that ran from beneath each of his eyes and down his cheeks to vanish into his beard made his smile into more of a rictus in Vala's opinion. It did not help that there was some of the same charcoal powder in the cracks of his teeth.

"Shaman Mytrov...I don't know how else to put this. I think my daughter might have been cursed."

The shaman turned his blackened face to her. His eyes glowed like white coals beneath the antlers and made her think about doodling his face as a bed of coals with the antlers as flames.

"What seems to be the problem? Please, come in. You know all dwarves are welcome in the Church of Dwarfish Origins." He stepped aside and gestured for them to enter. They complied and stepped from the gravel path outside to the packed-earth and stone floor within. The door clicked shut behind them with a heavy thud.

Shaman Mytrov led them to a simple wooden bench in front of the stone altar at the center of the room as Viktor explained all that had happened.

He said nothing during the explanation, although he did cast his bright blue, almost silver gaze at Vala each time the word magic was mentioned. His calm stoicism faltered somewhat when her father explained that they had taken Vala to see *that mage* before they had come to the church, but he held his tongue even then. In all likelihood, he was not surprised. Marma came to church sometimes, but she had never shown any great faith or adherence to the religion.

"So…what do you think?" her father asked when he had related all the events of the last few hours.

"You were right to come here," Shaman Mytrov said and licked his teeth but didn't dislodge any of the black between them. "The mage was incorrect, of course. Viktor, your instincts and faith in our ways are well-founded. I will lead a chant championing your faith on prayer day."

"Thank you," Viktor mumbled although he did not seem particularly pleased to have earned this honor. "We hoped you could tell us what might be happening to my daughter, oh Father of the Earth."

"We will pray for this curse to be lifted." Mytrov bowed his head and his painted face practically vanished beneath the horned wolf hood he wore.

"How do you know it's a curse?" Vala asked when the shaman did not immediately reappear from his mumbling withdrawal beneath his hood.

"It cannot be anything else," he replied and looked up slowly so the torchlight caught his teeth but not his eyes or his hooked nose.

"How can you know that?" she asked.

"Vala!" Viktor protested but he turned to Mytrov as well.

"A dwarf cannot have magic. If it were to happen, it would be a disaster for us all."

"A disaster? Why?" she asked.

"She has always been curious, Father of the Earth. You know this," her father said apologetically.

"There are prophecies—carefully guarded against our enemies for hundreds of years—that warn of such a thing. As your father knows, Vala, dwarves came from magic. We were created through the use of magic on normal humans. Our birth was intended to be a bloody one, but we gained wisdom that those who wished to be our masters did not have. They tried to cajole us and to force us to fight their war against the dragons, but we refused.

"They did not accept our words and instead, resorted to force. But when they did, they discovered that the very strength they endeavored to imbue us with protected us against them. Dragon fire —magic in nature—does not burn dwarf skin, but neither can mages use their powers against us effectively. Our greatest gift was not one the mages intended to give us at all. We have an incredible resistance to magic. This in turn means that dwarves cannot use magic. It does not flow through us. We are rooted to the Earth instead which makes us solid and foundational, not flighty magic creatures like the pixies."

"But it seems like I did use magic," she said into the silence that followed his speech. "Also, how can this be impossible if there's a prophecy that says it will happen?"

"You blaspheme in one breath and invoke the prophecy with the next?" Mytrov growled his displeasure.

"I didn't blast anything," Vala protested. "It was more like a weird activation of all the little electrical doo-dads. I would show you but…well, your aesthetic doesn't work with that." She waved her hands at the church all around them.

"Forgive me, Father of the Earth, for I do not understand," Viktor said in his most pious tone. It was—she noted—the same tone of voice he used when he had made her mother angry and she was baking a particularly rich-smelling pie. "If this is prophesied, isn't it possible that Vala is not cursed?"

"The prophecy heralds the end of us. If a dwarf wields magic, then magic can be wielded against us."

"But won't access to this new gift give us strength we didn't have before?" Vala asked. It was a common argument from her engineering classes.

Mytrov turned his hot gaze on her. "What hope do you think a few fledgling mages have against the hordes of dragons south of our border? If we are no longer impervious to magic, we are no longer impervious to dragon fire. Even if the dragons do not wish to take this country from us, what of the mages? They have long agitated for a land of their own. They would take the Earth from beneath our feet in a heartbeat. Mages cannot be trusted. You should never have gone to that...that *tinkerer* in town."

Vala bristled at this. Trevor had only ever been kind to her. Shaman Mytrov, on the other hand, had shamed her mother for installing a phone in their house. "As far as I can tell, Trevor was right. You haven't even checked to see if I am cursed. He tried to help. You're simply trying to scare us."

"I will not be spoken to in such a way by the daughter of a member of my congregation."

"Vala, please. Shaman Mytrov can help," Viktor pleaded but he looked like he had begun to realize that he was in way too deep.

"We will rid you of this affliction, Miss Gagnon. We have rituals for precisely this."

"Wait, rituals? Wouldn't any ritual that could remove magic necessarily have to be magic in nature?" She was outraged. The man was a hypocrite.

"Do not think you can blaspheme so freely in my church. You will submit to this ritual or you will be a dwarf no longer."

"Maybe that wouldn't be such a bad thing if part of what it means to be a dwarf is to contradict your own backward religion."

"Foolish child! You understand none of the words you vomit from your mouth. Do you think our scholars have never debated these very topics? There are entire treatises on these same questions and you think I have never heard them before. You are a child—a foolish child who does not know what she could spread through our people simply because of her ignorance. You will submit and we will cleanse your soul or—"

But Vala did not hear the rest of what Shaman Mytrov, Father of the Earth of the Seventh Branch of the Church of Dwarfish Origins said. She was distracted by something else.

B-riiiing!

She had felt a fury grow inside her as the shaman became more and more irate and lectured her about what she did not understand while he lived in a city lit up with electric lights he thought were magic.

B-riiiing!

Although it seemed his convictions were not quite as firm as she had always believed.

B-riiiing!

Unless she was severely mistaken, a telephone was ringing somewhere inside the church.

B-riiiing!

"Are…are you going to get that, Father?" Viktor asked.

"That-that is nothing of your concern," Shaman Mytrov stammered.

"You might want to get it," Vala said and pointed across the church. A telephone crawled up from the basement where the shaman slept. It threw its receiver up and out of the door, then used the accordion cord that connected the body to the receiver to haul the rest of it up.

B-riiiing!

Vala knew she should have been shocked that yet another piece of electrical equipment had come to life but she wasn't. She was pissed. What's more, she could feel the telephone. She could feel the tiny arm rattling the hammer that made the bell hidden inside its casing ring.

B-riiiing!

"You bring a monster into this simple house of earth and wood and stone," Shaman Mytrov said, frozen in place.

The telephone—perhaps fueled by Vala's rage at this ritual he wanted to perform on her—hurled its receiver at the shaman. It fell short but it dragged its body forward again. Behind it, the telephone cord that hooked the machine to the wall and let it receive calls whipped wildly, disconnected from the socket that should have provided the device with the modicum of energy it needed to ring.

While they all stood frozen and stared at it, something thunked at the door.

That jerked Shaman Mytrov from his state of shock. Flummoxed, he moved away from the phone and opened the door to what had been his sanctuary until moments before.

It was not a member of his congregation who had knocked, though. Instead, it was the remote-control car Vala had sent racing away from her earlier.

Except now, it seemed like it had an ax to grind with the shaman. It raced toward his leather boots and he shrieked and hopped on top of a wooden bench. The car raced around under it like a shark through bloody water. It did not occur to Mytrov that he could crush it with the single stamp of his foot. It was nothing but a plastic toy, after all.

"Leave this place. Now!"

"Not until you promise to leave me alone," Vala shouted.

"Vala, come on! Let's go," Viktor said and took her hand.

She let him lead her out of the church as Shaman Mytrov screamed at them from his perch atop the bench.

"You doom our race. You *doom* us! The prophecy says he who cannot protect himself cannot protect us. We will lose our powers and our uniqueness. We will lose *what makes us dwarves.* Pull the thread that will unravel us and in time, we will revert to the humans from whom we were made. You doom us, Vala Gagnon. Submit and be cleansed, or you will doom us all!"

Her father shut the door which thankfully stifled the next part of his impromptu sermon.

"Vala, I didn't realize. I thought he'd wave some crystals or perhaps recommend a type of mud to bathe in. I never thought… I'm sorry, my little sapling."

"I'm not a sapling anymore, Dad. I'm almost four feet tall."

"Don't I know it," he said and glanced at the church. As they had hurried away, the drone of the telephone had quieted and now, either they had moved far enough away that they couldn't hear it at all or it had fallen silent.

Mytrov prayed when Viktor and his cursed daughter left his church. He prayed for the demonic machine that zipped about below him to stop its infernal pursuit and for the telephone to stop ringing. Finally, he prayed for the ground to open up and swallow Vala Gagnon.

The Earth responded to the first two prayers, at least.

He opened his eyes and realized that the car was gone. The phone lay in the middle of his church as if to taunt him for bringing it into this holy place.

Still partially in shock, he stared and waited for it to animate again and attack him. Thankfully, it did not move. He clambered off the bench and approached the device, but it was utterly lifeless again. It made sense, of course. It was not the phone that possessed the magic but the girl. He had used it for years, his only compromise with modern technology—well, his only compromise inside the church—and it had never done anything like this before. It must surely be the girl and her curse.

The shaman marveled at how right Viktor Gagnon had been. His daughter truly was cursed but it was not the simple, delayed negative effect mages visited on each other and humans. That kind of curse would not work on a dwarf. No, Vala was deeply and truly cursed. She, like some dwarves in years past, had manifested the power that none of their kind should or could ever be born with naturally.

He had not had to deal with such an event in his community in his lifetime. He had heard of it happening—that was one of the reasons he kept the phone, after all—but he had not ever truly believed that such a horrible thing could happen to his people.

To Shaman Mytrov of the Seventh Branch of the Church of Dwarfish Origins, Vala manifesting the ability to use magic was nothing short of the bell that signaled the beginning of the extinction of his kind.

And she was out there, gallivanting about and doing only the Earth knew what to all these infernal devices around the city.

Infernal devices like the telephone that now lay limp on the floor.

Cautiously, he took a step closer but it did not move. He moved even closer and it remained inert.

When he snatched it off the floor, it did not resist or try to strangle him. But of course it didn't. The problem was not the device. Many other dwarves had them and nothing like this had happened to anyone before. The problem was the girl.

Mytrov hurried downstairs and plugged the phone into the jack in the wall he'd hidden carefully behind his handmade desk. Even reconnected to the electrical nervous system that empowered it to carry his voice across the land, it did not attack him.

But it wouldn't without the girl to inflict her magic upon it.

She was the problem, after all, not the phone.

He did not like electricity or gasoline-powered engines, but he could see they were different than magic. But what Vala had done? That was magic and it had to be stopped.

Shaman Mytrov picked his phone up and began to call some of the most trusted members of his congregation. These were dwarves who understood the threat magic truly posed, the kind he could trust to mention that he might call them on the phone one day even though he would continue to preach against modern conveniences in prayer days. They would not question him and would do as he commanded so he could save their kind.

CHAPTER ELEVEN

Vala and her father had only walked a few blocks when Shaman Mytrov caught up to them.

"It's not too late to save the soul of dwarf kind!" he yelled at them.

She tried to walk faster but her dad stopped and pulled insistently on her hand. Although it was the last thing she wanted to do, she stopped as well.

"What do you mean the soul of dwarf kind? Can't Vala sleep on it tonight?" Viktor asked.

"And risk it spreading to you or your wife? Your convictions might keep you safe, Viktor, but would Marma's? Bless her heart, but she's never been as devout as you and I."

Her father looked at her with fear in his eyes. "Vala, sweetie, can't we see what this ritual of his is all about?"

"No, Dad. I'm not broken."

"Right, of course." He nodded quickly but he did not look completely convinced.

"Viktor, if you walk away from me, you will not be welcome in the church. She is your daughter and therefore your responsibility. You must make her see that she is a danger to us all."

He turned to his daughter and his eyes filled with tears as he pleaded with her. "It won't take long, my little sapling. And when it's done, you'll be normal again."

"I don't want to be normal! I've never wanted to be normal!" She stormed away and left him standing there, wringing his hands until Mytrov went to him and embraced him. Although she could not hear what the creepy shaman said to him, she knew he was being twisted and his fear used to set his mind against his daughter.

Vala wished he would come with her, but he'd always been a sucker for Mytrov's teachings. It was part of his upbringing and even with Marma as his wife, he simply couldn't shake it.

The girl wasn't mad at him, merely disappointed. Still, she wished he had stopped Mytrov from yelling at her loudly enough to wake the dead.

Galen still had no idea how he could prove himself. His uncle Petrov had made it clear that trying to do something with the Steel Guard would not work, so that was out. They would hate Galen anyway, so there was little point even trying.

Plus, the Steel Guard were not the dragons he respected the most. Those were at the Lumos School. Tanya, Kylara, Karl Midnight, and even Jasmine—despite her being a mage—had helped him when he'd needed it most. What could he do to prove himself to them?

Canada seemed like an answer to that question. Kylara's Aunt Cassandra had lived in a hidden base there and Tanya had seemed impressed that he had managed to survive in the desert alone for so long. Maybe there, he could find a way to hide despite his uncle's tracking skills. Perhaps if it got too cold, there would be no trails for Petrov to follow. Still, while he considered all these and other vague possibilities, in the back of his mind, he thought that maybe he would find something that would appease his uncle.

He crossed into Canadian airspace and headed toward a town. While he knew he should probably avoid populated places, the lights were pretty in the darkness of the early night and no one should be able to see him up there anyway. He planned to completely skirt the town but shouts caught his ear.

"I don't want to be normal! I've never wanted to be normal!" a short, stocky woman—a dwarf, he realized belatedly—shouted at two equally stocky, equally short but decidedly more bearded men.

"Your wants are irrelevant, child," one of the bearded dwarves yelled at her. He wore a bizarre ensemble of clothes. Well, to the young dragon, calling what he wore clothing was being generous. The dwarf looked like he had donned the leftovers of a protein-rich meal. "You will come with me and you will be purified."

He knew he should simply fly on. This was dwarf country, after all. He had no right to be there and no right to interfere. This was inferior business, as his mother would say.

Except he did not want to be like his mother.

What he wanted was to be more like Tanya, who had helped him when he'd needed it not because she had sought political benefits or to curry favor with him. She had seen that he needed help and it had simply been the right thing to do.

Galen adjusted his flight path so he could fly lower and could continue to listen.

The dwarves yelled at each other about magic and rituals and some kind of sickness. He had no idea what they were talking about, nor could he read their auras since dwarves were resistant to the powers of dragons. Nevertheless, he could tell from the girl's body language that all she wanted to do was leave.

Because he wanted to be more like Tanya, he asked himself a simple question—what would Tanya do? The answer was obvious.

She would help, so he would too.

He tucked his wings and glided over the two male dwarves' heads to land between them and the girl they were following. Calmly, he turned toward the men and growled.

The dwarf who, from above, had looked like a mess of animal skins was even stranger from this angle. He wore a wolf pelt on his body and antlers on his head. His face was painted like he hoped to score a leading role in a B-rated movie.

"Back, you infernal beast!" the weird man shouted. "Return to wherever the girl summoned you from."

"Shaman Mytrov, Vala could not have done this!" the other dwarf said. In contrast to his companion, he wore extremely bland colors.

"She has," the wolf pelt wearer—Shaman Mytrov—shouted. "The proof is right in front of us, Viktor. Whether this beast is an illusion or one of her thralls matters not. Back, creature!"

Galen had never been called an illusion before, and the last person who had called him a thrall was an evil reanimated skeleton so he wasn't exactly pleased to be called either of these things. He did what dragons did when they were annoyed—he turned to the shaman and roared.

His voice was so loud that it shook leaves from the trees. The street beneath their feet rumbled and Viktor clamped his hands over his ears at the sound. When the shaman stumbled back, he stepped on the tail of the wolf pelt he wore and landed in an ungainly heap.

The young dragon smirked. "How's that for an illusion?"

While the two men stared at him in shock, he turned to the girl. One of the dwarves had called her Vala, he remembered.

"Are you all right?"

"I'm fine, yes." She seemed somewhat overwhelmed to have a dragon suddenly appear in front of her, but she reacted with more poise than either of the men had. Rather than fear or panic, she looked at him with something in her eyes that he couldn't quite place. Expectation? Hope? He wished he could read her aura. As it was, he could not tell if she wanted him to poof into nothingness or set the two bullies on fire.

When Galen had swooped down, he had not thought any further than stopping these dwarves from yelling at her in the street. He had no plan other than to disrupt what was happening but now, that seemed painfully shortsighted.

If he simply flew away, these two would continue to harass her. The weirdly dressed one might even assume that he truly was an illusion. He had never met a dwarf before but he had been in fights with dragons who could create illusions. They could also make sounds as often as they could make things appear.

Not at all sure if it was the right thing to do but not seeing any other option, he lowered a shoulder toward the girl.

"Vala, right?"

"Vala Gagnon, yes. And you are…"

"Galen Stormwing, at your service. Do you want a ride out of here?" he asked.

She bit her lip and looked at the two dwarves, although her attention seemed more focused on the plainly dressed one who attempted to untangle the shaman from his furs. After a long moment in which she seemed to consider something he assumed was relevant to her circumstances, she made her decision.

"Yes, that would be appreciated, thank you."

CHAPTER TWELVE

Vala had firmly believed that the decision to attend school to become an electrical engineer would be the most monumental of her life. She still remembered when she had finally worked up the courage to talk to her father about it. Her mother was already on board by that time, of course, and had been for a while, but her father had yet to know that she wanted to be something besides a woodsman.

The crazy thing was that she wasn't even sure she wanted to be an electrical engineer. She knew she liked machines, but what she liked most about them was thinking of the energy they had and the way they made themselves more than things to people. When she had spoken to her father, she had compared her interest in machines and their beauty and personalities in terms he would understand. She had spoken of trees and the timber hidden within, of cabinetry and how she had the support she needed to become a support beam for her community.

He had been horrified—although he might have been more horrified to learn that barely a year later, she was doodling in those classes more often than not. She certainly hadn't considered the possibility that she would surprise him again as much as she had that day.

Which meant that climbing onto the back of a dragon was a huge steppingstone in Vala's life. It felt bigger to her, and when she saw her dad's expression of horror, she knew that it felt bigger to him too.

But what else could she do? Let the shaman take her and allow this dragon to vanish as quickly as he had appeared?

No. He had arrived unexpectedly and she would take his help.

Still, when she approached and stepped onto his arm, her heart began to race with the confirmation that he was not an illusion. She had no reason to think she could create illusions, of course, but nothing about this day had made sense. It seemed entirely plausible to throw in a few more insane magic powers she had no knowledge of.

"Hold on," he said.

"To wh-aaaat?" Vala exclaimed as he launched upward, then pumped his wings and took them higher into the night sky.

For the first few moments, she was struck dumb as they ascended, propelled by the dragon's huge wings. It was like riding a living rocket. She could feel his muscles working in concert to take them higher into the heavens.

"Are you all right?"

"Wooohooo hooo hoo hoo!" she shouted in what was inarguably a less than elegant way to express herself.

Galen leveled out and her stomach—no longer pushed against the back of her spine—hopped into her throat. For only a moment, she was weightless.

In that moment, her excitement transformed into terror. She was appalled by what she had done. A random dragon had appeared in the middle of her town and offered her a ride and she had accepted. What was she thinking?

Dragons were not very common in Canada. One being up there, alone at night and looking for young, confused dwarf girls could not be a good sign. What if he tried to eat her? What if he incinerated her? Well, her dwarf skin should protect her against that. But still, what if he merely dumped her off his back so she could tumble to the Earth below?

Vala peeked over the side of the dragon and saw how far that was. Already, her town was nothing but motes of light and she felt closer to the stars than she did to the town she lived in.

"Are you nervous?" he asked.

The girl panicked and wondered if he could read her thoughts. She had been taught that dragons could read other beings' thoughts, or was it their emotions? It seemed important to know the difference. She thought that dwarves were supposed to be immune to such powers, but she had also thought that—as a rule—they were not typically picked up by dragons in the middle of an argument with the local shaman. Maybe this one was special, had sensed what she was, and had come for her. The girl wondered crazily if she should have gone with Shaman Mytrov after all.

"Vala?"

Oh. Right. He had asked her a question.

"Why do you ask?" She knew it was a wild thought, but maybe the dragon would reveal how he had been able to penetrate her dwarf defenses. Maybe it was as Shaman Mytrov said and she was already becoming less of a dwarf.

"I ask because you're gripping my scales tightly enough that they feel like they're about to pop off," the dragon answered, his tone both friendly and a little pained.

"Sorry!" She let go immediately—she knew from Trevor the tinkerer letting her touch some of his devices that the average dwarf grip was something above and beyond other people's. In the next moment, the wind caught her and she was almost ripped off the dragon's back.

She screamed and grasped the scales so firmly that she did indeed feel one of them crush in her grip.

"Youch!" he blurted.

That helped her to calm somewhat. Surely a serial-killer dwarf-eating dragon wouldn't say youch, right?

Vala selected a different, uncrushed scale, and was much more careful with her hold this time. As if to prove that he did not want her to tumble off his back and fall to her death so he could eat her, he slowed.

"Is that better?" The dragon—he had a name, she reminded herself, and it was Galen—asked.

"Yes, thank you," the girl responded.

"Did you know those guys?" he asked as he banked slightly. She could still see the lights of her town below. He seemed to be flying around the settlement in a wide circle. She decided that was another indication that he did not want to eat her. Surely, if her flesh was what he wanted, he would take her to some cavern stuffed with gold coins and jewels.

"One of them was my father and the other my shaman."

"Oh…uh, sorry. Were they trying to hurt you?" Galen asked. "I have crappy parents so I…uh…I get that family isn't always best."

Okay, so it seemed more likely that he was a runaway rather than a serial killer. Well, that was good. She was a runaway too now, except she didn't want to be.

"No. Yes? I don't know. They think something's wrong with me. Shaman Mytrov especially. They want to fix it."

"Is there something wrong with you?" he asked.

"Yes? No. I don't know! I…can you take me back down there?"

"Are you sure?" He sounded concerned.

Vala wasn't sure at all about anything that had happened today, but she knew she didn't want to run away. Her mom would be devastated and her dad…well, he could be a real moron but that didn't mean he didn't have her well-being at heart.

"Yeah. Our town's big enough that if you put me down in Wallace Park, I should be able to walk home without running into Mytrov."

"Sure," he agreed. "We'll go down now. Are you ready?"

She squeezed her legs a little tighter against his body and tried to not crack another of his scales, although the one she had shattered had already regrown. While she still felt bad that it had been damaged, she decided she wouldn't chide herself too much for it.

They descended toward the city. Blobs of light resolved themselves into over-lit parking lots or shopping centers. Streets appeared, then roofs and treetops. It truly was amazing to be up there, she thought.

"There's the park," Vala said and pointed out a dark-green patch nestled not too far from where she went to college.

The dragon coasted in, landed with only a small jolt, and lowered a shoulder for her to get off.

"I didn't mean to freak you out or anything," he said apologetically, which made her feel somewhat guilty for thinking he'd planned to eat her.

"Today's been a freaky day, so no worries," she said, climbed down, and stretched her legs which were both numb and exhausted from riding on his back.

"Yeah, what was going on back there?" he asked, except he was no longer a dragon but instead, a rather handsome young man. In a blink, mist had poured from his dragon form, enshrouded him, and vanished to leave a kid with stormy eyes who held what appeared to be a sword made of black stone.

I have magic. I'm the first dwarf with magic—maybe the only dwarf with magic, Vala wanted to blurt but she didn't. At this point in this disgustingly long day, she was all but convinced that she did have magic but had no idea what that meant.

Was she an abomination as Shaman Mytrov had claimed, a herald to the end of dwarf kind? If so, would this dragon share the beliefs of the shaman? Dwarves had been created a few centuries earlier but dragons had been around for millennia. It seemed likely that if there was any truth to what the shaman had said about her, the dragons would know it too.

So rather than explaining herself, Vala said something that might turn her only ally against her. "It's not their fault. They think I'll bring about the end of dwarf kind."

CHAPTER THIRTEEN

Shaman Mytrov looked at the most trusted members of his congregation. They understood the teachings of the Church of Dwarfish Origins as much as anyone in town did, unlike Viktor Gagnon who clung to his sermons without question.

The six dwarves seated on the benches of the seventh branch of the church were all dressed like Viktor had been in bland colors made of rough-spun cloth. They would never be seen using a cellphone in public, nor would they invite other dwarves to watch television—even if they did have a set tucked away somewhere inside their homes.

Each of them had been part of Mytrov's reason to get a phone. Some of these dwarves understood electricity as well as humans did and knew it was a power made of tools and machines, not magic. That understanding allowed them to use other, even more useful tools—like trucks and guns.

The religious leader hoped it would not come to that.

"Brothers of the Earth, you're probably wondering why I called you here today."

The six dwarves all quieted and turned their full attention to him—except for Roy, who never did anything quietly.

"I assume it has something to do with the toaster I saw hopping past my house earlier?"

No one reacted to this, which meant it was what they had all been discussing. That made sense to Mytrov, though. Despite Roy's zealous beliefs in the teachings of the church, he lived near the college in town. He must have seen some of the chaos when the girl had passed by.

"Indeed it does," he said. He had taken the time to reapply the charcoal streaks to his face so he knew his words would carry the weight that he needed them to.

"Now that's what I like to hear." Roy pushed the palm of one hand with his fist. "We've tolerated that filthy mage Trevor Miller for far too long. I, for one, think it's high time we show this town what it means to keep magic away from dwarves."

Shouts of, "Hear, hear!" and "It's 'bout time!" echoed off the timber roof and stone walls of the church.

Mytrov let them calm rather than calling for silence. He understood how power worked—hard and soft. It would not do for a shaman of the church to yell at his most trusted members.

"Brothers, there is a crisis even more dire than Miller's trinkets shop facing us—and indeed, all of dwarf kind."

He let that settle over them for a minute. The mage was a common target in his sermons. If this was worse than the immigrant magic-user working to destroy their economy and steal their gold, it must be bad indeed.

"You have helped to bring this church into the twenty-first century and have all helped your father see that what the humans do with electricity and gasoline are not the threat to our way of life like I had first thought. More importantly, you have all helped me to stay focused on the threat that was prophesied so long ago. Brothers, the time has finally come. We are being tested and I call on you in this moment of crisis."

"By the prophecy...you don't mean..."

"A dwarf has been seduced by magic. It has taken hold in her person. We knew this day would come, although I never thought it would happen now, nor in our town. We have been called upon to act and we. Will. Act.

"Viktor Gagnon—may the Earth bless where he walks—is being tested, brothers. His daughter Vala came to this holy place less than an hour ago. She was delirious, unable to think clearly, and not willing to see what she was inflicting on our people. Worse, she used magic to attack me."

Most of the dwarves paled. Roy cursed. All of them pulled their beards.

Mytrov could see he had them in the palm of his hand. Lately, he had not always touched his congregation with the full impact of his sermons. His faith had never shaken but he had struggled to express it fully to his congregation. But with a threat to unite them—a threat that he had preached about time and again—their eyes lit with the fervor of true believers. It felt right to have his congregation look at him like this. In fact, it felt wonderful.

"She left here crazed beyond reason. I was unable to stop her and did not wish to. Instead, I followed her to the edge of these hallowed grounds and recommended pieces of scripture to her father, and the girl used power I did not know even mages could wield."

He paused and as expected, Roy was unable to stay silent. "Did she hurt you, Father? Is it as you said? If a dwarf has magic, does that mean that the rest of us will lose our natural resistance to it?"

The other brothers muttered darkly at this, as well they should. Dwarfish resistance to magic, both of the mage and dragon varieties, was what kept Canada independent. If they could no longer resist, even small communities like theirs would have to go to the Steel Guard to settle their disputes with outsiders. Dwarves did not like magic, but they liked dragons even less. Which meant that what Shaman Mytrov said next would hopefully go off like the bombshell he intended it to be.

"Vala Gagnon, daughter of one of our own—a girl who was blessed with the dust of this very church on her name day— summoned a dragon to attack me."

The revelation didn't only send Roy into a titter. All six of the brothers began to shout and yelled questions over each other, demanding answers.

"I know, brothers, I know. It's a nightmare unlike any I have ever imagined," he said piously.

"How can you be sure the dragon is under the girl's control?" Roy countered.

Mytrov had assumed that the dragon had come because Vala had summoned it, but maybe Roy was right and there was more afoot than that. Was it possible that this was not the work of the prophecy at all but the work of the dragons?

"I'm not so sure that she is controlling the beast," he said, but his tone indicated that he was, in fact, quite certain about what was happening. "I know that when I was on the cusp of convincing her father to come here with me to pray, the dragon touched down but—as I said—no dwarf has ever been able to do such a thing. Controlling the minds of others is dragon's magic, and I fear that's what we're up against."

He drew a deep breath and went on. "Vala has manifested the ability to control magic, but the dragons are most certainly responsible for its occurrence." He was thinking on his feet now but it made a certain kind of sense. Where else had the dragon come from? "I don't know their relationship—if she was able to summon the dragon, or if he has simply watched over her and knew when to swoop in. Either way, he is how we will find her. She climbed on his back and abandoned her poor father in the street. We must find her, break her free from the dragon's hold over her, and cleanse her of her magic."

"But how?" one of the dwarves asked.

This was where everything became tricky. Shaman Mytrov did not have an answer for that. Nothing like this had ever happened and there was therefore no precedent. But that did not matter, not yet. First, they had to defeat the dragon and rescue the girl. "There's a ritual written about it in some of the first dwarf manuscripts. We will use it to free the girl of whatever the dragon has done to her."

The religious leader almost jumped through the ceiling when a phone rang. For a moment, he thought the girl had returned and summoned the red telephone to finish him, but one of the dwarves pulled a cell phone out of his pocket.

"Father, forgive me. I know the rules on phones," Gautier said. He was the most progressive of them all when it came to technology. "But my wife says her best friend's girlfriend's son posted a picture on social media of a dragon in Wallace Park."

"Then that's where we're headed, brothers," he said.

No cheer rose and no great battle cry rang out. These dwarves knew that this was not a war but an attempt to poison their culture. The dragons had long since agitated at their southern border and trespassed on their lands to apprehend mages or runaway dragons who had claimed asylum. No real dwarves loved mages.

Magic and dwarfhood simply clashed too much to make it possible, but there was not a dwarf alive who did not recognize the dragons as the power-hungry threat they were. There were those who thought the Steel Dragon and her Steel Guard were somehow better, but he and his congregation were not among them. A dragon in their town was not a good thing, and that it arrived on the same day that a dwarf had manifested magic did not bode well at all.

It was a stoic group that went outside and clambered into two pickup trucks. Shaman Mytrov normally asked his congregation to walk to church—their town wasn't huge with forty thousand souls at the most—but he was glad these dwarves had been able to look at the world around them and learn how to control these vehicles.

They were certainly impressive. Each had a flatbed in the back loaded with tools for mining or felling trees, as well as crates secured there and filled with items he had said might come in useful.

Mytrov climbed in the front of one of the trucks next to Roy. Two dwarves climbed into the bed behind them. Gautier drove the other truck and sat in the cab alone. The other two climbed into the back, where the tools they brought would be within easy reach.

The shaman had been in a truck before but not enough times for it to feel at all natural to him. He marveled at how quickly the vehicles could travel and how they could compress a walk that would have taken forty-five minutes into a fraction of that time. Sometimes, he felt foolish for preaching against these machines. If he had been a little more accepting of these human tools, perhaps they would not be in this mess at all. That would change after this. Now that he was faced with a true threat to dwarf kind, he would not shirk his duties.

"Let's go dark," Roy said into a kind of talk box mounted to the roof of the cab of the truck and in the next moment, the light shining out of the front turned off. Mytrov could see Wallace Park ahead. It was not lit by electric lights—something he had demanded that the city avoid doing—but under the light of the half-moon, he could see two figures in the center of the park.

The lights from Gautier's truck extinguished as well so when the two trucks turned, their headlights did not cut across the field ahead and reveal their presence.

They climbed out, careful to close the doors quietly behind them.

"What's the plan?" Roy whispered.

"I thought there was a dragon," one of the dwarves muttered.

"Oh, that's a dragon," Gautier said. "Look at his clothes and the way he holds himself."

The others nodded in agreement. All dwarves could detect a

dragon in human form, or at least, all those in Mytrov's congregation could. He often pointed out the techniques in his sermons so his congregation could make judgments without having to engage in talking to the intruder.

"What do you think that staff he has is?" another dwarf asked.

"Do you think that's how the dragon is controlling Vala?" Roy suggested.

"It must be," Mytrov said and seized the explanation. He had never seen anything like the black, slightly curved staff the boy held. It appeared to be made of stone and worked to an exquisite level of craftsmanship. He shuddered when he considered that it almost looked as if it had been grown.

"Stonework is the realm of dwarves," he said. "The dragon must be using that to control Vala."

"Is it too late, then?" Roy asked. "Because I brought what you asked for. I have it in the truck."

"Perhaps not yet," he whispered in return. "If we discover how his instrument works, perhaps we can use it to undo what's been done. Wait here. I will approach and try to listen."

His companions nodded and he crept forward. There were often deer in Wallace Park and indeed throughout much of the town, so his antlers would help to hide him in plain sight. He moved forward furtively until he could hear snatches of the conversation.

He heard the boy speaking first.

"How can you bring about the end of the dwarves?"

"I won't do it alone," Vala replied. "It will spread through my kind."

"It doesn't have to," the boy said and swung his staff—except it was not a staff. Now that Mytrov was closer, he could see it was a sword, one he had just used to show exactly what the dragons planned to do to the dwarf nation.

Satisfied that he had heard all he needed to hear, he retreated to the waiting dwarves.

"It's worse than I feared," he told the brothers. "The dragon plans to use the girl to exterminate all of us. She will be the fulcrum in the lever they use to steal our heritage and eradicate our people."

His cohorts looked furious at such a revelation. "What do you want us to do, Father?" Roy asked.

"It might be simplest to end them, but that might be rash," Mytrov said. "If the blade the dragon carries can be used to grant magic powers to dwarves, it can also be used to remove that power. That must be why he arrived when he did. He saw that his chess piece would be taken from him before he put his plan into place. If we can capture Vala and take that blade from the dragon, we can reverse the damage that's been done."

"So, we need to bring the girl in alive?" Gautier asked.

Mytrov nodded. For now, she needed to stay alive, at least until his theories could be tested.

"And what about the dragon?"

"If he won't release his instrument, we will do what we must to stop him," he said.

The dwarves all nodded and Roy moved to the truck to take something out of one of the crates.

The shaman considered telling him not to. After all, he was not completely sure about what was happening between Vala and this dragon but telling them to stop would reveal that he had doubts, which had no place in his religion or any other.

"Come. We will approach in the dark. When they see us, we will sing the hymn of purity and hope there is still enough of the girl's mind to see that we are on her side."

"And if there is not?" one of them asked.

"Roy has already prepared himself. I saw axes and hammers in the back of your trucks. Let us not face this dragon unarmed."

They armed themselves and together, with Mytrov at their head, they marched across the park toward the girl and the dragon.

CHAPTER FOURTEEN

Galen could tell something was wrong with Vala but not what it was. She had spent the last five minutes dancing around the topic.

"Okay…what did you mean when you said you believe you'll bring about the end of dwarf kind?" he asked.

"I don't believe that," she said hurriedly. "But some people do."

"Who? Why?" He tried to not get frustrated—after all, he had swooped in and interfered with her life—but it became more difficult with each moment.

"Them," Vala said and pointed across the park.

Even in his human form, his dragon eyes were able to easily recognize the shaman from the street. Not that it would have been hard even in fainter light. There could not be that many dwarves who walked around in a wolf pelt and antlers.

Behind him, the other six didn't wear animal pelts like the shaman but they weren't exactly threatening either. Four of them held their hands clasped chastely behind their back and the other two leaned on walking sticks that appeared to be reinforced to support their bulk. He had honestly begun to doubt his place in all this when the seven dwarves started to sing.

It was beautiful, a kind of choral chanting that was unusual in that the voices were all so deep. The harmonies were unlike anything the dragon had ever heard and made him think of heavy stone hearths, of crackling fires on cold days, of family, and of warmth and safety. It seemed unlikely that this church choir would do anything except pray for the girl.

"Vala, I need you to tell me exactly what you did."

"I didn't do anything!"

"Did you steal something? Or maybe you simply borrowed it? Not that I'm judging, but I need to understand what's going on here."

"I can do magic!"

That surprised Galen. He had believed that magic and dwarves did not mix, but growing up in Stormsiege had not exactly been illuminating about the lives of the other races.

"But that's…awesome," he said.

"Not to them. Dwarves aren't supposed to simply get magic."

"This only now happened to you?" he asked.

"It has been a crazy day," she exclaimed. "I wish it had never happened."

"Don't say that," he said. The dwarves continued to sing as they approached slowly. "I've seen dragons acquire new powers. In fact, it has happened to me. It's weird and honestly, it can turn out bad but most of the time I think, it's a real blessing."

"Not for dwarves, it's not."

"Well, why not? I went to a school where dragons acquired pixie powers and mages acquired dragon powers. A dwarf acquiring magic makes sense. I bet the headmaster would love it if you went to the Lumos School. You'd be the first dwarf there —ever."

"Yeah, well, dwarves don't feel that way," Vala said. The others were already halfway across the field and continued to move closer. "Most dwarves are proud of their anti-magic-ness. It's a point of cultural pride—part of our identity, and the reason we're independent from dragon and now mage rule."

"Things change, though. The Steel Dragon proved that."

"Not to them, it doesn't. Shaman Mytrov...he thinks me having magic is a virus or something and that it will run through dwarves. He wants to... I don't know exactly...perform some kind of ritual on me to cleanse me."

"It doesn't sound too bad."

"If it were merely some holy dust, I might be obliged to agree, but I got the sense that if the ritual didn't work, there would be other more lethal ways to solve the problem I have unwittingly become." Vala extended her arms so she could point at herself in a kind of curtsy. It might have been a cute gesture had it not been intended to indicate that she might be murdered.

But she must surely have jumped to conclusions. Not everyone was as bad as Galen's parents. They couldn't be. There wouldn't be any children left if that were the case.

"He said he would kill you?" the young dragon tried to confirm.

"Well, no, not exactly, not in front of my dad, but I very much got the sense he wouldn't hesitate if it was the only way to get rid of my magic. That was why I tried to get away from him and would very much like to get away from them again if you would be so kind?"

He couldn't make himself believe her. His mother had directly threatened his life and had given him three days to live. Period. Did these singing dwarves truly present such a threat? He did not think so.

While he knew his family was terrible, the majority of other dragons and mages he had met were excited about a more egalitarian future. Surely these dwarves were more like the dragons at the Lumos School than his bigoted parents? Galen knew that cross-species relationships were possible. He knew that if the world found out about Vala, she would be seen by many as a sign that things were changing and like Kylara Diamantine, Tanya, and the Steel Dragon herself, Vala would become a symbol for progress.

Someone merely had to make that clear to these dwarves.

"I need to talk to them," he said. "Tell them about the world outside this town and what you can represent out there."

"They're not interested in the world outside this town," Vala argued.

"Oh, yeah? Have you asked them?"

"Well, no. Honestly, I try to skip church with my mom as much as I can, but I'm telling you. A dwarf with magic is anathema to these guys."

"Then you can't even be certain," Galen said and tried to soothe her with his aura before he remembered that it had no effect on her. "Come on. Let's tell them about the Lumos School and explain that there's a place where you can learn to master this power."

"I don't think that's a good idea," she said but she followed him as he strode toward the seven dwarves.

CHAPTER FIFTEEN

"Hello! Shaman Mytrov, right? I'm Galen Stormwing," the young dragon said as he walked toward the dwarves and waved as cheerfully as he could. Despite knowing that they could not feel his aura, he tried to use it to cheer them up all the same. At the very least, it would make him feel better. "It seems like there's been a misunderstanding."

"Is that right, dragon?" the shaman replied and stopped a good twenty feet away from him. The other dwarves continued to hum as they approached and fanned out around their leader.

"You can call me Galen."

"Is that what you'll make me call you once you stab me with that magic staff of yours?" Mytrov grumbled.

"This?" He had almost forgotten that he was holding the Prairie King's claw. "This isn't magic. It's more of..." A weapon that could be used to stab someone from his family if they decided to come after him did not seem like a wise thing to say. He went with a far more enigmatic response instead. "An insurance policy. And it's not magic."

"It looks like a weapon, dragon."

Galen glanced at the other dwarves who had ceased their

approach once they formed a loose ring around him and Vala. He could see that those who had their hands clasped behind their back were, in fact, holding what appeared to be woodworking tools, and the two with heavy walking sticks were carrying massive sledgehammers. They had held them by the head of the tool so it had not been clear from afar.

"I can put it down if you tell your dwarves to put their tools down. Hammers and axes could be misconstrued as weapons, too."

"We're in dwarf country, dragon. We don't take orders from you."

"Let's go, Galen," Vala whispered.

"No. He's right. We are in dwarf country." He extended the claw, wedged the tip of it in the soil, and raised both his hands to show he was unarmed. "I only want to talk. There's a school for people like Vala. They can teach her how to use her magic."

"So this is how it's done, eh?" one of the other dwarves snapped. "You infect one of our children, then whisk them away to turn them to your side."

"Infect? No. I never met Vala before today."

"Your lies won't work on us, dragon," Mytrov said. "We know you dragons have long had your sights set on our territory. The Steel Dragon's Revolution merely gave you all a different excuse to take this land from us."

"No one wants this land." Galen snorted. "I only want to help Vala."

"Help her undermine the dwarf race!" the shaman shouted. "Admit it. That's your goal. You're part of the dragon conspiracy to undermine the dwarf race with magic. You'll weaken our bloodlines and then, whether in a year, or five, or ten, the dwarf race will be gone."

"What? No. There's no dragon conspiracy against dwarves." He felt reasonably confident that this was true. If there were some kind of push to enslave or destroy the dwarves, he was fairly certain his mother would want a piece of that genocidal action and he would have heard about it.

"Like you'd admit it," the other loud-mouthed dwarf said.

"We aren't here to make a compromise with a trespasser on our land who arrived on the very same day that one of ours became cursed with magic. We're here to help the girl. If you can…fix her with that sword of yours, you will do so now. Then you will leave and stop mucking about with dwarf lives." As Shaman Mytrov spoke, his voice swelled to an intimidating cadence. He was a leader in this community, the young dragon realized, accustomed to getting his way with only his words.

Galen could not help but feel that the right words were all that was needed to fix this, but they eluded him. "I want to help Vala too. I understand that her having magic is weird. One of my friends is a mage who can turn into a dragon or a pixie, so believe me, I know how confusing all this can be."

"We're not listening to a damn thing you say, lizard," the loud dwarf shouted.

The dragon knew there was a time where humans would have been killed for calling a dragon such a thing. His mother was still living in that time, or at least she tried to pretend like she was. But he did not want to be like his family. He honestly wanted to help.

"If you truly feel that way, I can take Vala away from here and you won't have to see her again. She can learn to control her powers at the Lumos School and your community can be safe from this magic virus or whatever." He rolled his eyes at the whole idea.

But Shaman Mytrov decided to take the sarcastic comment literally. "I knew it! You did infect her. Well, she's one of ours, dragon, and we won't let you steal her away to poison her against us. Brothers, for the Earth."

Vala yelped as two of the dwarves who had positioned themselves behind the dragon caught hold of her.

"No, please!" she screamed before one of them clamped a rag over her mouth.

"Let her go!" Galen demanded and lunged toward the two who held her by her arms.

He only made it halfway before a sledgehammer struck him in the chest, cracked a rib, and thrust the air from his lungs.

The young dragon landed hard on his back and tried to suck a breath in but was unable to. He couldn't breathe and felt like his lung had collapsed.

But he was still a dragon.

His healing power forced his lung to inflate and he dragged in a ragged breath. He rolled onto his chest.

The shaman was following the two dwarves who now hauled the unwilling Vala through the park. He muttered over her body as if he intended to exorcise a demon.

The other four dwarves—two armed with hammers, and two with axes—stood shoulder to shoulder between Galen and those who dragged her away.

Any doubts about whose side he should be on vanished in that moment. Where before, he had wondered how she had run afoul of these dwarves, what he saw now made it clear. They were zealots, freaks so blinded by their beliefs that they were willing to kidnap an unarmed girl simply because she had done something that hundreds of thousands had already done.

"Stay down, lizard," the loud-mouthed dwarf said. One of the others had given him one of the hammers.

"Let me pass," he said and pushed to his feet.

"Fat chance."

"You don't know who you're dealing with." He called on the power within him that he had possessed since he'd been born and that had been returned to him—the power of a dragon.

It did not come when he called it.

Having the wind knocked out of him and cracking a rib had

cost him more magic than he had realized. He didn't have the energy to transform instantly into a dragon.

Too bad he had already committed to attacking the dwarves.

He adjusted a split second before another hammer struck his chest and it caught him in the shoulder instead. The dwarf had put enough force behind the blow that he spun three times before he fell again.

"Like I said, stay down," the loudmouth with the hammer said and took a step forward.

Galen ignored him and scrambled to his feet.

His adversary grinned and swung with his hand ax. The boy dodged the first blow and the second, but his opponent was surprisingly fast. Galen barely managed to raise his forearm to stop the ax from striking him in the face.

Pain seared through the limb when the weapon pounded into it. Although it stopped at the bone, that was still a fair amount of flesh for it to cut through. He knew his dragon healing powers would handle it and rather than worry, he swung his foot to deliver a solid kick on the dwarf's chest. Even with it being augmented with dragon strength, it was not enough to knock his adversary over.

Instead, he stumbled back and the dwarf grinned.

"Get 'im, boys," he said.

They attacked together. Galen dodged the first two hammer blows and paid for it with the tip of an ax that sliced a gash across his chest. He dodged the next ax blow and was struck in the thigh by a hammer.

He stumbled and the other hammer struck him squarely in the chest and hurled him back. His head cracked against something and blood clouded his vision.

The dragon wiped blood from his face with one hand as his other felt for what he had collided with.

It was the claw of the Prairie King.

Galen yanked it free from where he had stabbed it into the

ground and managed to bring it in front of him before an ax blow caught him in the face.

The grunt of another dwarf alerted him to an approaching sledgehammer. He spun and managed to position the claw between him and the weapon. Part of him thought it would be the last defensive use of it—surely a sledgehammer could crack a dragon claw—but he was reminded that this was not normal dragon bone. The Prairie King's claw was practically indestructible. It had even been able to puncture Kylara's diamond scales.

The steel head of the sledgehammer stood no chance. He had turned the sharp edge of the claw toward it so when it struck with enough force to kill a dragon, it was simply cleaved in two.

The eyes of the dwarf who had been wielding it widened as he pulled the wooden handle back.

The other three dwarves gave no quarter, however. They surged into an attack and he was forced to whip the claw-turned-sword to every side to block their blows.

But Galen was no swordsman. Slicing the head of the hammer in half demonstrated what the sword might be capable of in more competent hands, but he was not able to replicate the blow again. It took everything he had to put any part of the claw between himself and his assailants. He did not have the skill to perfectly position the single cutting edge of the blade in the opposite direction of the vector of the attacking weapon. It meant he could block but not disarm as spectacularly as he had with his initial attempt.

Although, if he was honest, he didn't do a very good job of blocking either.

The remaining hammer swung past his defense, pushed him back, and ruined his stance.

An ax hit struck his back next which, quite frankly, hurt like hell.

Galen tried to stay on his feet and to keep moving. More than anything, he tried to keep the blade between him and his attackers.

The dwarves were better with their weapons than he was, but they were tiring. They had likely been trained to fight dragons in their human forms, but dragons did not use swords to fight. Their swings were now punctuated by increasingly louder grunts. Maybe he could outlast them.

Hope flared for a moment until he heard the sound of a gunshot and pain erupted in his gut.

He collapsed and held his belly with one hand and the claw with the other as hot blood streamed between his fingers.

This was not enough to satisfy the dwarves. A hammer blow crushed the bones in one of his ankles, and the two dwarves with hand axes readied them. He did not need to read their auras to know they wished to dismember him.

Galen did not have to let them, though. He could become a dragon and give these wounds time to heal.

With his lifeblood draining through his fingers and his ankle a mess of broken bones, he told his healing power to stop and he called on the magic that would let him transform into a dragon.

Mist poured from his mouth, his nostrils, and his wounds. It was the mist of a Stormwing transforming that he had not been able to summon when he'd been trapped as a mongrel. He had gained it again when he returned to the pixie realm with his friends and fought to reclaim it.

This was all lost on the dwarves, who plunged into it and began to hack and batter him with abandon.

CHAPTER SIXTEEN

As Galen's body took its dragon form, the dwarves continued to pummel him. Normally, he felt his power multiply when he did this but now, he only felt pain. He was not even sure he could complete his transformation. If he lost too much blood, he would pass out and given the condition of his powers, he would revert to his human form. He did not doubt that if that happened, the dwarves would murder him and his family would be happy to have a loose end snipped off so neatly. Or maybe they would try to burn this town to the ground in retribution. Some of his relatives would probably enjoy that.

Neither option sounded great to him.

He had already been so tired and now, he had to transform. While he hated to admit it even to himself, he did not know if he could do it or if he had the energy. But when he heard Vala scream, he knew he had to try. When Kylara had fought Boneclaw inside a bubble in the void, she had not given up. When Tanya had seen dragon skeletons attacking him, she had not given up.

The girl needed him and he would not give up.

With a labored roar, Galen completed his transformation. He

pushed against the earth, spread his wings, and whipped his tail so sharply it cracked. The movement would have been enough to hurl humans in every direction but it barely pushed the dwarves back. Only one of them fell, and it was more like a toddler landing on their bottom than them catapulting away, which was what he had hoped for. Dwarves had been built to face dragons, after all. It made sense that he couldn't simply knock them aside, even if it was frustrating.

"So you finally show your true colors, eh?" the loudmouth dwarf shouted before he brought a pistol to bear on him.

The dragon had no idea if the bullet would hurt him as badly as the first one had. It could be that he had only been injured because he was in his human form and not as strong as he had once been. But it was also quite possible that the dwarf had bullets made of dragon bone, in which case a single shot would rip through his dragon form as easily as it had his human one.

Even in this body, Galen's gut still ached from that wound. He could not afford another one.

Instinctively, he lashed out at his adversary with his tail and was quite pleased to see the claw of the Prairie King had become a barb at its tip. It sliced through the gun and severed the barrel from the grip to leave a look of surprise and horror on the wielder's face.

"Get 'im!" the dwarf shouted.

His three cohorts obeyed. The one with the hammer raised his weapon and raced toward the same foot whose ankle he had already crushed. In this form, the ankle still hurt and he was not about to let the dwarf hit him again. He swung his tail at the dwarf's chest with all his strength.

The blow landed squarely and his attacker hurtled away. He sighed with relief when the dwarf slammed into a tree, although his sense of victory dissipated when he simply found his feet and began to run into the battle again.

Pain brought Galen's attention to one of his front toes. A

dwarf was attempting to give him the world's most painful pedicure. He yanked his claw back and punched him. While he didn't go airborne like the other had, he tumbled end over end in a quite satisfying way. Again, when he stopped, he simply stood to rejoin the fray.

These dwarves truly were as sturdy as their reputations made them out to be.

Not sure what else to try, he knocked the other ax-wielder back and struck the loud-mouthed lout with his tail for good measure, but none of his blows inflicted any serious damage. The dwarves simply recovered almost instantly and resumed their attacks. It was like playing whack-a-mole, and he knew he didn't have the strength to keep playing all day any more than most kids had the quarters to.

"Galen!" Vala shouted.

The dragon looked over the short-statured dwarves with his long dragon neck and saw that the other three had dragged her almost to the trucks.

Galen did not know this area well, his gut hurt like hell, and he would have even less time in his dragon form thanks to his injuries. If they got her in the back of the truck, there was a very real possibility that they would get away.

Despite the predicament he was in, he was not about to let that happen.

He flapped his wings and managed to haul himself into the air but it wasn't easy. His ankle still hurt so he was not able to leap like he normally did. Plus, one of the strangely dense dwarves had grasped his tail.

Irritated now, he flapped a few times but was not able to shake his unwelcome passenger.

Thankfully, he remembered that he still had an insanely sharp barb at the tip of his tail. Rather than trying to knock his determined opponent loose, he twitched his tail and sliced his arm.

"The cursed dragon's got a stinger!" the dwarf shouted, stumbled back, and clutched his bloody arm.

That was enough separation for the dragon to get airborne. He pumped his wings and managed to get clear of the dwarves' reach. Even with their short height, that was not easy. His gut still hurt considerably. It was a painful lesson in anatomy. He had never realized how much a dragon used its core strength in flight and wondered why no one had ever mentioned it.

Still, he was clear. He pumped his wings through the pain until he was above the three dwarves who attempted to drag Vala away and let himself plunge earthward.

He pounded into the four of them and knocked the girl and her kidnappers over. He might have been concerned as the force of the impact could have crushed a human, but he had already learned a thing or two about dwarf resilience. Sure enough, she was fine and immediately scrambled to her feet.

"Get on my back!" he shouted.

She hesitated.

That gave the two dwarves who had held her captive time to run to the back of one of the trucks, where more tools awaited.

"Let's go!" he shouted again when one of them grabbed a pickax.

"You have no place here!" the shaman shouted.

The dragon upended him with his tail and was quite pleased to see that although the dwarf was not injured, he had at least broken the stupid antlers he wore on his head.

"He's not only talking to me, you know," he shouted at Vala.

The girl nodded, wiped a tear from her cheek, and climbed onto his back.

It took a tremendous amount of effort to get airborne again, but he managed. He spread his wings, coasted down the street, and glided between tall pine trees.

The dwarves wasted no time and scrambled into their trucks. Engines churned to life, tires squealed, and they gave chase.

"Can't you go any faster?" Vala asked.

"Not with you on my back and this wound in my gut." Galen grunted.

The vehicles were gaining.

"We can't outrun them!" she shrieked, terrified.

"We don't need to," he responded as the curtain of pine trees opened on the side of the road to reveal a body of water somewhere between a huge pond and a tiny lake.

He banked and flew out over the water.

The trucks screeched to a stop at the water's edge, unable to continue their pursuit. The harsh calls sent after them wafted over the water, music to his ears.

CHAPTER SEVENTEEN

The world raced past Vala and telephone wires, streetlights, and hundreds of branches all threatened to knock her off the back of a dragon—*a dragon!*—she could barely hold onto. Behind them, the curses of dwarves and the screech of their tires on the road grew louder as they gained on her. It seemed as if the world itself tried to stop her, to knock her down, and force her earthward until Galen glided out over a pond. The world opened before her and she was free.

Below them, the placid surface reflected her looking down from his back. Her hair was a mess and she had some of his blood on her, but she wore a wide grin.

In the next moment, her grin broke and she was crying.

It was too much. Only this morning, she had thought the highlight of her day would be the pancakes her mom had cooked for breakfast. She choked on a harsh laugh at how absurd that had been and at the naïveté of the person she had been only hours before.

Since that very ordinary breakfast, she had used magic to ruin an exam, arguably traumatized a roomful of students, and had a huge argument with her parents. She had been tested for magic by a mage and had her father embarrass her in front of him. As if that wasn't bad enough, she had been taken to the church, yelled at by a shaman, and had definitely traumatized him with more magic.

Except, she reasoned, he could not have been all that traumatized by the jumping magical phone because he had been able to turn her father against her as he yelled at her on the street. Then a dragon—a fire breathing, flying, transforming dragon with claws, teeth, and a tail—had arrived but had unaccountably been on her side, and she had flown higher than any bird she had ever seen

All that would have been more than enough to make this the weirdest day in history, but she had then been attacked in the park by Shaman Mytrov and almost kidnapped. A fricking dragon had come to her rescue, but he was badly hurt and they'd almost been captured by trucks full of religious zealots—which she had thought was totally against the precepts of her father's religion. Now, they glided over this beautiful, pristine lake and the world was so quiet that it seemed like none of that could be real. But, she reminded herself, it had to be real because she was on the back of a dragon.

"So, is this your first time being driven into the wilderness by people you had only ever hoped to impress?" Galen asked as the wind whipped Vala's tears from her face into the lake beneath them. "Because I have to say, you're taking it very well."

"If you want to know the truth, I'm crying up here so no, I'm not taking it that well," she said.

"I realized you were crying. That's why I said something," he responded after a moment.

"Because you could feel my aura, right?" the girl asked.

"No. Dragons can't feel dwarf auras at all. I merely assumed you were crying because I've been where you've been."

"You have not been a dwarf who manifested magic despite her

dad belonging to a religion that says a dwarf developing magic would be the end of our kind."

Galen chuckled darkly. They had reached the end of the lake, so he pumped his wings to get up over the trees. It did not seem effortless and in fact, it felt as if he had to work a fair amount to gain only another few feet.

"I might not be a dwarf but I know what it's like to be expected to be a certain way and fail. I'm a Stormwing. I should be able to make hurricanes but I can't. I'm a runt. Then, when I gained the power to raise the dead, I threw it all away to impress a girl and her friends. Now, my family… Well, let's say that if I never see them again it will be too soon."

"You're that dragon? We heard about that up here. You brought some big bad dude back, right? Lord Boner?"

He laughed loudly at that, but it was not wise to do so. He was injured on one side and favored a wing, and the effort of laughing unbalanced him with a sudden jerk of pain.

"You're hurt. Is it bad?" Vala asked.

The dragon grunted. "I should be able to heal it but this form takes too much energy. I need to land and change into my human form. Some food and sleep wouldn't hurt either."

"Food, huh? Well, my parents always have something hot on the stove."

"I wouldn't want to impose."

"No, like, literally. There is always soup on the stove."

His stomach grumbled so loudly it almost knocked her loose from her perch on his back.

"But your dad…isn't he angry you're a mage?"

"Maybe? But he loves me and I trust him. He won't call Shaman Mytrov. We only now discovered that he had a phone. If they arrive, my mom will keep them out. They might know how to fight a dragon but she is a whole other nightmare."

"You don't think—you know what? Forget it. Let's go to your folks."

Vala nodded before she remembered that the person she was conversing with couldn't see her since he was a fricking dragon and she was riding on his back. "Do you see that clock tower? That's the university. My folks are only a couple of blocks north of there, more toward the outskirts of town. Can you make it that far?"

Galen grunted. "Yeah. I think so, but I hope we don't run into your church friends again."

He adjusted his course but didn't fly directly toward her parents, as that would take them across the brighter downtown area. She wondered if he was serious about being out in the wilderness. He seemed to have an instinct to avoid being seen although she couldn't imagine how anyone could see them out there in the night, away from the lights of the town.

"So. You truly are that kid who brought Lord Boner back?"

"Lord Boneclaw, yeah. That was me. My family wanted me to be the Necroboner Lord, I guess, and I said no. They never forgave me for giving that power up."

"Huh." Vala snorted. "You said we're the same but we're opposites. Your parents were mad that you lost a power. My parents are upset that I gained one."

"If you think your parents will keep you safe despite this mess you've caused, we truly are opposites," he said, which killed the conversation fairly effectively.

They continued in silence. Conflicting emotions of awe at flying and fear of what awaited her on the ground battled for dominance in her mind. The dragon seemed to have a similar struggle as he said nothing while they flew, although she wondered if that might simply be because he had been the recipient of the gunshot she had heard in the park.

She didn't know how wise it was, but she decided that she trusted him. He had saved her not once, but twice, and she did not know why he would have lied to her about the things he had said about his family. She felt like she had spent her entire life trying to understand how things worked, and here was someone who was willing to tell her exactly that.

Vala appreciated the honesty.

And then there was the fact that he knew more about magic than anyone she had ever met. Trevor Miller was a mage, but he was also quick to point out the limits of his power. Meanwhile, Galen had been able to summon skeletons. If her memory served, he had been able to summon a large number of them as well. Was that so different than what she had done with machines? Would he be able to help her control that ability, or if he couldn't, would he be able to help her get rid of it?

"That's my house." She pointed to one of the widely spaced houses on their dark street. Her father had never wanted to leave the forest for even a small town like this one. Her mom and he had agreed to it only after they found a piece of well-wooded property.

"There's a clearing a little way back from the house where my dad felled a big red cedar to make our house and furniture. You should be able to land there."

"I see it," he said, but his speech sounded heavier than before.

They flew over and around the clearing before he caught the wind and tried to put them down. He succeeded but it was a rough landing and although he didn't spill her from his back, it was only because he used a much smaller cedar than the one her father had logged to stop his momentum. The collision seemed to hurt him far more than it hurt the tree.

"Thank you so much," Vala said as soon as she had clambered off his back. "If you can change into your...uh, boy body, that might be better."

Galen nodded but he did not transform. "You're safe now so I will leave."

"No, Galen, you're hurt!"

"I'll be all right. I'll go catch a moose or something and I'll be fine."

"No. Absolutely not. You said you needed to change into your human form and get some food and rest. That's what we'll do. If you leave, I'll come with you."

"That can't happen. My family…well, they're not done with me. If they find you with me, they'll kill you without even wondering how we ended up together."

"You've risked your life to help me. I can't simply abandon you like this."

"I'm not giving you a choice," he said.

"Oh, really? I can see you're still limping on that ankle. Did you plan to jump into the air or would you make another weak lift-off like you did at the park? Because if that's all you can manage, I'm very sure I can hold your tail and keep you from going anywhere."

"You don't understand. These church guys want to cleanse you. My family wants me dead. They gave me three days, Vala. Three days to prove myself or die."

"And you said I was the lucky one? Shaman Mytrov didn't give me three minutes."

Galen snorted, which made him wince and clutch his side.

"Can you transform into the cute boy version and come inside and have some soup?"

"Fine," he said. "But then I'll leave."

"Have you ever been inside a custom-built dwarf house? We have about six spare bedrooms and you're crazy if you think my mom will let you leave before you get some sleep."

He drew a deep breath and sighed. "One night."

Vala was not about to let him run off simply so his family could murder him, but she knew that now was not the time to belabor the point. She simply muttered what he would assume was positive affirmation and waited for him to transform.

Mist poured from his nose and enshrouded him but before it could completely eclipse the dragon, it seemed to slow. Galen coughed harshly and some of it dissipated. He took a deep breath and managed to create more. This time, it enshrouded him completely and in the next moment, it was gone and the young man with stormy eyes was there again.

"Just for the record, you calling me cute has nothing to do with me saying yes."

"Oh, don't flatter yourself. Your naked cheeks make you look like a six-year-old."

"Wait—six-year-old dwarves grow beards?"

"Not in reality, no, but compared to you they do."

The dragon smirked and fell into step beside her. He did not look good and held his stomach tightly, and his shirt was a mess. Normally, dragons had a pristine appearance about them. Or, at least, that's what it said in the field guides. Vala had never met one but she had learned that because they could transform with their clothes, they could leave the dirt and grime behind. Or something. Dwarves did not understand dragons at all. They only knew how to recognize one if they arrived in their territory.

But she could use that. His coat didn't have any blood on it at all. Even his shirt was unstained, despite having a bullet hole in it. If he could hide that they should be all right.

"When we go inside, do you think you can keep your coat on?" she asked. "I'd rather not tell my mom you're a dragon straight away."

"It makes sense to me." He nodded and pulled his coat tighter.

"Okay, now don't take this the wrong way, but no one has perfectly tousled hair like that except for dragons. Here…" She picked up a pinecone, rubbed the sap all over her hands, and smeared it in Galen's hair. "That should do it. My mom will be happy that I brought a friend home from school."

Galen nodded, followed her around the house, and limped to the front door. Vala could smell soup from outside and that steeled her resolve to help him, even though her nerves all screamed to run into the woods and never look back.

CHAPTER EIGHTEEN

When the dragon flew out over the lake, Shaman Mytrov gave the order to return to the church. The energy was high in the two trucks. Roy and Gautier drove like maniacs and raced each other head-to-head while the dwarves in the beds jumped from one vehicle to the other. It might have been a dangerous thing for a human to do but for a dwarf, falling from a vehicle traveling fifty kilometers an hour wouldn't necessarily be a disaster. Their skin could resist dragon fire and their bones had proved to be strong enough to withstand a dragon knocking them around. The worst that would happen to them was road rash.

Shaman Mytrov let them have their fun. None of them had ever fought a dragon before and they had done well enough. They had emerged unscathed and Roy had returned to the car with some of the dragon's blood spattered on his hands. Still, they had ultimately failed to prevent the girl from escaping. He would let them have their moment of fun now so that he could end their glee once they were back in his domain.

"Should I park a few streets over like usual?" Roy asked as they neared the Seventh Branch of the Church of Dwarfish Origins.

"Our time of hiding from technology is over," the shaman replied. "Vala's curse has made it clear that we need to embrace everything we have available to combat the atrocity that is magic. You may park in front of the church."

"I guess the jig is up on that, huh?" Roy mused. "Half the town might have seen us driving around."

"Indeed," he agreed.

The other dwarf parked, looked uneasily at their leader, then climbed out of the car.

Mytrov said nothing. He walked into the church and took his place at the altar at the very center of the stone and timber structure.

"Please, be seated," he said to the six dwarves as they filed in.

They exchanged a few glances—they were still excited—but they held their tongues.

The shaman took his time and let the men stew in their thoughts as he removed the broken headdress. Beneath the wolf hood, his hair was tied in braids that were fastened with pieces of bone. He looked in the water in a bowl made of half of a massive geode and reapplied the dark lines beneath his eyes, then sucked the excess off, knowing some would get stuck in his teeth.

Confident that he looked like a shaman should, he turned to the six dwarves.

"You would all make your mothers proud," he said loudly enough to echo off the stone walls. They could not help but whoop and cheer at this. It was as he had anticipated. He wanted them to feel their jubilation taken from them.

"But I am your father."

As expected, they quieted and focused on their religious leader.

"If our goal had been to rough a dragonling up, I would be quite proud."

Their eyes widened.

"If our goal had been to overturn decades of our religious

practice without so much as a sermon to explain it, I would be elated."

Six butts scooted back in their seats.

"If our goal had been to let the future of our race slip through our fingers, I would be ecstatic."

The inside of the church was so quiet, you could have heard a pin drop.

"But none of that was our goal. Our goal—the only one that matters—was to capture the girl. We failed at that today—we failed to capture her and we failed to stop the dragon who stole her away. Worse, we failed to learn anything about the dragon conspiracy to steal our future and rob us of our ability to defend ourselves.

"The fault is not all yours. As your father, I take responsibility for these shortcomings. I should have acted faster when Viktor brought her to me and been better prepared for the dragons to make this prophecy come to fruition. I should have seen that the...technology you have all embraced is not our enemy but a tool we can use in the war against the magic these dragons would seek to poison us with."

"It was my responsibility to free her from this curse. Your failure is my failure."

Silence hung over the six dwarves and their religious leader, but Roy was unable to keep quiet for long. He coughed, which was the quietest thing he knew how to do.

"What, Roy?" Shaman Mytrov demanded.

"Sorry, Father. I mean no offense. It's only...well...you said we would capture her and cleanse her."

"That is correct."

"Right, but...uh, how?"

Shaman Mytrov felt his face flush under his black makeup. "There is a ritual!"

"How does it work?" Gautier asked.

"I...I've never done it before." He had read of the ritual, of course, but he had never learned how to do it. As far as he knew, no one had. After all, no dwarf had manifested magic powers in their community before. This was all like a virgin forest to them.

"Was that stone sword the boy had involved?" Roy asked.

"I believe it was." As always, he latched onto the beliefs of his followers and tried to amplify them, as any religious leader should. "I believe the dragons used that to make poor Vala into an abomination. I don't know how it works, however, or how we can undo the damage that has been done to her."

Truthfully, he had no idea if the black sword had anything at all to do with the girl's magic, but he was not about to admit that. Besides, it seemed obvious that the girl was part of some kind of dragon plot. How else would she have manifested magic? Why else would the dragon have appeared when it did?

"What we must do is fight the source of whatever is doing this to her. Dwarves have been around for hundreds of years and never once has a dwarf mage been born. Something must have caused this to happen. If we let her go"—Mytrov almost said go free but he caught himself at the last second—"go about the world with this affliction, it could spread to other dwarves. Worse, if the dragon has the power to inflict others with the curse of magic, he will do it again. He must be stopped and the girl must be purified."

"But...you don't know how to do the ritual?" Gautier asked.

"No dwarf knows how to do such a thing because no dwarf has ever had to do it." The shaman's mind spun. He knew he had to provide answers and needed to present them with a plan. That was why people came to his church—they needed meaning when there was none. It was important for them to know they were part of something greater, even if they couldn't understand it. While he did not understand what was happening, he had to pretend he did for their sake.

"What we need to do is determine exactly what was done to the girl and then learn how to undo whatever damage was caused. This will take time as I will need to study her, learn what was done to her, and decipher how to undo it."

"You're saying we can't do it at the church, right, Father?" Gautier asked.

Mytrov seized on the question. "That is correct, brother. It may take days to unravel the curse the dragon has put on her. I will not be able to simply snap my fingers and undo it. Taking the black sword from the dragon may help, but we must focus on capturing the girl and making sure the magic inside her does not spread through our community."

"I...uh, I think I know a place," Roy said. "Outside of town would be better, right? That way, the magic won't be able to spread to anyone nearby?"

"Indeed, brother Roy. Please, tell us more."

"Well...some of the boys have already been out there."

Most of the other dwarves nodded.

Roy continued. "Gautier has a hunting lodge in the woods. It's a fair way out of town with no neighbors and best of all, it's built on top of a cave entrance. We could go underground. It's solid and secure and no one comes to bug us, and there's no one to overhear us, either."

It sounded perfect to Shaman Mytrov. A place like that would give them the privacy they needed to cure her, and if they couldn't...well, he wondered how deep this cave went.

"Father Earth provides," he said piously.

"Father Earth provides," the dwarves all replied in unison.

"Where do we find her, though?" Gautier asked.

"We start at her home. Vala has never left the city. She won't leave without saying goodbye to her parents."

"Do we take the trucks, sir?" Roy asked.

"We do. We are facing a threat to our very existence and will use all the tools this congregation has."

"All of them?" Roy asked with a grin.

"We will not hurt Viktor's daughter unless we have to. But if we see the dragon, we will stop him by whatever means we have available to us."

The six dwarves nodded eagerly. They might not understand the particulars this plan would eventually need, but they understood exactly what they had to do next.

CHAPTER NINETEEN

The dwarf woman who opened the door was the spitting image of Vala, but instead of a frizzy head of hair, she had two braids that looked quite tame. She narrowed her eyes at Galen, who understood almost immediately that her daughter's proposed deception would not last two minutes against her.

"Vala! You're back. And you have a friend! What happened to your father?"

"We were...separated," the girl said. "Mom, this is Galen... Stevens. He's in my engineering class. Galen, this is my mom, Marma Gagnon."

"A pleasure to meet you, Lady Gagnon." He bowed politely.

"Oh, a pleasure to meet you as well, Galen. Please, call me Marma. All the boys around here do. Such good manners you have. Not at all like the locals."

He shrugged and decided it was time to keep his mouth shut.

"Mom, Galen hoped he could come in for some soup."

"Oh! Of course. Sure. Now, Galen, this is dwarf food. It can be a little...tougher than humans are used to."

"Honestly, ma'am, it smells amazing. I've never had dwarf food before."

"Seriously? Not once this whole semester?"

Galen shrugged and turned to Vala, who responded with a peal of awkward laughter.

"Well, I'll get the soup," her mother said and vanished.

"This way." The girl led him out of the entry room, down a wood-paneled hallway, and into a room with a massive dining room table that was so well worked, it would not have been out of place in Stormsiege.

A moment later, Marma placed a bowl of soup that looked more like an urn than a bowl on the table.

The smell of herbs, meat, and root vegetables made his mouth water. While Vala told her mom what had happened at the church—she had animated a telephone?—he ate the entire bowl she'd served for him.

When her daughter reached the part where a dragon landed, her mother turned to Galen.

"That's good soup, isn't it, Galen?"

"Yes, ma'am, it was."

"It's odd, though. I've never seen a human eat that much before. Ever. Vala, what was it you were saying about a dragon?"

He grinned into the last scraping of soup as the girl began to mumble something about how the dragon had swooped in and saved her and they'd flown away.

"And what happened to this noble dragon?" Marma asked, rubbed her chin, and darted another pointed glance at Galen, who had lifted his bowl to drain the very last of the contents.

"He, er…"

The dragon had never seen someone quite so bad at lying before. Stormwings were trained to hide their feelings and even their auras. He had never been particularly good at it and it was almost impossible to fool everyone at once in the grand hall at Stormsiege, but he had managed to lie to his mother successfully a few times, although never about anything of much consequence.

"Galen, did you like the dandelion roots and moose bones in there? Most humans don't normally crunch through them like you did."

He grinned. "They were great, ma'am, and gave me the energy I needed." He decided the charade was over. The only person who still believed Vala's thin story was the girl herself.

Calmly, he opened his coat, revealed the bruise and barely closed gunshot wound, and poured his magic into the wound. He had already managed to stop the bleeding by the time they landed but had done little else to heal it.

Now, though, the flesh re-knitted, the muscles reattached themselves and tightened, and a mass of scar tissue formed where the bullet had punched through his abdomen. He had already dumped a ton of magic into fixing his intestines and burning out any bacteria that had escaped. This took less magic than he'd used during the fight but it still almost knocked him out. He slumped in his chair.

"Vala, you silly girl, I don't know who you were trying to fool. Go fetch the turkey from yesterday. Dragons need meat." She turned to him. "I'm grateful you stepped in to save my daughter, but you should understand she wasn't in any danger. Shaman Mytrov is harmless."

"Who do you think gave me this wound, ma'am?" He grunted with the effort of speech.

The look of realization on her face might have been cute if it did not reveal how ignorant she was about the people in her town. "Vala, how did Galen get hurt?"

The girl returned with a huge wooden cutting board with most of a roast turkey on top of it. "It was Shaman Mytrov, Mom. Well, not literally, but it was someone from the Church of Dwarfish Origins and he was there. Mom, he...he tried to kidnap me. They tried to throw me in the back of a truck. I...I wouldn't be here if not for Galen."

"Oh, Vala, that's terrible. And Galen...how do I say thank you?"

"The turkey's fine, ma'am, thanks," he said around a large mouthful.

Marma's calm motherly demeanor was gone, replaced in an instant with the ferociousness of a mother grizzly bear. "I never trusted Mytrov. Vala, I'm so sorry I didn't come with you to the church. I knew that was a bad idea. And he came after you in a truck? The cursed hypocrite. Where was Viktor in all this?" The question felt more loaded than the gun that had shot Galen.

The dragon's ears pricked up and he stood in a heartbeat, although the effort hurt his freshly healed gut wound. It was better but still not good and he reminded himself that it would take time to heal a wound like this.

"Vala? Vala, are you home? Marma, hon, everything went wrong. Vala...she's missing. She ran off with some dragon she summoned or something." Viktor entered the dining room and his mouth fell open. "Vala! You're all right."

He rushed to her and hugged her. "Oh, my little sapling, I was so worried. I can't believe you took off like that on a dragon. That's dangerous, Vala. You know that. Shaman Mytrov only wanted to help you. I know it was a little scary, but he explained that he only wants this curse on you—wherever it came from—to be lifted. He knows it's not your fault. We all know you don't want this. We'll help you find a solution."

"Dad...Shaman Mytrov followed me."

"As well he should have. You were on a dragon!"

"He tried to kidnap me."

"No. No, he wouldn't do that. He was trying to save you."

"I beg to differ, sir," Galen said and drew the dwarf's attention to him for the first time.

The color drained from her father's face when he realized who this human boy in his home was. "You! What do you think you're doing here, dragon?"

"Protecting your daughter from those goons," he said forcefully and immediately regretted it. Even the effort of speaking that loudly was too much right now.

"Protecting her? Shaman Mytrov wants to cure her."

"Magic is not a curse, not if the mage who has it understands it. It is a gift and with proper training, Vala can be something special. I can take her to the Lumos School. It's a place for people like her." If he kept his voice level, his gut didn't hurt as badly.

"You're not taking my daughter to some freakshow!" Viktor roared.

"The Lumos School is not a freakshow. The professors there have helped my friends do amazing things."

"And what about you? What are you doing here in dwarf country? Huh?"

Galen didn't have an answer for that and Viktor seized the moment.

"No one asked you to come here. No one wants your forced intervention here. If it wasn't for your meddling, Shaman Mytrov would have already fixed my daughter."

"No offense, sir, but you have no idea what you're talking about. Magic is something you are, not something you can fix."

"No offense? *No offense?* How dare you speak to me like this in my own house, you cold-blooded cretin. If we can't get this...this curse off Vala, her life will be a nightmare. She will be different than every dwarf who has ever existed. And you come into my home and tell me I have no idea about my own culture? The arrogance of you dragons."

Galen wisely remained silent. It had been a mistake to say what he had and he couldn't think of anything that wouldn't be misconstrued in the same way.

Marma put a hand on her husband's shoulder and he looked at her before he drew a deep breath. Her hand seemed to calm him, so it was in a more relaxed tone that he addressed the boy again. "Look...I appreciate what you did. Or what you thought you were doing. I can only imagine what it must be like to see a shaman of the Church of Dwarfish Origins in their ceremonial gear, and you happened to arrive when Mytrov was all worked up. You tried to protect our daughter. That was…good of you. But now, it's time for you to leave."

"Dad, Galen can help," Vala pleaded.

"He certainly can. He can get out of here and let us get back to our lives."

"No, Dad. He can help me."

"Vala, I know this is overwhelming but clinging to a dragon who is trespassing on our land is not how to get us through this."

"He's right, Vala," Galen said. "My staying here will only make things more complicated for everyone."

"I like complicated," she begged. "Please, Galen, don't go."

"Maybe we need to each face the problems of our own world," he said and forced himself to stand. "Alone."

"Galen," she implored as Viktor put a hand on the dragon's shoulder and led him to the front door. "Galen!" she cried behind him. He heard her start to cry but what was he supposed to do? Fly her to the Lumos School so his uncle Petrov could kill him as soon as he arrived? He knew she was in danger, but she had said she would be safe there for the night. That was better than he could promise her. For all he knew, his uncle might be waiting outside, ready to murder a dragon who had tried to help a dwarf when his family would have preferred him to bury their town in an unseasonal blizzard.

"Thanks for leaving, young man. I know it's always odd to see a foreign culture. I went to the United States once and the things I saw there…" Viktor forced a chuckle. "People driving distances in automobiles when they could walk them in less than an hour. Living in homes made of all kinds of materials instead of only wood. You can imagine my shock."

Viktor put his hand on the door latch—made of wood, Galen noted—and pulled the door open.

At that precise moment, two pickup trucks pulled up in front of the house.

Galen pushed the door shut. "Did you call them?"

"What? No. I don't know anyone who drives a car."

"Look again," he snapped.

The dwarf opened a little porthole on the front door and slammed it shut hastily. "That's Shaman Mytrov—what...what is he doing in a truck? And was that a phone in Roy's hand? I don't understand."

The shock and hurt in his voice almost made the dragon feel sorry for him but he needed this wake-up call. More importantly, Vala needed him to have it. From where Galen stood, it looked like her life might depend on it.

"They are hunting your daughter." He lifted his shirt to reveal the freshly healed bullet wound and the bright red skin around it. "And they have the tools to finish the job—like the gun one of them used to give me this."

CHAPTER TWENTY

"We have to get Vala out of here," the dragon said.

Viktor nodded dumbly, threw a wooden bar across the door, and followed him to the dining room.

Galen did not wait for him to explain his religious leader's arrival. The dwarf looked like he was still in shock over seeing his friends using technology. He wanted to roll his eyes at that but there wasn't time. "Vala, our friends from earlier are here."

A couple of hard knocks at the door accentuated the truth of this statement.

"You told them I was here?" Vala bolted upright so fast it knocked over the chair she had been seated in.

"No, Vala, of course not! How could I? I only found out you were here a few minutes ago," her father said.

Galen could not read his aura but he didn't think the dwarf was lying. He had seemed thoroughly distressed when the dwarves had appeared at the door.

His daughter, however, did not seem convinced. "You want me fixed, exactly like Shaman Mytrov."

The new arrivals pounded at the door again, harder and more insistent than before.

"No, Vala, I don't. Well, I did, but I've seen who they are now. Shaman Mytrov drove here in a truck. The dwarves with him have phones and guns," her father said. With every word, his voice grew angrier. The shock was fading into fury at having been deceived. "I saw what they did to the dragon, too. With their gun."

"He has a name, Dad!"

Viktor looked like he almost had something constructive to add, but another demanding tattoo came from the door and pushed whatever he had been about to say from his mind.

"Viktor, is everything all right? Open the door or we'll knock it down…uh, for your safety." Roy's voice carried quite easily through the wooden door. Galen got the sense that Viktor had built the house for aesthetics and comfort, not for security. *How very un-dragon-like of him*, he thought darkly.

"I hate to eat and run, but I have to go," he said. "I can't fight them, not without rest."

"I can't believe you did this," Vala said, although she sounded less sure of herself now that she was faced with the look of terror on her dad's face.

"My little sapling, you know I've always been bad with words. So I'll prove it to you. You two get out of here and I'll hold them off as long as I can."

"Wait, you will?"

"Go, Vala. Your dad may not be good with words but I certainly am." Marma drew herself to her full height, such as it was, and marched to the front door. "Roy, that had better not be you knocking dents in my door. I had that repainted only a few weeks ago."

"Mrs. Gagnon, if you could open it, we can talk." Roy's voice echoed down the hallway.

"Vala, I never should have taken you to Mytrov. I'm sorry. But you have to go now."

She nodded and pointed down a hall. "That way to the back," she told Galen and he nodded and hurried in that direction.

The girl began to follow but paused. "I'm sorry too, Dad," she said and moved quickly to hug her father.

Galen saw a tear roll down the man's cheek and he promised to himself that he would somehow get this girl back to the parents who truly loved her.

"Turn up ahead," Vala said, wiped her tears, and directed him from behind.

In moments, they were outside, hidden from the moon by the trees on the Gagnon property.

"I'll get us out of here," he said and called on his reserves of magic.

Unfortunately, it seemed they weren't there. A paltry amount of mist appeared around him but it took nothing but the gentlest of breezes to blow it all away.

"Now would be good, Galen." Vala's foot tapped furiously.

"Right." He closed his eyes and tried again. When he reached deep, he found a trickle of magic but pulling on it only made his side ache. He understood his powers well enough to know when he was beaten. After all, he'd spent months in the desert subsisting off only a tiny modicum of power. He felt like he had even less than that at this moment.

A crash from the front of the house indicated that the dwarves had broken Marma's recently painted door down.

"What on Earth was that for, Roy? I was unlatching it, wasn't I?"

"You were doing no such thing, Marma."

"It is *Mrs. Gagnon* to hooligans who break my door down, thank you very much!" she roared.

Galen didn't know who was louder, Marma or Roy. He imagined that the whole neighborhood would hear their fight, but decided that must be the point. As long as they yelled at each other, they wouldn't search the house and discover that Vala had returned there and left again.

He tried again to transform but he already knew it wouldn't work. He'd been running on fumes since he'd met Vala and there was no reserve left to draw from.

"We have to get out of here," he said and turned to her. "But I'm out of power."

She did not answer. Magic crackled off the tips of her fingertips and her frizzy hair whipped wildly.

"They will not hurt my parents."

CHAPTER TWENTY-ONE

Vala was furious. Her mom had never liked her dad's religion and now, they had come and broken her door down? They would pay.

She lashed out with the fury inside her and felt for a vessel, something to pour it into. There wasn't much inside her parents' house. Her mom's hairdryer, a toaster her dad had begrudgingly allowed into the house, and a few things hidden in her room. None of it seemed right or like it could handle what she wanted to do.

Her magic found one of the trucks parked in front of her parents' house. Without consciously knowing what she was doing, she dumped the fury churning within her into the vehicle.

She felt her rage leave her but it was immediately replaced by terror when she heard the squeal of the truck's tires, the race of its engine, and the crash when it bulldozed into the front of the Gagnon residence.

"No!" she screamed. She turned to race inside to check on her parents but Galen blocked her path.

"Wait!"

"They could be dead. I have to make sure they're not dead!" she said, her panic rising.

"They're dwarves, Vala. I knocked one of them fifty feet and he wasn't even stunned. Your parents are fine. Please, listen."

Sure enough, a moment later, the sound of timber being shuffled about was followed by Marma yelling at full blast.

"You ignorant morons! Which one of you will pay for this? And Shaman Mytrov—don't you dare say you can't afford it when my husband has paid for the roof over your head for years."

"Where's your daughter, Marma?" Roy bellowed in return.

"Not here, you damn fool!" Viktor shouted.

"See? They're fine," Galen said. "Now come on. We have to go."

"We can't simply go. It sounds like one of them drove a truck into the front of our house," she said. She knew she had done something to the truck, but she had not wanted it to crash into her parents' home.

"Vala...that was you. You know it was."

She sighed and nodded. Yes, she did know. She could not deny that. Exactly like she couldn't deny the appliances or the telephone. "But I didn't mean to."

"That's why we need to get out of here." He limped away from the house. "You have an incredible power, but you need to learn how to control it. You're in danger until you learn how to direct it properly, and so are your parents if we stay here."

"They're dwarves. Magic can't affect them," Vala said, half by reflex and half because she wanted it to be true.

"Sure, exactly like dwarves can't have magic despite the fact that you most certainly do?" He gestured for her to come with him.

"That's different. Just because I did this doesn't mean my parents have changed. They're fine."

And she knew they were. She could hear her mother and father yelling at the intruders in their home at the tops of their lungs. They were angry but they were well enough to shout, which counted for something.

"And their house? Are you sure you won't activate that other truck and drive it into their house as well?"

"I didn't want to do that," Vala said weakly.

"I know you didn't. That's why we need to go somewhere you can practice."

"You can help me then? Can you help me learn to control this?"

Galen paused and turned to her, bit his lip, and winced. "Yes. Yes, I think I can," he said finally. "At least, I can get you started in the right direction and get you to the Lumos School."

"I won't abandon my parents."

"That shaman doesn't want your parents. He wants you. The best thing you can do is get away, learn to control yourself, and come back when you can protect them."

Vala reluctantly agreed that it made more sense than her plan to make her mom's hairdryer attack the dwarves.

"Okay," she conceded. "I'll come with you so you can teach me. But if you can't fly us out of here, what's the plan?"

"For starters, getting away from them," he said and continued to limp toward the back of the Gagnon property.

The girl nodded and caught up to him easily despite his greater height. She put an arm around him to help support his weaker side.

"I'm fine," he muttered as they moved deeper into the woods and away from the shouts coming from the house. It sounded like Mytrov and his goons were tearing the place apart looking for Vala.

"You are not. If you're going to help me, you have to let me help you."

"Fine," the dragon said and leaned more of his weight on her.

They had reached the fence along the back of the property

before the back door of the Gagnon house opened and cast a long rectangle of yellow, electric light into the woods.

"I see tracks!" a dwarf shouted, and Galen cursed.

"I can't jump this fence."

"No problem." Vala put him on her shoulders heaved him over. He landed harder than she had wanted but he didn't cry out, only grunted and clenched his teeth.

"You're stronger than you look," he muttered as he pushed to his feet.

"You too, but with smarts," she said as she led him through the woods behind her parents' house and around toward town.

She tried to focus on where they could go to let him get some rest rather than the sounds coming from her parents' house. Most of all, she tried not to think about the damage she had caused.

CHAPTER TWENTY-TWO

Vala had a dwarf's resilience, so despite the hour being late, she had more than enough energy to traipse through the woods while she tried to think of a place where they could take refuge.

Galen didn't look very good but kept pace with her, although he had to use his big black sword-thingy as a walking stick to stay upright. He held his other hand against his stomach as if he were worried that his guts might spill out onto the forest floor if he let them.

"They're following us," he wheezed at one point. "They breathe so loudly I could fight them in the dark."

"You can't fight anything right now," she retorted bluntly, which only earned her a grimace from him. "But you're right, we won't lose them in the dark. Roy and some of the others like to hunt. They would be able to track us through the woods even if we tried to not leave a trail."

He grunted. "Do you have any suggestions?"

"Yeah, this way." Vala had not wanted to point out that the dwarves would be able to track them through the woods. She had not seen the point in worrying him. Besides, she had a plan.

It had become increasingly clear that despite all their anti-tech rhetoric, the followers of the Church of the Dwarfish Origins were not anti-tech at all. Still, she had rarely seen them in the city center or the couple of coffee shops near the university, nor had she ever seen their trucks there. She felt confident that she could lose them on the asphalt streets where they would not make tracks.

They broke cover from the forest, hurried through a few suburban streets, and reached the university.

"Be careful to not step on any grass. If they get even one footprint, they'll be able to tell what direction we're traveling in."

"Great, so they're hard to stop and good at hunting us. The best of both worlds," Galen said. "The guns are merely a bonus after all that."

"Yeah. Hypocrisy has its perks," Vala said and led him across campus. She had to help him up a flight of stairs and when they reached the central green, she had to keep a firm hand on him to make him use the sidewalk on the perimeter instead of letting him walk straight across the center field.

He protested and sounded tired. "Are you sure they can track us through grass?"

"You're a flying dragon. What do you know about tracks?" Vala asked querulously.

Galen did not answer but let her keep leading him.

They crossed the campus to a section of the city that appealed almost exclusively to college students. She hurried toward one of the more crowded shops with a sign above it with a picture of an owl wearing a helmet and holding a cup of coffee in one talon and comically exaggerated eyes. Outside, she hesitated.

"Can you leave that sword of yours outside?"

"It's a claw from the Prairie King."

"What?"

"No. I won't leave it outside. It's not an umbrella."

"Fair enough, I guess. But don't stab anyone with it."

"I'll do my best."

Vala knew they needed to get off the street, so she led him inside the Knight Owl without further argument. She knew the barista there, so she waved, put some money on the counter, and asked for the usual without feeling too guilty about being rude and hurried past crowded tables toward the nook behind the bar. Not only did it have comfy couches but it could not be seen from the street. She hoped that the lights, moody electronic music, and students staring into computer screens would all work as dwarf-religious-zealot-repellent.

Unfortunately, the couches were taken.

Normally, she would have crowded up against the counter or looked for a classmate she recognized so she could ask for table space, but there was nothing normal about their current situation.

"Can we please sit here?" she asked the dwarf sprawled on the couch watching a vapid comedy on a laptop.

"Nope."

She ground her teeth. They did not have time for this. "Get up."

"Was my nope not clear?"

"Did you hear about the room of appliances that went crazy during a final on campus today?" she asked.

"Yeah! There's no footage, though. Can you believe that?"

"Maybe you can see it happen for yourself," she said and his screen began to flicker.

That did the trick. He slammed his laptop closed, stood quickly, and was gone from the coffee shop before she had time to usher Galen to a seat.

"You know, when you're trying to keep a low profile, it's best to not show off the power people are hunting you for," he said once he'd collapsed onto the couch.

"I'm new to this whole running for my life situation," Vala said.

"Lucky for you, I'm a real-life social pariah."

She chuckled and turned her attention to the other patrons. If they had created any hubbub with their entrance, it did not show. Everyone had their gazes fixed on their screens, or were engaged in their conversations about finals, parties, or any of the other topics she wished she could share again. How could her life have changed so much? It had not even been twenty-four hours and in that time, she had become a mage, met a dragon, almost been kidnapped by a church congregation, and drove a truck through the front of her parents' house without even touching it.

"Is everything all right?" the barista asked when he arrived a few minutes later with two cups of coffee on a platter. He nodded pointedly to Galen, who Vala only now realized had fallen asleep on the couch.

"Yeah, thanks, Gene. I appreciate it."

"Are you sure? He doesn't look like an engineering student." He leaned closer conspiratorially. "I think that might be a dragon claw he's carrying."

"Yeah, I'm sure I'm not in any danger from the dragon passed out on the couch next to me."

Gene nodded. Fortunately, he did not seem particularly offended by her rather curt answer. "Does he have anything to do with the dragon who was seen over town today? The story is it arrived unexpectedly and has an ax to grind with the Dwarf Origin people."

Vala knew she should probably keep her mouth shut, but she also knew that he had no love for her father's church either. They were strict believers in dwarfish purity, which meant they had no patience for dwarves like Gene who made no secret that he dated men and women, of either the human or dwarf persuasion.

"We're on the run from them," she blurted.

The barista's eyes widened but he brought his shock under control quickly. He knew a thing or two about keeping secrets, far more than Vala did.

"If anyone comes asking, I'll make sure to say I saw you two go into the shop down the street."

"You'd do that for me?"

"They claim their pastries are vegan but they are most definitely not vegan. They deserve what they get." He winked and returned to minding the front of the shop.

Vala was not exactly sure what to do. She knew they should probably keep moving but Galen needed sleep. The Knight Owl was open until three in the morning, and although Gene often made a show of kicking any stragglers out, she doubted he would do that to them tonight, not with so much secret gossip on the line.

She was about halfway through the cup of coffee when Galen's eyes jerked open and he sat like he had been shocked.

"Where are we?"

"The Knight Owl. It's a coffee shop."

"So that's—"

"Coffee. Yes."

He snatched the mug gratefully from the low table in front of them and emptied it one swallow. His eyes widened and almost resembled the sign out front.

"That's...wow."

"I take it you've never had dwarf coffee before?"

"It's strong," he managed although his teeth had begun to chatter less. "Do your people use dirt for a filter?"

"Peat, but yeah, I love the earthy notes."

The dragon leaned back and looked around. "Coming here was smart, but we shouldn't stay long. If they saw us...well, I don't want to think what your magic would do with a milk steamer."

"You're not exactly discreet either. What's with the sword anyway? The barista said it looked like a dragon claw."

"Did he?" Galen craned his neck to see the barista but of course, the wall behind them was in the way. "Well, remind me to leave him a tip on the way out. Those dwarves chasing us thought it was a sword."

"You used it like a sword," she pointed out.

"Hardly," he said. "It's not very useful in this form."

"It's different when you're a dragon?"

"Yeah, it certainly is," Galen straightened and did not seem to hold his wound quite as tenaciously as he had when they had been running. Vala thought those were good signs.

"When I'm a dragon, it turns into a claw, one of my horns, or the spike at the tip of my tail. It's from the Prairie King. I got it when I brought him back from the dead." He did not sound particularly proud of that admission. "I had hidden it in the desert so no one could use it but well, with my family, I thought I might need it. Plus...well, never mind."

"Plus what?"

The dragon bit his lip but he finally took a deep breath and explained. "I was ashamed of what I did when I had the power to raise the dead. I am still ashamed of it, but I don't know...it's different now. I no longer want to hurt people. I won't hurt people, but knowing this claw was out there and gathering dust in the desert didn't seem right either. I retrieved it because I wanted it to be a reminder of what I have done so I won't do it again if that makes sense."

Vala nodded. "It does. Still...it is awkward in your human form."

He smirked. "I guess you're not the only one that needs practice."

She was more than willing to let the conversation shift and focus on her. "Do you truly think I can learn to control my magic?"

"Absolutely," he said, his expression serious. "In fact, you must learn to control it. Mages—human mages anyway, but it might be different for you—have to learn to control their magic or it can blow them to pieces."

The girl forced out a hollow laugh. "You're joking."

Galen clenched his jaw and stared at her.

"Okay, great. So yeah, let's get training."

"We must and we will. But we'll need somewhere safe where you can learn the basics."

"What about the woods near my parents' house? Once the dwarves find we're not there, they shouldn't go back."

"Yeah, you're extremely bad at hiding. You already went back to your parents' house once and they found you. We can be certain almost they will be watching them. We can't go anywhere near them, at least not until you're strong enough to…well, what do you want to do?"

"That's a huge question."

Galen grinned. "Don't I know it. My whole life—well, once it became clear that I wouldn't gain the ability to control the storms —was essentially designed for me to serve the Stormwing clan. I thought that maybe school would change that, but it didn't work out either. Religious freaks aside and knowing that you absolutely cannot ignore your magic, what do you want to do with it?"

"Use it?" Vala said tentatively, but she found that the words felt honest. "I want to master it. I've always been interested in how things work, but engineering didn't quite deliver. I think that's why I was always doodling in class. There was this energy missing from engineering that I could never explain. Drawing felt like the closest way to express that."

"That energy was magic," he said. "All dragons know that feeling."

"So you can train me on how to use mine?"

"Not exactly, no, but I sat through enough of Professor Sharra's class that I think I can at least show you the basics. Still, we need to be somewhere fairly remote—somewhere no one will hear any explosions."

"Explosions?" She laughed. "Seriously?"

"You drove a truck into your parents' house and you doubt that you can make things go boom?"

"Boom?" she asked, more frightened by the stone-cold expression on his face than anything else.

"There's no guarantee you can create fire, of course. Some mages have particular predispositions and yours might be—"

"Appliances?"

The dragon laughed. "That wasn't what I intended to say, but yeah. Maybe you're an appliance witch. Either way, we need to be somewhere you can practice without breaking anything or hurting anyone."

Vala was crestfallen. "You made magic sound like it's a gift but I don't want to hurt anyone."

"Magic is a gift. It's a power unlike any other in the world but like all power, it doesn't come free. You have to learn how to control it."

"What if I can't?"

He paused to consider the question carefully. "There are ways to lose powers—or, at least, there are for dragons. I lost one and I'm relieved I did. But is that what you want? Do you want to go back to being merely a dwarf and doodling during your engineering classes?"

She did not have to think before she answered. "No. I want to control it. I want to use this power."

Galen nodded. "Then I want to help you use it."

Suddenly, an idea popped into her head. "I think I know where we can train. Wait, do you think you can fly us there?"

He poked at his side and winced but only slightly before he nodded. "I think I can. Where do you have in mind?"

"There's an old lumber yard a little out of town. It has a couple of warehouses and a huge workshop, so we could practice inside where no one would see us."

"Are you sure it's private?"

"No one goes there except for photography students and they

all stay outside to take 'the forest taking back industry' pictures. Even then, it's only the most pretentious ones."

"But you've been there."

"I never said I wasn't pretentious." She smirked. "I might have a few doodles of trees battling saws."

"It sounds good. The place I mean. A tree would beat a saw, though."

"What? No. Trees can't move."

"You should meet my friends," he said enigmatically. Before she could ask what that was supposed to mean, he retrieved his claw, pushed up, and steadied himself on his dragon relic turned walking stick. "Shall we?"

"Are you sure you're ready?"

He responded with a massive yawn. "I need more sleep, so the sooner we get there, the better." Maybe the dwarf coffee wasn't that strong.

"It works for me," Vala said.

She showed him out the back of the coffee shop. In the alley, Galen transformed and only grunted minimally to do so.

The dwarf climbed on his back and they took to the skies.

CHAPTER TWENTY-THREE

Amy Williams willed the skateboard beneath her feet to push her faster through the air. She wondered if any of the dwarves below had any idea that the world's most powerful mage was flying over their heads in the dark. Probably not. It wasn't like they could sense magic—or so she thought. Thinking of what lay ahead pushed her to even greater speed.

She leaned forward so she moved almost horizontally like an action figure of a superhero that still had the plastic holder connected to its feet while a kid played with it.

Except she wasn't stuck to her skateboard. Lately, she had practiced ways to augment her magic. A geometric pattern ran beneath all magic, and by using her telekinesis to whip her board around, she could increase her speed while using less magic—or more precisely, using magic more efficiently.

That meant—in practical terms—that she busted a double kickflip and exactly like the video games she used to play, rocketed forward at greater speed.

She was fully horizontal now and had to let the burst of magic dissipate or risk being ripped off her board by the wind. Unfortunately, she could not use her telekinesis on herself. In that way, she was like the dwarves below.

Amy had a soft spot for the dwarves in Canada. When she had manifested her magical powers, her mother had called a group of dwarves who had taken her in despite a team of dragons being hot on her tail.

Looking back on those fateful days, she could see why the dragons had been afraid of her. She had killed not one but two without even meaning to. That didn't give them license to hunt and kill her like a rabid animal as they had tried to do, but it certainly warranted looking into.

Although it had taken her a long time to recognize even that. It had not been until her best friend Kristen Hall had become head of the Dragon Council and founded her global police organization that the mage had been able to come to terms with the need to investigate strange new magical occurrences.

Now that she was an officer of the Steel Guard—and more importantly, now that there was an organization like the Steel Guard that tried to solve disputes by putting all races on an equal footing instead of prioritizing dragons—she felt especially responsible for young mages manifesting their powers.

When Amy did not have specific duties to perform for Kristen, she was given free rein to pursue her own cases. She had spent months traveling across North America developing mage contacts to help her find these runaway mages and while she wanted to get to Europe, South America, and the world beyond, a crisis always pulled her home. Even though the world was becoming more accepting of mages—slowly but inexorably—a teenager waking one morning and discovering they could light fires or pick their parents' car up with their mind was still a source of chaos.

It was a cruel trick that magic tended to manifest in people in their teenage years. Teens were already pumped full of hormones, developing independence from their parents, and forging their paths despite brains that tried to develop. It was too much to add magic to that as well, but such was life. She knew that better than anyone.

Amy and her growing network of mages had already been able to help a couple of dozen people come to terms with their latent magic powers but she had never received a call like she had last evening.

That was why she was hundreds of meters above Canada, flying toward the mage's address in a small town she had never heard of as fast as she could.

Trevor Miller had told her that a young dwarf had manifested magical powers.

It was still almost impossible to believe.

Humans did live in Canada. Trevor Miller was an example of that simple fact. Amy wondered if he had perhaps been mistaken. She had experience with dwarves and she knew how magic worked on them—or rather how it didn't. When she had fled to Canada, the dwarves had taken her in largely because even if she accidentally lashed out at them, there was little she could do to harm them.

Her primary power was telekinesis. She could lift cars, boulders, trees, and even whole buildings if she was well-rested and in a particularly pissed-off mood. But she could not lift a dwarf. Magic sloughed off them like oil on water.

But she would not let her preconceived notions of how magic worked stop her from investigating.

She crouched and leapt off her board as she flicked her ankles with perfect precision. The skateboard spun both laterally and radially, which meant—in skateboard parlance—she had performed the impossible. The geometric symmetry of the spin augmented the magic she used to push the board through the sky. It slammed into her feet and she crouched into a stiffy grab and held on for dear life.

If she was ripped from her board by the wind, she wouldn't

plummet to her death. Despite being unable to use her telekinesis on herself, she could use her magic to lift her baggy hoodie or her skate shoes, but compared to using the skateboard, carrying herself by her clothes was a messy, imprecise, and uncomfortable affair.

Plus, she liked this board. Its deck was covered with stylized lipstick kisses she hadn't worn away to nothing yet, and the trucks were sprayed with rose-gold paint. It might have been a little girly for her but for some reason, it simply worked. Despite the grip tape being "diamond studded"—and thus extra sparkly—she didn't think she would be able to find the skateboard if it landed a couple of hundred meters away in the piney forests of Canada.

Although that was not strictly true. There were methods of detection she could use with her magic but they would take time she was worried she did not have.

She did a triple kickflip and felt her magic rocket her even faster across the landscape.

Amy reached the address Trevor had given her later than she would have liked. Was it midnight there or had she traveled to a different time zone? It didn't matter either way. She remembered that he had a little magic trinket shop and lived in a modest apartment above it. The lights were on in the apartment, so she guided her board down and landed on a tiny patio.

Immediately, the sound of the TV inside went quiet.

Concerned, she slid the sliding door open.

"I have every right to live here!" he shouted from the darkness. "I know magic will slide off you, but I have a frying pan enchanted to beat anyone who hurts me senseless. It won't stop until I tell it to, which means if you kill me, you'll be haunted forever."

"Trevor?" she said into the dark room. "It's me, Amy Williams. You called?"

The lights turned on to reveal the mage standing in his

pajamas with a frying pan clutched in one hand. He was skinny—almost uncomfortably so—and his pajamas hung loosely on him. Unlike many mages, he did not have any tattoos to augment his magic, but that made sense given where he lived.

This was dwarf country. Tattoos didn't stick to the incredibly tough dwarf skin, so they were rare. He had lived there a long time, so he had probably decided long ago that being able to fit in on the street was worth more than whatever modicum of extra power some tattoos would have afforded him. His eyes looked red and swollen from crying and his thin blonde mustache trembled.

"Oh, Amy, thank goodness you're here!" He dropped the frying pan, ran to her, and wrapped her in a hug that reminded her of how skinny he was.

"It's all right," she said and patted him on the back. They had only met once before, so the hug was a little forward, but she had long since accepted that her reputation preceded her and that after decades of dragon oppression, she was a hero to many mages. Plus, it seemed like he'd had a very rough day. "Are you all right?"

"I'm fine, yes. Sorry, it's been a terrible night."

"You mentioned that a dwarf you knew came here with magic powers? Did she try to hurt you? Is that why you enchanted the frying pan?"

Trevor responded with a single harsh sobbed laugh. "The frying pan isn't enchanted. I don't have the power to make it follow someone around for a day, let alone a lifetime. Most dwarves around here fear frying pans because their wives use them to knock sense into them. It was merely a bluff."

"Are you always awake at night in your pajamas, waiting for a dwarf to break in?"

The mage's laugh was harsh and rough and cut off almost immediately. "No. Like I said, it's been a rough night. Vala came here—she's the dwarf I told you about—gosh, it feels like days ago at this point. Since then, the local congregation of religious nuts has learned the news. They've been driving around town with banners on their truck that say, *No place for magic*. I…mages are tolerated here but aren't exactly welcome. I would never have moved here if I knew there was one of those churches in this town. Unfortunately, I had already bought the shop and redone this apartment before I found out."

"Okay, Trevor. It'll be all right." Amy used her telekinesis to take a cup from the cupboard, filled it with water, and levitated it to him.

The display of power worked in the way she had hoped— Trevor was amazed. Lifting a glass was easy enough but she had twisted a knob she had never seen and thus only sensed with her mind, filled the cup, and made it levitate through a room she had also not seen. This wasn't something most mages could do.

"Are you truly as strong as they say?" he asked and perked up slightly.

She snorted. "I just flew hundreds of miles through the sky on my skateboard." She grinned. "And I'm still fresh enough to want to know everything that happened, all right?"

Trevor nodded hurriedly and proceeded to tell her everything. In a rush, he explained how Vala Gagnon had said she had activated some electronic devices and how he had tested her for curses and not found any. Instead, he'd only found magic potential—her magic potential—and how her dad had not liked that at all.

"Her dad's one of these religious types?" she asked when he started to ramble.

"They're called Originists and…yes? Many of the dwarves in town go to the shaman's services, but I don't think most are true believers. Vala has certainly been to her fair share and she isn't committed to the church. They preach against magic and even regular human technology—although it seems they gave up on that. Now that a dwarf with magic is running around, they're more than happy to drive around in their trucks. They have these flags—"

"You mentioned it, Trevor. Do you have any idea where Vala is now?"

He shook his head. "She left with her parents. Viktor—that's her father—wanted to take her to the church, but I can't imagine her still being there if these guys are driving all over town."

Amy nodded. "Do you have her parents' address?"

"I do." He found a piece of paper, scribbled an address, and described the part of town it was in.

"Is there anything else you can tell me?"

"I think that's it. The Originists don't like magic, Amy. Not at all. They've protested in front of my shop simply because I'm a mage. But they also don't fully understand magic. They're more afraid of it than anything else. I think they would have destroyed my property a dozen times already if they weren't afraid that most of the junk I keep behind the counter would attack them if they tried."

"That's good to know, thank you, Trevor. You did well by calling me. It sounds like this is a real powder keg."

He nodded. "I wish I could have helped her myself, but...well, I don't have that much power. I'm very glad you're here. I simply thought...I don't know, having someone who knows their stuff helping the girl makes sense."

"You did well. If you see anything else or think you're in danger, you call me, all right? I'll let you know if I leave town."

"Where are you going now?"

"The parents' house."

"Viktor's a lumberjack and a woodworker. He'll be asleep."

"I hope so. That would mean Vala is safe and sound. If she isn't, her parents will be up."

Amy arrived at the Gagnon residence perhaps fifteen minutes later—or what was left of the home, anyway. Even from the end of the street, it was obvious that something had happened to their house. It wasn't only the police cars parked out front with red and blue lights to alert anyone who might still be awake that all was not well. The house looked like a giant had taken a swipe out of it.

She skated closer, kickflipped off her board, caught it in the air, and walked up to the police who watched the perimeter of the building.

"What's up?"

"Ma'am, you need to stop and take a step back," the human police officer said.

"Aye, lassie. This is no place for skate heads." Despite the dwarf's words, he studied her lipstick board with a knowing glance. Between that look and the gemstone studs in one of his ears, she decided he was the proverbial good cop.

She flashed her Steel Guard badge at him so quickly that his human partner wasn't able to make out what it was and walked past the perimeter.

"Ma'am, you can't go in there. Ma'am!" the human hollered but was quickly shushed and likely held back by the dwarf.

"That's Amy Williams, you fool! She's here on the behalf of the Steel Dragon herself."

"Should we tell the detective?"

"Nah. He fancies himself a skater and is always going on about how much he knows about the south. Let him work it out for himself."

Okay, so maybe it wasn't her board that had caught the dwarf's eye but her reputation. Amy thought it was a good sign that he let her through. It meant that despite some of the local dwarves having taken umbrage at magic users, the sentiment was not the default. This was a good sign and something she needed to know. If those who had done this to the house were still at large, this mess would get a whole lot messier.

She walked through what was left of the front door. The frame was still loosely in place, but barely. The wall next to it had taken most of the damage from what she assumed must be one of the trucks Trevor had been afraid of.

"Hello? Steel Guard. I'm here to help," Amy said as she moved deeper into the house. It was a pity that the building had suffered the fairly extensive damage visible. She had grown up in a tiny town in Maine so she had seen her fair share of handmade cabins, but this one put them all to shame.

It looked like every piece of wood had been carefully chosen and selected to add to the overall look of the house. Now, however, patterns in the grain that must have spanned the entire hallway were all splintered. She wondered if Timeflash could do something about it and made a note to ask the dwarves, but Vala was still the priority. Clean-up would come later.

Amy stepped into a living room where two adult dwarves whom she assumed were the Gagnons huddled together on a couch. Each clutched a cup of tea in their hands and seemed to cower behind the police officer who was in the room. He was a short dwarf with no beard and instead, his mustache was so large that it covered the lower part of his face entirely except for the very tip of his chin. He held a club in one hand and looked ready to face whatever came through the hallway, be it a rude commanding officer or a rhinoceros.

"Steel Guard? Funny. I've never seen one of them come this way before. I'll need to get a feel for your badge."

She flashed it like she had the police on the street, but he did not budge from his place in front of the Gagnons. "Did I mumble? I'll need to touch your badge. No offense, lady, but it's been quite a night and I wouldn't put it past some mage to come in here with an illusion or whatever they do."

"From what I heard, mages aren't the problem here," she replied but she took her badge out and offered it to the officer for inspection. He took it, pushed it so far inside his mustache that it practically vanished, and gave it a couple of good strong sniffs.

Satisfied, he handed it to her. "That's good Detroit Steel, that is. I can tell from the coal and the temperature the furnace had to be to get steel like that. Detroit, through and through. In fact—"

"You did your due diligence, Trudeau. If this young lady is truly from the Steel Guard, we'd like to speak to her about what happened," Mrs. Gagnon said.

"It's not time to brag about your little hobby," Mr. Gagnon snapped. It didn't take a dragon's ability to read auras to tell the dwarf was upset.

"Mr. and Mrs. Gagnon, I presume?" Amy asked.

"This is Viktor and please, call me Marma. Are you here to help our little girl?"

"Yes, ma'am. My name is Amy Williams and from the sound of things, your daughter is going through the same thing I did. Can you tell me when her powers first manifested?"

"We can't be certain that's what's happening," Viktor blurted, although the effort drained him and his eyes welled with tears.

"Oh, hush, Viktor. You'll have to forgive him, dear. He's having something of a religious crisis."

"Dwarves aren't supposed to have magic," he retorted miserably.

"And our house wasn't supposed to get destroyed tonight either. Yet here we are."

Marma clucked in triumph, and the mage got the sense that this was an argument the two of them had already been through a few times today.

"If you could tell me what happened to your daughter, starting with the first…uh, occurrence, that would be great."

"Well, you must know something or you wouldn't be here. We don't know where she is if that's what you're asking," Vala's mother said, her tone slightly offended.

"No, ma'am." Amy tried to stay polite and formal like Kristen had taught her. "I've heard an account of what happened but I'd like to hear yours as well. All of it. My hope is that it will save me time in the long run."

In reality, she thought that asking multiple witnesses the same questions was a huge waste of her time, but it was something Kristen insisted on. Despite being the head of the Dragon Council, she had been trained as a cop and she expected her head mage to follow protocols that sometimes felt less than expedient. Still, Kristen had proven time and again that it paid to do research, so she listened closely while Marma explained the events of the day.

She corroborated almost everything Trevor had said—although she did downplay her husband's temper at the mage, which was a good sign that Trevor had told the truth. Amy barely managed to maintain a poker face when Viktor cut into his wife's telling of the events to complain about a dragon carrying his daughter away.

The mage filed the question away and let the woman finish. She began to grow increasingly curious about what was happening when Marma mentioned her daughter arriving with a boy. She made it sound like she had not expected him to be a dragon but of course, Amy had listened for what happened to the dragon ever since Vala's father had mentioned it.

"And then, they showed up here—Shaman Mytrov and some of his most trusted congregants—and destroyed our home," Viktor interjected, apparently assuming that she was not interested in Marma describing the boy eating soup, even though she was very interested so she could glean a description of the dragon's human form. Blonde and messy, with eyes like storm clouds was what she had so far.

She would come back to that but first, she addressed Mr. Gagnon's concerns. "What exactly did they do to your house?"

"Well, when they discovered Vala was gone, they trashed it." He fumed and his facial hair bristled. "They destroyed every dang appliance we had here, then turned their truck on the front of the building."

"I don't know, dear..." Marma said doubtfully.

"What do you think happened?" Amy asked.

"Well, Vala can make things come to life. That was why they came through the house. Oh, you should have seen Mytrov's face! Dwarves can resist dragon fire yet he acted like a toaster hopping after him would do him in."

"So, they broke everything?"

The dwarf woman nodded. "They destroyed it all because they thought Vala was after them. I think...well, they might have been right. I think she sent the truck through the front of the house."

"She would never do such a thing, Marma! Not our Vala!" Viktor protested but his heart wasn't in it. He slumped on his couch, totally drained.

Amy nodded as if either could be correct, even though she thought Marma's guess was the most likely. It made sense and certainly sounded like the kind of chaos a mage's burgeoning magic abilities could cause.

"But they didn't find Vala, correct?"

"No. One of them followed her and that dragon out back, but they didn't catch either one of them."

"That was the boy you fed the dwarf stew to?" she asked.

Marma nodded. "I didn't see him transform but he had to be one. He had a bruise that he healed."

"What can you tell me about him? Did you get a name?"

"You see, Viktor, I told you I knew the boy was a dragon, didn't I?"

"Vala wouldn't associate with one of them under normal circumstances, you understand," Mr. Gagnon grumbled.

"My best friend is a dragon, so no, I'm not quite sure I understand what you're talking about," Amy snapped without meaning to. Sometimes, her words got away from her. She was so different now that she had all this power. A younger Amy would never have said something so rude but she saw the value in expediency. She wasn't sure if that was something she liked about what the job was doing to her, but she didn't know what else to do. Their daughter was in danger and they could deal with a few bruised feelings.

"Do you want to explain your prejudices against dragons to me, or do you want to tell me what you can about this one so I can help find your daughter?"

Viktor didn't seem to know what to do with that, but Marma was quick to answer.

"We'll help however we can, of course. He, uh...he said his name was Galen. I think I mentioned his hair and stormy eyes. He was skinny—still muscular, you understand, like all dragons are, but skinny too."

"Galen?" she asked.

"Aye. Yes, ma'am."

"You're sure? Not Gabe? Or Gary?"

"It was Galen, ma'am. I'm quite certain. It's not every day that you have a dragon in your house— Well, pardon me I suppose it might be every day for you, but I did make a note of his name. Is that...all right?"

"It might be a lucky break," the mage said. "I know a young dragon with stormy eyes named Galen."

"But that's great!" Viktor perked up as if the case had been solved.

"Is it?" Marma asked.

"Galen has something of a troubled past," Amy said.

The woman nodded and took it in stride but her husband wilted and huddled on the couch.

She knew she shouldn't say anything as an officer of the Steel Guard, but this wasn't a shoplifter or graffiti artist she was talking about. It was Galen Stormwing—the same Galen Stormwing who had summoned a horde of dragon skeletons and hurled them at her as if she were nothing but another body to be claimed. It was he who had brought Lord Boneclaw back, the dragon who had almost killed Kristen who knew how many times.

"He's working on it, though," she said to reassure both herself and the Gagnons. "In fact, only recently, he proved that he has turned over a new leaf."

"You don't sound convinced," Marma said carefully.

Amy allowed herself a small chuckle. "It's for the best, truly. I've met Galen, which will help me find them. That is unless you know where they are?"

"I already asked them that," Trudeau said. He had poured himself a cup of tea and had watched the entire exchange. While he didn't have pen and paper, it still seemed that he had been taking notes.

"And?" Amy asked.

"I can't say for certain," Marma said slowly, "but if it was up to Vala—and Galen was in such a bad condition when they left that I think it may have been—I think she might have headed to campus."

"You didn't say any of that to me," Trudeau protested and stiffened as he glared at her.

"You came in and demanded to know where my daughter was like you thought I was hiding her in my home. Why do you think we called you?" Viktor roared.

"Right. That's a fair point," Trudeau said and sat.

"Why campus?" Amy asked.

"Vala's a student at the local university. She knows the area and spends time there."

"Would she have any friends she might trust enough to try to hide out with?"

Marma's face was tight. "She's a bright girl, you understand, but she never quite fit in here."

"She liked the fool of a mage more than she liked most of her classmates." Viktor snorted before he remembered who he was talking to. "No offense."

"Where on campus?"

"I don't know. There are a few coffee shops she would talk

about. One, in particular, was open late. The, uh…Owl of the night? Something along those lines. I'm sorry I can't be of more help."

"There's no need to apologize, ma'am. These things happen."

"Not to dwarves, they don't," Viktor groused and folded his arms but he didn't look as if he had any more to say.

"It can be a confusing time for humans and I can only imagine that it must be even more so for your daughter. I will do everything I can to make sure she's safe, all right?"

Marma nodded. "And what about the dragon, Galen? I don't think he meant her any harm."

"But if he did—"

"Galen's landed himself in messes before but I think his heart's in the right place," she said. "I want to get him out of this before he gets in any deeper, though. I assume that's Vala on the wall there?" She nodded at a painting of their daughter.

"We had that done last year, yes," Marma said.

Amy nodded. "All right. If there's anything else, call me. I'll leave my number with Trudeau here."

The Gagnons nodded and she saw herself out.

She had almost finished asking a few questions about this Shaman Mytrov character with the police out front when Trudeau rushed out of their house.

"Will you work this investigation while you're in town?" he asked.

The mage nodded. "No one else seems to be."

"Well, see, I am working it too." His gaze settled on her skateboard. "I think we should team up."

It took an effort to not roll her eyes. She had been through this before on other cases. It was normally with a mage, though.

"Look, if you want to ask me a few questions when this is all done, by all means, let's get coffee. But until then—"

"Ask you a few questions? I want to help find Vala."

"You mean...you don't merely want to ask the world's most powerful mage how she does her job?" she asked.

"The who?"

"You've honestly never heard of me?"

"Should I have?"

The other two officers doubled over with laughter. She wasn't sure if they were laughing at her for presuming to be famous or at Trudeau for not knowing who she was despite a reputation for following worldly events.

"Look. I admire your commitment to your case and I'm sure nothing like this ever happens around here, but I can't handle going slower, even if you could help with your...uh, sniffing ability." She had meant it to be a polite dismissal but he seized on the compliment like a rat from a sinking ship finding a piece of driftwood.

"It absolutely can help, and if that's your ride, well..." Trudeau gestured at the levitating lipstick board—quite obviously the vehicle of a mage—and moved to one of the police cars. He returned a minute later wearing what looked like a Viking's helmet that had been painted day-glow green and with a skateboard tucked under his arm. It was so scratched that she could not even guess what had once been on the face.

Amy snorted. She could see she wouldn't be able to talk him out of this. Having a local could be useful, though, and he would probably quit of his own accord the second they got moving.

"Are you sure?" she asked, dropped her skateboard on the ground, and climbed on.

"Yes. Affirmative." Trudeau mounted his.

The mage rocketed them both into the air. He managed to not only not fall off but also not scream as they elevated sharply above the town.

"Where to?" he yelled over the wind and grinned so widely that she could see a few teeth poking through his mustache.

"The university. Do you know the coffee shops?"

"Of course!"

"Great." With Trudeau's help, she might be able to find Vala—and Galen—before the shaman caught up with them.

She didn't know if that worried her more or if the young dragon's bad luck did.

CHAPTER TWENTY-FOUR

Even though it took them less than ten minutes to fly to the abandoned lumber yard, Vala was not sure they would make it.

Halfway through, Galen's wingbeats became more labored and he began to grunt each time he had to flap his wings. Still, he soldiered on and finally set them down between the two huge warehouses.

Even at this late hour, a few students still hung out there and attempted to capture moths flying around the few lights—until Galen flew over. They pointed their cameras hastily at the dragon, artistry forgotten as they played the part of hungry paparazzi.

But once he took his human form, their interest waned. Vala led him behind one of the warehouses in search of an entrance.

They found one that was almost overgrown with vines, but she pushed through and he followed her.

"I can't believe you'll help me with magic," she said. After everything that had happened, she was so excited that something good would finally come of all this. Maybe the coffee was partly responsible, but she felt like she could stay up all night. She was hungry for knowledge about magic, not sleep. "Can we get started right now?"

He nodded, although he looked completely drained. "I need sleep but I'd rest better if I knew you at least had some of the basics."

"Yeah, that sounds great," she agreed.

"All right. So magic...it's like a river inside you except it's not in everyone. But it is in you."

"Right. I know that," she said.

"Of course you do. So...like, magic flows. Okay? So, one thing you need to do is focus on it flowing."

"I'm not sure I understand."

Galen scrunched his face in frustration. "Do what I do."

He led her in a kind of flowing dance. She had seen something like it at the university gym before, although she didn't dare call what he was doing tai-chi. Still, there was a way to how he kept his body moving through specific formations that reminded her of the classes she had seen.

"You have to feel the magic," the dragon tried to explain while they moved.

"How?"

"You should simply be able to."

"But I can't."

"Then you need to try harder."

"Sure. How?"

Galen sighed. "Everything has power inside—humans, animals, plants, and dragons. What makes mages, dragons, pixies, and you so special is that you can move that energy outside your body. Does that make sense?"

"No."

He grimaced and fought his impatience.

"If everything has magic, why can't other dwarves use magic?"

"They can. Their power is to make magic flow off them."

"But then they can't use it."

"You know what? Can you give me a minute?"

Vala nodded and felt like she wanted to apologize but didn't go so far as to say she was sorry. He was not doing a very good job of explaining how it was supposed to work and now, he was texting? She honestly didn't see how that was supposed to be useful at all. Why couldn't he simply show her more of those motions?

Maybe she should keep practicing, but it didn't feel like it was working. So instead of simply standing there and watching him text, she went to explore the warehouse.

There was a type of conveyor system in the middle that looked like it was designed for turning logs into lumber. It was one of the machines that had put people like her father out of work, only it had soon become obsolete.

She could almost feel that it could still work, though.

"What if I practice on this?" she asked and thought back to how she had made so many different devices turn on. She was an engineering student, after all. Maybe that knowledge, combined with her penchant for art, somehow made her magic work.

Galen didn't answer. She turned to see if he had finally decided to call someone instead of dither over his text, but he had not. The dragon who had faced Shaman Mytrov and a group of armed dwarves had fallen asleep on a pile of sawdust.

Vala Gagnon turned her attention to the line of machines running down the middle of the room and tried to feel the energy flowing through them.

CHAPTER TWENTY-FIVE

Motes of dust floated in the morning light. Most of the windows of the warehouse were dirty or overgrown with vines, but the broken ones allowed sunlight to stream in and illuminate decades' worth of sawdust in the air.

Galen pushed up and the movement made even more sawdust flurry around him. He could see why photography students would like this location. Something was enchanting about the old building made of cinderblocks, thin timbers, and glass. For a moment, he wondered if there was a magic equivalent. A dragon at school could make illusions. Would she be able to learn from the beauty there? Could she make an illusion that felt as calm and as peaceful as this warehouse? His still-awakening mind thought it would be nice to ask her.

"Oh, you're up!"

He startled and turned to someone who was most certainly not a dragon.

Vala Gagnon strode toward him from a line of machines that ran down the middle of the room. Each step of her booted feet kicked more sawdust up. The events of the last night, week, month, and year all came back to him. He groaned from the weight of it all and flopped into the pile of sawdust again. The makeshift bed had been comfortable enough to give him dreams that allowed him to forget the nightmare that his life had become. A plume billowed around him, but the motes now seemed choking rather than beautiful.

"You should have woken me sooner," he said once she stopped her approach.

"I tried at dawn but you didn't move. The next time, you reached for that." She pointed at the claw of the Prairie King in his hand.

He stared dumbly at it and didn't remember reaching for it. Had he slept with it in his hand all night long? He supposed he had. There was a time when he might have found that an ominous sign but now, he saw it as a reasonable precaution. It was likely the only thing that could save him when his uncle came for him.

That thought woke him fully.

"How long have you been up?"

"I slept for a few hours."

"You should have tried to get more rest."

"I feel like I've been asleep for my whole life. If I truly have magic, I want to know how to use it."

Galen nodded. He understood that. The thought reminded him of his phone. He pulled it out of his pocket and checked to see if Tanya had responded to his text to her last night, asking if she could have Jasmine send him a PDF of some simple magic texts.

Her one-word response—*ya*—was less than he had hoped for.

He stood slowly. "Well, should we get started?"

"I would love to."

"Did you have any success last night?" Galen asked.

Vala shook her head. "I've focused on trying to make my magic flow through these machines but I can't seem to get them to work."

"Let me see what you've been doing."

"Well, sure, but I haven't accomplished anything." She led him toward the row of machines in the center of the room. He studied the interconnected system that included all kinds of conveyor belts, groups of rollers, and machines that looked like they did little beyond move tree trunks through their transition into lumber. Between all these machines dedicated to motion, there were saws and sanders of various sizes.

Vala seemed to be focused on one in particular. It was fairly small compared to some, perhaps two feet across, although half of it was hidden beneath the surface of the table it was mounted vertically in the middle of.

The dragon knew next to nothing about machines. He did not know much about magic either, but compared to what he knew about machines, he was practically a wizard. Still, the saw seemed like a good choice. It was not as rusty as most of the others, which he assumed meant it was newer. Of course, that did not mean that it was new. Nothing in this place looked new and he wondered if that might be affecting her success or lack thereof.

"All right. So, can you make the table dance or whatever?"

"I've focused on getting the saw blade to spin, not making the table move," Vala replied.

"Great. So have at it," he said.

The girl nodded and began to move through some of the motions he had shown her the night before.

He tried to keep a smile on his face as he gave her words of encouragement, but it was not exactly easy to fake his optimism about her skills. She tried her best with each move and held her muscles tightly but moved smoothly, exactly as he had told her. Despite this, it seemed off. He didn't know if it was because she was still new to it or because she was a dwarf, and either her proportions were off since she was so short or it was the way her magic worked.

Galen let her try for a good ten minutes before he told her to stop. She had worked up a sweat and now clenched her teeth in evident frustration.

"I don't get it! I'm doing the moves you showed me. Why doesn't it work?"

"Magic is about intention," he explained. "You have to imagine the energy flowing into the machine."

"Is that how you made those bones come to life?" she asked. She made it sound so innocent—like she was asking for help with homework.

The young dragon paused and the claw felt heavy in his hand. Would this be what he was forever remembered for? No. He would not let that define him. Still, he could not act like it had never happened either. It was part of his life, part of who he was, and—hopefully—who he had been. If he could use that experience to help others, perhaps that would make everything worth it.

"When I first took control of those revenants, it was because I was afraid. I didn't want to be a failure to my family—that was what pushed me into the swamp—but in that moment, it was even more pressing than that. I feared for my life and reacted. I let my emotions guide me."

Vala nodded. "Well, I'm frustrated. Can I use that?"

"Sure, yeah," he said and nodded for her to try again.

She did, forced herself through the motions he had shown her, and looked thoroughly miserable doing it. He knew the feeling from when he had tried to summon storms hundreds of times and failed in each and every instance.

"You know what? I don't think that'll work," he said after she completed another round of the exercises.

"Yeah, no kidding. It'd be easier to fill my tummy with mouse meat than get that blade to spin."

"Mouse meat?"

"Sorry." Vala shook her head. "My mom has all these weird expressions about animals."

"It's fine," Galen said and his stomach grumbled.

"Oh, my God, you dragons can eat," she muttered.

"Keep practicing, all right? I'm going to find a snack."

She nodded and he left her to the routines. He checked his phone again as he went outside but had still received nothing from Tanya. His initial hope had been that the warehouse simply had very bad reception and that she had already tried to contact him, but he was not so lucky. No more texts came in and no missed calls displayed.

Not far from the warehouse, he saw a herd of deer. His stomach grumbled at their presence. Finally, he had found enough meat for him to eat properly. He grasped the claw tightly and raced toward the herd.

He closed the gap quicker than they could react. They raced into the woods, but he had expected that. He darted to one side with his dragon speed, outpaced them, and cut off one of the bigger ones with no antlers. When he veered in front of it, the animal reared. He swung at it with the claw but only grazed it. A moment later, its hoofs struck him in the chest and knocked him over before it ran toward the warehouse.

The boy pushed to his feet and gave chase. He closed the distance between him and the deer quickly but fumbled again when it was time to deliver the finishing strike. Annoyed and hungry, he changed into his dragon form and thrust a foot on top of the deer to spear its chest with the claw that was now part of his dragon body.

Victorious, he began to eat.

"That's how you eat?" Vala sounded outraged.

"Huh?" Galen looked up, his dragon mouth filled with a deer leg.

"That was a mother! That's her fawn right behind her."

He swallowed the piece of deer leg and turned to where a fawn peered out from the woods. A little confused, he turned to his companion. "Do you want me to eat that one too?"

"No! Even human hunters know you're not supposed to kill the mothers. How will there be any deer next season if you do that? You're supposed to kill the bucks."

"The what?"

"The ones with antlers."

"They're animals, Vala. The girls are made of as much meat as the boys."

"They still deserve our respect."

A sound came from inside the warehouse. "Vala," he said quietly.

"This is what my dad always said was so wrong with dragons. You believe any action you take is justified simply because of your position in society. Well, it's not."

"Vala, listen."

"I get it, you need to eat meat. I'm not saying you can't eat meat any more than a wolf can't eat meat, but you can at least learn enough about the world around you to know how to help the animals you consume rather than hurt them."

"Vala, what is that sound coming from inside the warehouse?"

She turned and listened, but the sound immediately began to fade and she raced inside.

He swallowed the rest of the deer hastily before he took his human form and followed her.

The girl stood in front of the saw on the table with a wide grin.

"It was spinning, Galen. When I came in, it was still spinning."

"That's great," he said, aware that this was perhaps not the most useful thing he could have said.

"But I don't get it. I wasn't doing any movements. I wasn't feeling my inner magic either."

"No, you weren't. You seemed pissed off." That gave him an idea. "Wait, Vala, how did you feel when those dwarves bullied your parents?"

"Are you serious? I was furious."

He nodded. "And what about when that shaman called you an abomination or whatever? Did that make you happy?"

"Of course not."

"And before that. You were probably totally calm when you almost killed all those other students."

"I didn't almost kill them!" Vala shouted.

The table saw began to spin.

She yelped when it did and it immediately started to slow. "What happened? Did I do that? Galen, I think I did that."

"I think you did."

"But how?"

"You must use emotion to power your magic. Think about it. Every time it has happened, how have you felt?"

"Angrier than a bag of ferrets."

"I don't know what a ferret is but that sounds good. This has to be the key to your powers, Vala."

"Rage? I'm a rage witch? I don't want to be a rage witch."

"With practice, you shouldn't need to become enraged to make it work, but using that emotion seems like it might be the key to getting you started."

The girl nodded, although she didn't seem exactly thrilled at the prospect. That annoyed him somewhat. What he would give to have magic that was activated by his anger. If him being angry would grant him powers, he would have knocked his mother from her seat at Stormsiege long before. If anger could give him strength, he would have defeated Boneclaw himself.

"Try it. Make yourself become angry and channel that anger into the saw blade."

Vala nodded. She furrowed her brow, clenched her fists, and mumbled something to herself. Nothing happened and she mumbled something about foxes in hen houses. It did not work.

"It's no use. I can't make myself mad for no reason."

"No reason?" That was a little much for him. "You have no reason to be angry? Seriously?"

"I can't simply throw myself into a fury!" she protested.

"Oh, so you don't care about your parents who care about you?" Galen snapped. He knew she would not like it, but they had less than no time. This was the only way.

"What is that supposed to mean?" she demanded. There it was —an edge of passion in her tone.

"It means that your parents might be dead because of you. You drove a truck through the front of their house, Vala. Doesn't the thought of their death make you mad?"

"You said that they must be fine. They are dwarves. A little wood falling on them wouldn't—"

"And you're sure the shaman let them be? You said your dad didn't go with them. Does this wacko normally let members of his congregation refuse him?"

"I don't care about what Mytrov thinks.!" Her voice was stronger and angrier. Good. He merely had to push her a little more.

"Well, he cares about you, Vala. He's hunting you right now. He intends to kill you not because of what you are but because of what he thinks you are. And you're fine with that? You get worked up over a stupid dead deer but a man hunting you is fine? What is wrong with you?"

"You could have killed a different deer," Vala screamed and the saw behind her spun to life. "You could have shown it mercy instead of wounding it like a stupid savage."

"Vala, you did it!" he said.

"I did?" She turned toward the table saw and it began to slow, robbed of its source of magic when her mood improved.

"You did it because you cared more about that deer than your parents," he snapped. While he felt nasty for saying it, he saw no other expedient way.

Sure enough, the saw reactivated. "I don't care about a deer more than my parents. We eat deer." The saw increased in speed. "I simply think you dragons are too arrogant for your own good, exactly like Mytrov. He thinks he has all the answers but he's like a turtle in winter, buried in the ice."

The saw spun even faster. It threw sparks now and had begun to rattle.

"Good, Vala, you're doing it. Focus on Mytrov!"

"I can't stand him. I was never allowed to talk to Trevor because of him. We never even got a computer because my dad said Mytrov wouldn't allow it. And then he arrives in a truck? Who does he think he is?"

The saw spun faster until something snapped and it became airborne. It lodged itself in the ceiling and quivered there.

Vala stared at it. "I did it."

"Now, we need to work on consistency. I don't want to have to yell at you about your parents every time we're in trouble."

"I think part of it was that this table saw is so old. And maybe if there was something smaller, it might take less energy?"

It sounded good to Galen, and he latched onto the idea. "Yes. That makes sense. If you can practice channeling your emotions into one of those spinny things with the spike, maybe you can work your way up to a truck again."

"You mean a drill?" She snorted.

The dragon shrugged. "I don't know. Use your rage over the arrogance of dragons or whatever."

"All right. We need to find some hand tools."

"You need to find some hand tools."

"What? Why me?"

"If you think dragons are arrogant and privileged and that pisses you off enough to launch a metal blade across this room, I'm not about to dispel this notion. Besides, you're right. I should have killed that deer in one blow. I need to practice with this claw."

"So, you won't help?"

"I won't, dwarf."

Vala frowned, but when she realized he was helping her, she grinned. She was so friendly that this would take a while.

But after a few hours of work, both had begun to improve. She had focused on how anger truly felt to her. It seemed the feeling of wrongness in her gut was similar to magic, and she was able to direct it in more specific ways.

Galen had also practiced. He knew it was unconventional but he couldn't help wanting to be better with the claw. So, while she practiced pouring her rage into tools, he practiced striking with the claw.

It was probably a good thing that she was so focused on practicing or she might have been jealous of how much more quickly he had progressed. The thing was, she was working with an utterly foreign power. She was doing something that she had not only never done before, but no dwarf ever had either. It made it difficult.

In contrast, he was practicing how to fight. That was something dragons had done for thousands of years and he had done his entire life. He enjoyed using the weapon as an extension of himself to move, strike, recoil, and strike again. It did not hurt that his dragon speed, strength, and agility made him a natural with the blade.

Although that might have been a factor too. The weapon in his hand was sharp—sharper than any piece of steel—but it was not a blade. It was a claw, a part of a dragon that he had used as a part of his own body. Even when he held it in his hands, he felt as if it were a part of him, as if his inner magic or whatever—he didn't particularly subscribe to all that inner magic crap—flowed through the claw.

Vala had improved too. She currently sent her electricity in and out of another saw to turn it on and off without much difficulty. It didn't seem like much to the dragon, but she seemed pleased with herself so he considered it a success. He was still worried about his uncle arriving, but he had another thirty-six hours. His plan was to use that time to convince Vala to go to the Lumos School. He didn't know how to explain it but he was certain she was important and that in a way, the shaman was right. She would change what it meant to be a dwarf and he wanted to help make sure that happened.

Which seemed less likely when the crackle-snap of magic outside the warehouse caught his attention.

Vala looked up, concerned but not fully understanding what this could mean.

Galen sprang into action. He raced forward and sliced the brick wall in front of him with the claw. Then, he kicked at the gouge the claw had made in the bricks as if they were nothing but foam blocks. Bricks exploded outward and he stepped through the hole into the outdoors.

"Stay behind me," he said as the ball of magic expanded and turned into a magical gate.

He had no idea who this might be but he suspected his family. They had employed mages before and he wouldn't put it past them to use any tool at their disposal to reach him.

Well, they could try, anyway. He was not about to go down without a fight.

CHAPTER TWENTY-SIX

Galen grasped the claw tightly and braced himself to attack, then grinned when Tanya Fastwing stepped through.

She smiled and looked as beautiful as ever in one of her trademark Victorian-style dresses. He didn't honestly know what a Victorian-style dress was, but he didn't know what else to call the multi-layered, tight-waisted puffy-butted dresses she always wore. All he knew was that he had said she looked Victorian in one once and she had smiled and thanked him, so he simply stuck with that.

"Galen, is that any way to greet a friend?" she said and looked at the claw.

"Uh. Sorry?" he said and lowered his weapon.

She looked back through the portal and made eye contact with someone who was invisible to Galen from his angle. "Can you pick me up in an hour, Ky? Thanks!"

In the next moment, she stepped through and hugged him as the portal snapped shut behind her.

"I thought you would text me a PDF," he said as she released him.

"That was the plan, but when I asked Jasmine about it, she

started on this tangent about digital media not being able to hold magic well. I told her it was for you, not a mage, but she insisted we go to the library. Anyway, I got a couple of books for you—the basics, like you asked for. Why did you want them anyway?"

"How did you find me?"

"Your text said you were in a lumberyard near a small town in Canada. I Googled you and found it. It turns out this location has its own hashtag. Who knew? Anyway, I asked the headmaster if I could go and she agreed, although she did say I'm supposed to be back in an hour.

"But listen to me! Here I am rambling. Why did you need magic books? Did you find a way to impress your parents? Because I don't think hiding in this lumberyard exactly counts as keeping a low profile."

"I—"

"Ah! I can't believe you're here. Come here, give me another —" Tanya spread her arms for a hug but she stopped abruptly. "You didn't say you had a friend."

"Oh, yeah…uh, Vala, this is—"

"Tanya Fastwing, charmed." Tanya did not sound at all charmed.

"Tanya, this is Vala Gagnon who I texted you about. She's a dwarf but she can do magic. It's incredible. Last night, she made a truck drive itself."

"You didn't mention anything about anyone else," the other dragon said slowly.

"I didn't? Sorry. We were up fairly late."

"You were?"

"Dinner, then coffee, and I met some of Vala's…church members."

"Galen, can I speak to you for a moment?"

"Yeah, of course."

"In private."

He turned to Vala, who shrugged.

"Sure, yeah. Vala, give me a minute. I'll be right back."

In silence, he followed Tanya away from the warehouse and closer to the street. Two students gaped at them—likely because of her dress—and snapped a few photos.

"Galen, I thought you were supposed to go into hiding or prove yourself to your family."

"I was. But then I met Vala, and well…Tanya, she's amazing."

He felt a flush of irritation from her aura. It was weird but he had to explain what was going on. "She's special, Tanya, more special than anyone since…well, Kylara."

"Kylara?" The flush of irritation flared again, except it seemed to edge toward anger now.

"Yeah, she can do magic. No dwarf has ever been able to do that before. That's what I wanted the books for."

"Galen, I came up here because I thought you were in trouble, not because some dwarf needs help making a pen float or whatever."

"No, Tanya, Vala is not merely some dwarf. She's magic. There's never been anyone like her before."

Tanya's aura shifted. "No one's ever been like me before either." Fear emanated from her, along with betrayal. He was so confused. What was wrong with her? She had come to help so what had she expected? Why would she feel betrayed?

"I want Vala to go to the Lumos School. I want to introduce her to Kylara and everyone else."

"You want to…introduce her to them?" Tanya's rage returned.

"What is with you?" Galen demanded and immediately regretted it.

"What is with me? It's more like what is with you?" she said. "You sent me a text in the middle of the night that explains nothing. I came here hoping you'd found a way to use magic and maybe stop your family from hunting you and instead, you're what? Playing house with a dwarf?"

"Playing house? What is that supposed to mean? I wanted her to have those books so she could learn about magic."

"Oh, how stupid of me to assume it was anything else."

"Yeah, it was," Galen said, relieved that she had finally admitted that she was being a dolt.

Her rage struck like a lightning bolt. "Well, fine!" She took a step toward him and shoved the books into his arms. "Here's your delivery. I guess Jasmine was wrong. I should have simply sent a PDF."

He managed to not drop the books but in the time it took to balance them, she had already pulled her phone out and placed a call.

"Ky? Yeah, it's me. No. We won't have a visitor. I was wrong—horribly wrong. No. No, I'm not overreacting. Can you please open a portal? I want to come back to school." She hung up.

"Tanya, I don't think you understand."

"No, I don't, Galen. I thought you came to see me because I was something special to you. I thought you had called because you had found a way that we could…that is, you and me…"

"We can be together." That finally earned the smile he had expected this entire time. "And Vala too."

She sighed and a portal blazed into existence behind her.

"I'm glad I could help you with your new friend," she said in a voice so phony he was sure every dragon in Stormsiege would have recognized it for the lie it was.

"Tanya, please. What's wrong? Why are you acting so crazy?"

But that wasn't the right thing to say either. Tanya didn't answer and simply turned on her heel and marched through the portal. She looked back the second before it closed and he felt disappointment and heartbreak from her aura, then she was gone.

Galen stood alone in front of the old lumberyard warehouse and held a stack of magic books he would gladly have traded to understand what was going through Tanya's head.

CHAPTER TWENTY-SEVEN

Feelings of confusion and rage battled in Galen's chest as he stormed into the warehouse.

What was wrong with Tanya? She hadn't listened to a word he'd said or even tried to understand why he was helping Vala. And what was even more annoying was that he was only helping the dwarf because he had thought about what she would have done in his situation. He had seen someone who needed help and he had helped them. While he hadn't exactly expected to win an award, he had certainly not expected that a show of kindness would be met by such...such insanity!

"Here are some books for you. Maybe these can help you do something useful." He shoved the books into Vala's hands.

"Oh, great—wow! I had no idea there were entire books written about magic." She flipped through the pages.

"Of course there are books written about it. The whole world uses magic. Not everyone is stuck in the past like you dwarves."

"Technically, magic is older than technology so I wouldn't say we're stuck in the past. That's like blaming beavers for refusing to build skyscrapers."

"That's stupid and doesn't make any sense," he said. How

dumb was she? Couldn't she read his aura and tell he was pissed off?

"It's only an expression, but you're right. It's not important. Who was that?"

"Tanya. I told you."

"Right, yeah, but where did she come from? Is she a dragon? Her dress was very cool but if she was a dragon, why did she have those books? Where is she?"

"Gone."

"Oh. Is that her power or something?"

"Will you please shut up?" Galen roared.

Vala froze. Her stupid face didn't show any more emotion than her aura did. He hated that he could not read her emotions. It reminded him of when he had been trapped in the mongrel body, half-human and half-dragon, without the full powers of either form. Everyone had been cut off to him, inscrutable and unreadable. He had been alone for so long but he had made it through. He had met Tanya again and she had helped him and he'd thought he would never have to be alone like that again.

Now, he could see that he was wrong.

Tanya had abandoned him with Vala. She had left him alone with this block of a person who couldn't even tell that he was in a foul mood.

"What's your problem?" the dwarf demanded.

"My problem? You're asking me what my problem is? You! You're my problem. I should never have swooped down to save you."

"Are you trying to activate my magic again?" she asked cautiously.

"I don't care about your magic and I don't care about you. You're merely a dumb dwarf who I thought I could help so my friends wouldn't hate me. Look how that turned out."

"Why are you talking to me like this?" Her eyes welled with tears.

"Because you have ruined my life. I was supposed to go into hiding and now I'm here, stuck with a dumb dwarf who can make saw tables spin."

"Table saws."

"Will you please shut up?" He used dragon power to augment his voice. "I came here to hide. Don't you get that? You've ruined everything."

"Don't talk to me that way. I never asked for your help," Vala said quietly.

"I'll talk to you however I damn well please. I'm a dragon from the Stormwing clan. You're a runty dwarf whose people want to neuter her."

"I said don't talk to me that way," she said and the saw behind her began to spin.

"Or what? You'll convince me to walk over there and lay on that table so you can saw me in half? Admit it, you're pathetic."

"At least I'm not some woe-is-me snot of a dragon. You think your family doesn't like you because you don't have powers? They don't like you because you're a whiny little baby who can't communicate to save his life." Conveyor belts clicked on and a pulley on tracks on the ceiling that he had not previously noticed lurched to life and rolled toward him.

"You don't know anything about my family," he said and marched forward. He towered over her.

"I know they have good reason to want you gone." She didn't so much as take a single step back. Instead, she stood there and held her books as if he were nothing.

"You take that back," Galen said.

"Make me."

He shoved her then, or he tried to, but she was too sturdy and did not budge.

"Like a mouse trying to move a moose," Vala sneered.

"Oh yeah?" He roared and put all his dragon strength into pushing her over.

It worked and she careened away and crashed through one of the conveyor belts to destroy it.

Galen almost felt bad. He had not wanted to hurt her and had only intended to show her that he was not weak. Before he could say anything, she pushed to her feet as if nothing had happened. The pieces of machinery all around her continued to move, despite no longer being connected to each other.

"Oh, wow, so strong! You pushed a dwarf over," she snapped sardonically. "Do you want to try your fire breath next?"

"You owe me your life."

"Get bent," she said and gathered the magic books. She stormed toward him. He didn't move out of her way, of course, and she didn't bother to go around. She merely threw a shoulder into him as she passed, upended, and spilled the books from her hands in the collision.

The dragon scrambled to his feet and in the process, his hands settled on one of the magic books. He held it up between them. A peace treaty? A threat? He wasn't sure.

Vala didn't seem to have any more of an idea than he did. "Keep it," she said finally after she'd stared at him for a long moment. She took the other two books and marched out of the hole in the warehouse he had made with the claw.

"Where do you think you're going?" he demanded.

"Away from you. I'll be better off on my own."

"Fine!"

"You don't get a choice, Galen. I'm going."

He scowled but she didn't see it as her back was turned. Unlike Tanya, she never looked back.

CHAPTER TWENTY-EIGHT

Galen watched the dwarf go. He was beyond furious. If he had Vala's power to channel rage into magic, he had no doubt that he would create a hurricane, even in the middle of Canada. He would create a tornado and use it to scour this worthless town from the Earth or he would make a blizzard that would bury it so deeply that it could never be found.

The dragon sagged and sat on the floor. What was he thinking? He didn't want to hurt anyone. Even before he had powers, when he had fantasized about being something more than a runty vanilla dragon who was an embarrassment to his family, he had never dreamed of hurting people. He wanted respect, honor, and even prestige, but he didn't want to hurt others.

Unfortunately, he had never been good with words. What had happened with Tanya made that clear. He should have explained what he was trying to do with Vala and that he wanted to help her to prove to Tanya—not his family—what kind of a dragon he truly was. In hindsight, he wished he had explained that better instead of merely fumbling over his words.

What was worse, though, was what he had said to the dwarf. He had been upset with Tanya—whom he knew was capable of forgiving acts that did not deserve to be forgiven—and he had taken it out on Vala. He liked her and he wanted to help her but he didn't know her. She didn't deserve to be spoken to that way and didn't deserve him being so nasty to her any more than she had deserved the shaman and his cronies attacking her.

And now—because of him—she was wandering out there alone. They had found the perfect place for her to practice her skill and he had driven her off. He felt like a jerk. Honestly, he conceded, he was a jerk.

Galen sighed and pushed to his feet when he decided he should go after her. He knew he had said horrible things but that didn't mean he couldn't try to make it right. Those dwarves were still out there and despite her improvement, she still had considerable ground to cover. She could not stand up to them alone.

He retrieved the claw. She would need his help. After a moment's thought, he picked up the magic book that she had left behind. She would need more help than his. He had to reach her, make sure she was safe, and find a way to explain everything that had happened with Tanya. She would cool off and he would make it right—he hoped.

His mind made up, he stepped outside. He didn't know the area particularly well but he was a dragon and therefore reasonably certain that he could catch up to a stubby-legged dwarf. The thought drew a rueful smile. It was probably saying things like "stubby-legged dwarf" that made others so mad.

He could do better and while he worked to improve himself, he could help Vala get to safety. It might be difficult to apologize but he was strong enough. If he had been able to go to Tanya when he had still been a mongrel, he could face the dwarf now.

An inner prompting made him look into the sky and he drew a deep breath and froze.

Only moments before, the sky had been clear and blue but now, a bank of gray clouds moved in. At the very edge of the front was a dragon.

Petrov Stormwing circled once and landed in his path.

Galen—still reluctant to reveal the Prairie King's claw—transformed into his dragon form.

"Are you going somewhere?" Uncle Petrov asked.

"Yes. I'm working on proving myself to the family exactly as Lady Stormwing ordered me to."

His uncle flashed annoyance at him and he realized his mistake.

"Uncle," he said and bowed in a tacit show of respect.

Petrov snorted and began to pace around him while he sniffed the air. "You stink, Galen."

"I have been too busy working to bathe, dear Uncle."

"You stink of dwarf, you little brat."

"This is dwarf country, Uncle."

"You stink of dwarf because you have been cavorting with one since last night. Why, Galen? Why waste what little time you have left with a mage experiment gone wrong?"

"Vala is not a waste of time."

Petrov snorted. "Oh, dear. You've gone soft on her. It's as I expected. Why prolong this? Why not surrender your little toy to me now and hope it's enough?"

"My...toy?"

The older dragon lunged before he realized what was even happening. He drove into him, sank his claws into his armpit where the scales were weak, and dug into the nerves to make his arm go numb.

Easily, as if plucking an apple from a branch, Petrov lifted the hand that had absorbed the black claw.

"You hid this well the last time we met. But I saw it this time."

"It's nothing!"

His uncle tsked in disapproval. "It is the only reason I have not killed you yet. Do not discount its utility so easily."

Galen shifted under the weight of the older dragon's form and tried to position himself in such a way that he could throw him off. "But Uncle, it's only been forty-eight hours. I was given three days, not two."

Petrov could tell what he was doing and dug into even deeper the wound he had inflicted. Then, almost casually, he plucked the magic book off the ground. "And you hope to earn the family's respect by gathering trinkets? A claw and a magic book. How pathetic."

"I have more time." He grunted and strained to free himself.

The older dragon finally released his hold. "More time to waste. You're an embarrassment, Galen. I have long argued that you are not worth the meat it takes to feed you. Still, you're right. My sister has a soft spot for you and we will respect her wishes and let you live a while longer."

Petrov climbed off him. "These things you have will not be enough to spare your life. Do you understand this?"

"I still have another day—"

"Yes, yes. You can count. How nice for you. I will return tomorrow evening and you will show me how you have proven yourself. And if you cannot, I will take that claw and the hand it's connected to."

Galen stood slowly and his uncle snorted in disgust. It seemed he could not even stand in the right way.

"And if you need motivation…" Petrov inhaled and breathed a great plume of fire onto the book of magic.

The text must have had some kind of protection and it resisted the flames admirably, but only for about ten seconds before the cover started to blacken and the edges of the paper began to curl inward. Whatever magic had protected it failed and it was reduced to ash.

"I will return tomorrow. If you have nothing to show for your efforts, I will relish turning you into mincemeat."

The dragon laughed and braced himself to leap into the sky but paused.

"Do you value your life, Galen?"

"Of course I—"

"I'm not so sure you do. I think your time spent as a freak wandering the desert made you realize how worthless you truly are. Perhaps you failed to earn the honor of your clan thus far because you know you do not deserve to return to Stormsiege. Still, I have faith in you, boy, even if you do not have it in yourself. All you need is motivation." He drew a deep breath and his nephew braced himself.

But it wasn't a breath, Galen realized. He was sniffing.

"She does stink, does she not?"

"What are you talking about?"

"Not the Fastwing girl, if that's what you're worried about. She brought honor to her clan, as inferior as they are. It is the stench of the dwarf that I am concerned is a distraction to you. Instead, let her motivate you. Fail, and she dies but perhaps not in front of you. I look forward to snuffing you out too much for that but she will die, Galen."

"That was not the agreement!" he roared and charged toward his uncle.

Petrov knocked him back without even turning to him.

He pushed to his feet but the older dragon did not so much as flinch although his body was held ready to attack. Honestly, he did not think he had ever fought a dragon like him.

"If you wish her to live, you have until tomorrow as my sister promised you." Finally, he leapt skyward and flew away, although he left the foul weather behind. That suited the young dragon's mood perfectly.

CHAPTER TWENTY-NINE

Vala continued to walk despite her tears, although she had no plan and no idea where she should go next or what she should do. She had two magic books and had tried to look through them, but she couldn't understand half the words, let alone the diagrams.

To make matters worse, it looked like someone had doodled all kinds of weird patterns in the margins of the pages. She wondered if the magic book was cursing her for all the doodles she had drawn on pages. Did it know she was a fraud? Did it know she was a dwarf when a human should be holding these books?

She wiped her tears and drew a deep breath. Maybe she could hitch a ride to town. She needed to check on her parents and make sure they were okay. Once she was sure they weren't hurt, she would attempt to reach the southern border. Galen had talked about that school and maybe she could get there.

But of course, thinking about the school brought her mind back to the dragon. What had happened with him? Everything had been going so well until that girl had arrived and it all exploded. Was she an enemy of some kind? Someone from his family? But no, he had introduced her as Fastwing, not Stormwing. Plus, she had brought the magic books. So why had her appearance made everything go so wrong?

The girl looked over her shoulder and down the long street that led to the lumberyard. She did not know how long she'd been walking, only that the sky overhead had grown dark and stormy. Still, she could see a long way and Galen was not on the road following her. Nor was he flying above. She had hoped that —despite their fight—he would come after her.

Now, however, she saw how foolish she had been and sighed. At least that helped her make her mind up. She would check on her parents and head south alone.

Was that the right thing to do, though? He had said some horrible things but he had also saved her life the night before. In fact, he had risked everything for her. Maybe she should head back and apologize. He might not have followed her because he hoped she would return. Maybe he didn't want to abandon their temporary safe house because he was concerned that they wouldn't be able to find each other.

Vala sighed. She felt like a fool but she already knew she would be the first one to apologize. If he continued to be a jerk, that would change things, but he was worth another attempt.

She turned and had to hold a hand up to block the lights of an approaching car. It passed and she lowered her hand, but a second vehicle followed the first. This one's high beams were on and completely blinded her.

That should have been her first clue but she failed to notice it.

A moment later, the car that had passed her braked sharply and screeched to a halt. She recognized it now as a truck with a damaged front end and a flag flying from the back of it.

"Vala—thank Father Earth we found you!" Dwarves scrambled out of both vehicles to surround her.

"Leave me alone!" she shouted and summoned her rage like Galen had taught her.

"You're not thinking clearly, my child," Shaman Mytrov said. She turned toward his voice but the other truck had moved so she was now trapped between the headlights of both, blinded and unable to see.

But that was not a problem for her. She focused on her magic and sent it into the trucks to extinguish their lights and plunge them all into darkness.

"She's going to attack!"

"I won't. Please, leave me alone," Vala responded.

One of the dwarves caught hold of her and it only served to make her madder. She let her anger pour into one of the trucks—the one that had not been damaged yet. Even with the little practice she'd had, she could understand it better than she had before. She could feel how the engine craved its valves to be opened so more gasoline could pour in and how the steering column demanded to be used.

Happy to oblige it, she turned the wheels toward three dwarves who approached through the dark.

"Let. Me. Go!" she shouted and gasoline poured into the engine and lurched the vehicle forward.

But Vala was not the only one to remember what she had been able to do with the truck. The three dwarves not only managed to dive out of the way but they flung themselves toward her.

They drove into her, smothered her, and pushed her face against the asphalt.

She couldn't move as Galen had taught her but she could still feel the truck. As she tried to remain calm, she summoned it and urged it to return to her. She almost felt like she could get it right and could make it ram these three dwarves off her and hurl them away. Then, she could shove the one who had grabbed her off and—

Something struck the back of her head and she felt her control over the vehicle slip as pain exploded.

"Don't hurt her!"

"She's still conscious!"

"She's a dwarf, you fools!" That was Shaman Mytrov, her fuzzy mind told her. "She can take another blow."

Pain exploded a second time and her face thumped on the street. The last thing she felt before she slipped from consciousness was the truck sliding out of her control. Its horn honked, its light flashed, and music blared from the radio. Help...she needed help...and the truck could guide someone to her.

But despite the sounds of the horn, the radio, and the flashing lights, she fell from consciousness. The vehicle became silent and dark when it was freed from her magical touch and she sank into a place where there was only darkness.

CHAPTER THIRTY

All Galen had wanted to do was to help Vala and now, he had put her in more danger than she would have been without him. He no longer doubted if finding her was the right decision. He had to find her if only so they could decide how to keep her away from his uncle. He wouldn't pretend he could escape his ability to track, but maybe he could distract him long enough for her to get to safety. Petrov couldn't be in two places at once and they could use that. It was all they had.

But first, he had to find her. He looked at the sky again and wondered where his uncle was hiding behind those clouds, but he decided it did not matter much. If he wished to hurt Vala, he could track her better than the young dragon could. Why use him to locate her? The only option was to find her and think of a way to get her to safety while he somehow dealt with Petrov.

Conscious that a fair amount of time had already passed since she left, he took his dragon form and launched skyward. After a day spent training in his human body, the deer, and a decent amount of sleep, he didn't feel nearly as fatigued in this form as he had before. A small blessing, he thought grimly.

He flew to the street and assumed that she would probably

follow it one way or the other. She seemed more comfortable on the streets than the woods so hopefully, she was using them rather than the forest. Logic said she was probably on her way home despite the fact that she was already being hunted. The smart thing for her to do would be to get out of town as quickly as possible.

Galen did not think she had done that for a minute. He banked to follow the road to town and hoped she had stuck to it.

To his dismay, it appeared she had.

About a mile ahead, two trucks were parked across the road. As he flew closer, one of them lurched into life, then both flashed their lights and honked their horns.

"Vala." He grunted and urged himself to fly faster.

Abruptly, the lights cut out. One of the dwarves lifted Vala and put her inside the cab of one of the vehicles.

For a moment, he cursed himself for wasting time moping instead of going after her, then made a choice he hated despite his certainty that it was the right one.

When he saw his friend in peril, Galen Stormwing vanished into the bank of clouds above him.

He knew there was a time in his life when he would have called any dragon a coward for doing exactly what he had done. He was wiser now, though, if only a little.

There were at least eight dwarves down there. That meant eight bodies with bones he could not break and skin that would not blister under dragon flame. They had already proven themselves experienced in dealing with dragons. Plus, he had seen guns.

It might be too much to assume that these dwarves from deep in the middle of nowhere had dragon bullets but to assume that they did not have any was akin to suicide. If only one struck him, it could be the end. He still did not have full control of his powers. There was no telling what a bullet made of dragon parts would do to him.

The dragon felt better in this body than he had in a while but still, something was missing, something he didn't quite understand about his body. He had felt it a few times when training but had not been able to determine what it was before had Tanya interrupted him.

Galen shook his head. It was not the time to think about Tanya but to focus on Vala.

He lowered his altitude enough to poke his head out from the clouds.

The dwarves were moving but slower than he had expected. They took a turn that led them out into the countryside. He had assumed that they would return to their church, but that couldn't be their plan.

They followed this smaller road for a time before they turned onto another even smaller one. It wasn't paved at all and seemed to head up what he wanted to call a mountain in this landscape, despite it being much smaller than most of the peaks in New Mexico.

The cloud bank gave way—hopefully a sign that Petrov was not following him too closely and would rely on his vaunted tracking abilities—so he flew higher. With enough height, he knew he would practically vanish, especially when viewed from the back of a vehicle moving over an unpaved road.

In his new position, he followed and waited for the trucks to stop, but they continued even higher. He was a dragon so he knew a thing or two about remote bases. Stormsiege had been the Stormwing's seat of power but his parents had other pieces of property spread out for different purposes.

None of those purposes had ever sat particularly well with him. Now, he could not help but think that the dwarves being out here was not a good sign.

He considered moving ahead of them and blasting fire to fell some trees and make the road impassable but wasn't sure that would slow them. They were strong and extremely resistant to fire so might even be able to deadlift a burning tree trunk. Finally, after he'd considered and discarded other possibilities, the dwarves came to a stop.

Galen circled twice as they unloaded. They truly were strong, stalwart creatures. Each of them put more on their back than he had ever seen a human carry. Eventually, Shaman Mytrov reached into the cab of one of the vehicles. He seemed to struggle for a moment before he dragged a now conscious Vala out.

"You ferrets and foxes! You stoats and toads!"

The religious leader forced a gag in her mouth.

Furious, the young dragon almost attacked then and there but he calmed himself. The dwarves were taking her somewhere specific, but where? If he failed to rescue her, he very much doubted that they would let him tag along to discover the location of their base. He knew he had made many people angry but he could still call Tanya once he knew where they were headed. If he failed, she would come—he hoped.

But he would need to have somewhere to send her.

When no other option presented itself, he took a risk and landed on the dirt road the dwarves had used but about a kilometer back and beyond a bend in the dirt road where the trees would hide him from sight. As soon as his talons touched the ground, he changed into his human shape and ducked into the woods.

His quarry did not sound any different. They didn't yell about him and still seemed to be talking about unpacking their supplies. He assumed that meant they had not seen or heard him. With the black claw grasped tightly in one hand, he moved through the forest toward them.

He had expected the terrain to be difficult compared to the desert, but the pine needles on the forest floor did a good job of muffling his footsteps. Thankfully, he was able to move through the woods and get close enough to the dwarves to see them before they left the vehicles.

It was lucky he managed to come that close. Once his quarry started to move, they did so with surprising speed. Despite being weighed down with packs, tools, and weapons, they did not seem significantly encumbered at all and advanced up a dirt path at a quick trot. Vala seemed to give the shaman some difficulty, but whatever the dwarves had in their packs did not include electronic devices. He waited for one of the packs to explode to life with an animated machine of some kind but it never happened.

It seemed her powers had convinced them to return to their troglodyte roots. He understood that. Fear was a powerful motivator and combined with ignorance, there was nothing more powerful.

Galen tried to stay focused on the task at hand as he followed them but it was difficult. He wished he knew more about dwarves, both about their beliefs and their capabilities. There had been classes about their culture at the Lumos School but he had been too full of himself and his family's racist values to ever sign up for one of those.

Everything he knew about dwarves came in the form of practical combat advice from his mother and father. They had lived in Seattle—a little south of dwarf country—so they had planned on the eventuality of fighting them. As a kid, he had thought they were talking about being attacked but as he grew older, he had come to understand that their tips and techniques were for attacking the dwarves.

Although he wasn't sure if any of them would be of any use. Dwarves were supposed to be strangely dense—something he had confirmed—so could not be lifted to the heights necessary to drop them and crack their thick skulls. Fire was reputedly not much good and neither were brute attacks.

For most of the Stormwing family, the solution had been to lure them to a low position and summon a storm to drown them. He didn't have that ability and even if he did, it wouldn't work in this situation. If he tried to attack the group, he'd hurt Vala. That was not an option.

Galen looked ahead and saw that although he was ostensibly there for the girl, he had lost sight of her captors. They had been directly ahead of him. He hurried and paused as he neared a clearing that formed almost a semicircle around a rock face on the side of the "mountain" he was climbing.

Panic began to rise in his chest as he searched for signs of them but saw nothing. The path they had used came to this clearing and seemed to vanish.

But then he heard a voice, faint and reverberant as if it had echoed down a long hall. "Murderous moose!"

He looked across the clearing from his position in the forest and again, saw nothing.

"Forget it." He broke cover and moved out into the field toward the voice he had heard. Despite his careful scrutiny of the area, he found no signs of their presence. He had half-expected a tent to be hidden in plain sight or to stumble across a trap of some kind but seemed doomed to disappointment. It was like Vala had vanished into the rock itself.

The thought made him pause.

The dragon approached the rockface. A few deep fissures traced through it, likely caused by water getting in, freezing, and cracking it continuously over the years. Could the dwarves have vanished into one of these? Cautiously, he moved down the rock face and peered into each of them until he found one that was large enough for him to slip inside.

He ducked and went down a narrow passage but after only a few feet, it opened into a kind of underground room. His gaze swept over an old chair, some blankets, and strips of jerky hanging on one wall. If that was not enough to convince him, he also found a strip of paper. On it was an illustration of a table saw, although it had been given eyes and was feeding pieces of wood to its spinning blade using its electrical cord as a hand.

"Nice job, Vala," he murmured. The piece of paper was in front of another crack that led even deeper into the earth. That was where the dwarves must be but the gap was extremely narrow.

Galen would have no hope of transforming into his dragon form once he entered, nor would he stand much of a chance in his human body if they had guns. Even with dragon healing powers, a bullet in the brain was an effective way to kill a dragon. There were some—Kristen Hall and Kylara Diamantine—whose powers could stop normal bullets, but he was not one of them.

The young dragon could admit that he had come as far as he could by himself. He retreated into the woods and although he hated himself for it, he knew it was the only option. Once in the safety of the trees, he pulled his phone out, bit his lip, and called Tanya.

The phone didn't ring. He looked at it and groaned when he saw there was no service. Wherever the dwarves had taken Vala, it truly was in the middle of nowhere.

He tried again but the call still did not go through.

Galen sat on the pine needles and tried to decide what to do next. If Tanya couldn't help, who else was there? None of her friends, certainly. If she was mad at him, none of the others would help him either.

Which meant he would have to think of a way to rescue Vala himself. He cracked his knuckles, looked at the gap in the wall, and wondered if he could lure them out somehow. It seemed unlikely but he honestly had no idea what else to try.

Stifled by indecision, he crouched in the woods and searched for a solution he could not see.

CHAPTER THIRTY-ONE

Amy Williams had never expected a single dwarf to be so hard to find. In retrospect, that seemed foolish of her—after all, dwarves were resistant to magic so any attempts to sense Vala's aura had failed. Still, she was accustomed to being able to follow the trail an unpracticed mage left behind them. This was an entirely different kind of challenge.

"Still, nothing, huh?" Trudeau asked from the back of his beat-up skateboard.

"Still nothing," she confirmed.

She had to admit, she was somewhat impressed with the dwarf. In all honesty, she had expected him to chicken out and beg for mercy as soon as she launched him into the air, but he had clung to his board and never asked for her to slow.

Trudeau—true to his word—had led her to the coffeeshops around the university area and they had even found the one Vala had gone to but after that, the trail had gone cold. It seemed her companion was a notoriously bad tipper and the barista didn't have any trust for the Steel Guard so was less than helpful. She had considered a little destruction—she had learned how to put things back together, although it wasn't easy and she had not been able to fix the Gagnon residence—but decided it would cause more harm than good.

They had already looked everywhere on campus, the shops close to it, and the classrooms where Vala attended class. After all that, they still had nothing.

When her phone rang, she answered it.

"Aren't we supposed to be on the case?" Trudeau asked.

Amy stopped using her telekinesis to levitate his board and he plummeted toward his death.

"Woo-hoo-hoo! Yeah!" Trudeau shouted as he fell and picked up speed. He truly was unflappable. With a sigh, she caught him with her magic again and he cheered.

She rolled her eyes and answered the phone as she descended to ground level to stand beside the dwarf, who—despite plunging a hundred feet—was still calm enough to practice kickflips in the parking lot she had landed in.

"Amy Williams, Steel Guard. Talk to me."

"Amy, er—Mage Williams? It's Tanya Fastwing."

"I know, Tanya. I have caller ID. Have you heard of it?" She knew she shouldn't snap at kids or make dwarves fear for their lives as she dropped them from the sky, but she had never faced a case like this before. She needed a break.

"Uh. Yeah. My phone has it too," the girl replied awkwardly.

The mage cursed her attitude. Being snappy with her was costing her time. "What do you need, Tanya? This is not a great time to talk about magic." It truly wasn't. Besides, it was the middle of the night. Why was Tanya calling now?

"It's Galen."

If she had still been in the air, she knew that hearing that name would have caused her to fall. As it was, she sat heavily on her board.

"What is it? Did you get a lead? Is this our lucky break?" Trudeau asked and skated closer.

She motioned for him to shut up. He knew exactly what it

meant as she'd done it so many times and he simply nodded with a wide grin.

"What about him?" she asked and hoped it wasn't too rude.

"Well, I can't get hold of him."

Her hope withered. "When was the last time you talked to him?"

"I saw him this morning."

Hope bloomed instantly in response. She was so excited that she had failed to pay attention to everything Tanya was saying.

"—was acting like she was so amazing, and I was… Well, I don't want to say jealous, but I couldn't understand why he felt this way. But I think it makes sense now. He only wants to help and I shouldn't have been so mad at him."

"Where did you say you saw him?" Amy asked and hoped she hadn't missed it.

"He's at a warehouse outside of… I don't remember the name of the town."

"That's fine, I'm here. What kind of warehouse?"

"Wait, what? You're there? Is Galen all right?"

"I'm trying to make sure he is," she replied. "This warehouse—tell me more."

"Oh, yeah. There were two of them and both were fairly over-grown. I can send a pin if that would help."

"That would be great, yes. Send me a pin. Trudeau, do you know a place with two overgrown warehouses?"

"The old lumberyard?" he asked.

The mage asked Tanya to confirm and she did. "I think I heard machinery in the background."

"That's impossible," Trudeau said. She had put Tanya on speaker now that the officer had proved useful. "It hasn't had service in years."

"But Vala can make machines work with her magic," she said. "Tanya, thank you for this. Do you have anything else?"

"No. Sorry. Like I said, Kylara portaled me in and we had a… fight, I guess, and I left. I haven't been able to reach him since."

"Okay. If you do, call me right away, all right?"

"You got it."

Amy hung up.

"The lumberyard. Which way?"

Trudeau pointed.

"I hope you're ready to go fast."

"Do you mean you've been holding back on me?" He was already grinning.

"Hold on tight." She launched them both into the air. Minutes later, they set down at the lumberyard.

The officer went and poked his head inside. He emerged a moment later, his expression tight. "Nothing. No sign of them."

"That's good. If they left something else behind, those dwarves might have been able to track them."

"Something else?" he asked.

"Magic was used here." She closed her eyes and let the energy of the property flow over her. "I can sense Kylara."

"Who?" Trudeau asked aloud.

"The girl who made the portal to get Tanya here. Yes…I can feel that…but there was more inside." She moved toward the warehouse.

It was odd. She had flown over the town all day and felt nothing and still, even in this place where she knew Vala had been, the magic was almost nonexistent…although that wasn't quite right. There was magic there, although not of the variety she was used to dealing with.

All magic was essentially the same—a kind of energy that flowed through the universe—but it was harnessed in different ways. Amy thought about it like sound. Every magic had a partic-ular type of sound to it, but not all magic users could hear all the same sounds. It was much like a bat could discern sounds that were too high for humans to hear but dogs could hear them fine, or how whales could make sounds so low it took special tools to hear them.

There was magic in this room but the vibration of it—the frequency—was different than anything she had ever encountered before.

But it was still magic.

The mage moved through the room and was immediately drawn to a row of machines that had served a purpose long before but no longer did. They were covered in equal parts dust and rust, except for two. One of those had been destroyed and something about the broken components called to Amy. She picked a gear up, turned it in her hands, and was almost able to feel something move through it but not quite.

A table saw also caught her attention. She approached it and noticed that the blade was missing. Almost without thought, she rested a hand on the tool and suddenly, she felt it.

It was as if a whole lake of magic had been poured into this table.

Feeling it transformed what Amy thought was possible. She could sense the magic that mages created easily enough. It had taken practice but under Larry Brockton's tutelage, she had mastered the skill. Dragon magic was trickier but it could also be detected, especially when it was used on the landscape. Pixie magic was the easiest of the non-mage types of magic to sense as it was wild and uncontrolled.

This was different than all the others. It was solid in a way that she had not experienced before. She got the sense that the magic in this table would linger for a long time. It meant that Vala's ability to activate objects would probably be easier if she repeated it on the same things. Now that she could sense it, though, she could also sense its user. The girl had been in this room for quite a while. But what had she been doing?

Fortunately, she knew how to make the secrets of the past become clear.

Trudeau gasped as she extended her arms and filled the entire room with mist. At first, nothing moved but after a moment, two shapes came in through a back door.

"Ghosts!" The dwarf pointed.

"Not ghosts. Memories. Vala's magic helped to leave an imprint. This was last night, I think." She pushed harder, and the two figures—little more than impressions in the white mist—moved through the space.

They seemed to converse for a while— perhaps Galen was explaining something. He certainly did more of the talking than his companion. Then, to Amy's surprise, he led the dwarf through a magical warm-up routine that she knew they taught at the Lumos School.

"Well, I'll be. Galen's trying to help her," she muttered.

"I wouldn't be so sure," Trudeau said. The dragon's silhouette turned away from the activity and pulled something out—his phone, most likely, but it was hard to tell—then passed out. The mage had been impressed but him sleeping in the middle of the training session diminished some of that feeling.

Vala's shorter and rounder silhouette continued to work for a while before she slumbered too.

Amy fast-forwarded the vision and resumed it once Galen awakened. They talked for a while and ran through more of the routines, then he left. Amy thought that might be the end of it, but he returned shortly after. Some kind of altercation seemed to flare between the two of them—the dwarf's body language indicated that she was quite upset, but Galen was so far away that it was hard to see what he was doing in his dragon body. They stopped their fight and came in.

Vala now focused on the saw and the mist made it look like she had finally realized how to make it work.

"Well, I'll be. The kid did get her to do some magic."

Although again, trouble seemed to interfere between the two. Tanya appeared—it must have been her given the shape of her massive dress—and her body language made it clear that she was upset before she left abruptly. After what appeared to be another rather intense disagreement, Vala strode down the road. A short while later, the young dragon followed.

"Great, let's follow it!" Trudeau said.

"She stops using her magic there. Come on, let's try to pick her trail up."

"Can't you simply misty-magic the whole town?"

"Not if you want me to keep carrying you around on that skateboard."

He wisely did not push the issue.

They skated down the road. It was hard to see much in the dark but after a while, they reached a location that seemed to suggest that something had happened.

"A truck left the road here." Trudeau had noticed it first. "And another. See the tracks?"

Amy had not but she nodded all the same and got off her board. She reached out with her power and felt Vala's magic there as well.

"Before I try to sense where they've gone, can you tell me anything about it? Do their trucks give you any clues?"

He shook his head. "Many people around here have trucks. I can't even be sure it's them. What's the problem? The other officers said you're a big deal. You've carried us all over town. Do the misty thing again."

"I will, but it's a difficult type of magic for me to use. We'll be on our boards after this. I assume we'll need to convince these dwarves to let Vala go by force. If that's the case, I need to be rested. This will wipe me out."

"We can't save her if we don't know where she is. I say go for it."

The mage nodded. She had thought the same thing but was worried about how weak this would leave her. If it came to a fight, it would not be pretty.

"Here goes."

The magic was harder to use this time, despite Vala's presence there as well. Still, she had the strength necessary to fill the road with mist. She immediately recognized the dwarf's shape trudging down the road.

The girl seemed surprised when two trucks pulled up, one on either side of her. After a brief conversation, the brutes attacked the poor girl. Amy felt a flash of power as one of the trucks was animated by Vala, but a dwarf struck her on the back of the head and that was it.

Unconscious, she no longer left any traces of magic and the vision faded.

But that was not enough. She returned to the very end of the memory of the location and focused on the truck Vala had infused with magic. The girl certainly had an unusual ability. She suffused the entire machine with her energy. While everything else in the misty vision was little more than a vague anti-space, the truck positively glowed as if the mist around it were denser and illuminated from within.

Even though her head had begun to hurt and she could feel the capillaries in her nose burst from the exertion, she pushed harder. She could see details on the truck that normally remained hidden in the mist like the tools tied the racks in its flatbed, a high-powered rifle, and both axes and pickaxes.

And she could see the license plate.

The mage gasped and raised her hand to her nose. It came away bloody. She had not overextended herself that much in a long time. All mages had a particular power that they were best at. Hers was picking heavy stuff up and beating people with it. That was what had earned her reputation as the world's strongest mage. Other powers, though—like this ability to recreate the memory of places—were more difficult for her. That was why her nose was bleeding and why she would need to rest if she didn't want to get a splitting headache the next time she tried to club someone with a tree.

"They went that way, then," Trudeau said. "Can we follow them? Oh, dear, Amy!" he blurted when he noticed the blood dripping from her nose. "Are you all right?"

"I'll be fine. It's only a nosebleed," Amy assured him. "But like I said, I'll need to recharge." She took her phone out.

"You…can use electricity?" He practically danced up and down with excitement. "Well, there's a hardware store in town. There are enough batteries there for you to have an entire feast!"

"I don't use electricity, you goober. I was calling a friend to help us track the plates and dig up some dirt on these dwarves."

"Oh, right. Of course. That makes way more sense." He blushed behind his thick mustache.

The phone rang only once before Brian Hall—Kristen's brother and communications extraordinaire—answered.

"If this is about paintball, Butters told me to tell you that you're banned."

"What? No."

"He says he should have shot you but you made his ammo miss."

"That's not important right now."

"She says it's not important!" Brian yelled, presumably to Butters. "Uh-huh. He says it is important and that—"

"Brian, I'm working right now and trying to stop a dwarf from having some kind of magical exorcism done on her. Can we talk paintball later?"

"Exorcism, huh? That's a new one. What do you need?" He still sounded lighthearted—he always sounded lighthearted—but there was quickness to how he spoke now. Like many of the core members of the Steel Guard, Brian was never entirely off duty. If she had told him she was working, he would help. That was simply how it had to be.

"I have a license plate—a big jacked-up truck in Canada." She gave him the plate number.

"You want to know if it pops up?"

"I think that might be wishful thinking, but God, yes. Please let me know if any CCTVs catch it."

"Hack into a foreign country's security systems to stop a dwarf exorcism? This is so going on the resume." In the background, she could hear his fingers flying over his keyboard. He could type faster than he could talk and had likely already found her using GPS and scrubbed any nearby video he could get his hands on.

Amy waited.

"Mmm...I don't get much. Oh, dang, it looks like our friend Galen got tagged like a dozen times on social media up there."

"Yeah, I'd like to track him too. Anything recent?"

"Not since yesterday, no. He was near a lumberyard. Hashtag old mill? But nothing since then. Did that help?"

"I've already been there."

"Dang. Yeah, there are no cameras around. Let me see what I can do about the owner of that truck." More typing followed. "Okay. Yeah. It's owned by someone with the last name Gautier. Mark Gautier, I think. I'm not a hundred percent sure of that. There are quite a few dwarves with that name there. He also owns a property in town."

"What about any other property?" Trudeau asked. "They won't take her into town. While they might try the church, there is no way they'll go to a normal house for whatever they want to do."

"Brian?" Amy asked and waited while she counted the seconds and dared to hope. "Anything else?"

"No...sorry, Amy. That's all I can find. He has a squeaky-clean record."

"Dang it," she said instead of the string of much stronger curses going through her head. "We could have used a break."

"I'll let you know if I find anything else, all right?"

"Please do. And Brian?"

"Yeah?"

"Tell Butters I don't need to block people with lousy aim."

"If you don't hear from me again, it's because he murdered me over that. Brian out." He hung up.

"What now?" Trudeau asked.

"I don't know. I had hoped that would be our break, but I guess not."

"And your misty thing—"

"Is out."

The officer nodded. "Then we follow this road and hope that one of those trucks leaves it so we can see its tread. Does that sound good?"

"It's better than anything I have."

Trudeau nodded. "Come on. I'll show you how to skate without telekinetic powers."

That at least pushed some of her fatigue aside. "I don't need magic to skate."

"Prove it." The dwarf shoved forward on his board and she followed. She was glad he was there. If not for him, she might have given up already.

They skated down the dark road and scanned the edges for some sign of the heavy trucks. Truthfully, she had now begun to worry. She was not a tracker. Normally, she could sense a mage's powers and follow them like a homing beacon but she didn't seem to be able to do that with Vala. The dwarf didn't radiate energy the way most mages did. Instead, she infused things.

"Wait a minute," she said and stopped abruptly.

"What is it? Have you found something?"

"I think I've gone about this all wrong." She got off her board and tried to simply feel for magic. She didn't activate her mist power, nor did she try to sense for Vala specifically. Instead, she felt for magic itself.

That was when she sensed the truck. "How could I have missed this?"

"Missed what?"

"The truck. Vala used the truck against the dwarves so she left her mark on it. I can follow them."

"What are we waiting for?"

It was a lucky thing, too. A short way down the path, the magic signature turned up a dirt road. About a hundred meters in, Trudeau located some tracks, but they would never have seen them from the road. The first section was all gravel and even he admitted that he hadn't seen anything.

They got off their boards and hurried up the winding path. Amy could feel her strength returning. She still was not ready for a fight but moving on foot—even at a fast pace over less than perfect terrain—was easier than flying. Soon, she'd be back to combat strength. She still didn't know what that could do against a group of dwarves, but she would have to work it out. For now, she had to catch up to the trucks and Vala.

Around a bend in the road, two trucks were parked and even now, presumably hours later, she could feel magic infusing the vehicle.

"Are you ready? Trudeau asked.

"Ready enough," Amy said and crouched off the road in the woods so the dwarves wouldn't see them. "Our priority has to be to rescue Vala. We get her out—"

"Then we go for arrests. Right. It sounds good."

The mage nodded. She should probably wait but time was of the essence. They moved through the woods as close to the trucks as they could and sprinted out into the field.

A moment later, they discovered that the vehicles were abandoned.

"No!" Amy said. She touched one and it wasn't warm at all.

They had been there for quite some time and the girl could be anywhere. "There's no way Brian will be able to help out here."

"We might not need his help," Trudeau said and knelt to study the soil. "Heavy dwarves make deep footprints." He pointed up another, smaller path that she might never have noticed. "This way."

CHAPTER THIRTY-TWO

Vala was only able to drop two illustrations before the Originists noticed what she was doing.

"What's this, then?" one of them demanded and pulled a piece of paper from her notebook. It featured a blender that snatched ingredients to make a smoothie.

"The breakfast appliance we all deserve?" she said.

"You're trying to make a trail," the dwarf said. Perhaps he was not a fan of smoothies.

"If anyone's tracking us, a scrap of paper ain't going to matter much," Gautier said. "We left tracks on the way in but down here, we'll be harder to find. These tunnels are part of an old mining complex—a real maze unless you know your way."

"Which that dragon of yours doesn't," Shaman Mytrov said. "We need a chamber, somewhere large enough for us to pray. Can you take us to one, Gautier?"

"Oh, yeah. That room up top is a place to catch our breath. I have a real nice place for us."

The tunnel forked twice. Vala noted which way they were going but she didn't see how it would matter. She didn't have a phone—her parents had never allowed her one—so how could she possibly get a message to anyone with the directions? Still, she didn't know what else to do. The dwarf who carried her paid much closer attention to her hands, so she couldn't drag another piece of paper out of her pocket.

"It's a little farther ahead. This way," Gautier said and pointed down another fork.

"Very good. Charles, Benoit, go to the entrance and stand guard."

"Won't that give us away, Father?" Gautier asked. "If someone is tracking her, they'll see the guards."

"If they get this far, it will be because they are using the taint of the girl's magic to track her."

"For the sake of a woodpecker's egg, I have a name," Vala said.

Mytrov licked his blackened teeth when she said that, studied her coldly, then turned away. "Lead us deeper, Gautier."

"Right," the dwarf said and proceeded down another passage.

"How did you find me anyway?" she asked as they carried her along.

"We have our methods," Shaman Mytrov said enigmatically.

"Yeah, hashtag-forest-fights-back."

"Hashtag? What are you—" Vala finally understood. "One of you has a social media account? I thought you didn't believe in using electricity?"

"Doctrine's a living thing," the leader said.

"I loved the pictures of the dragon coming in with you on his back, by the way. It's not something you see every day, a young, respected dwarf completely selling her cultural heritage out." Roy's grin was vicious. "We might not have recognized you, what with the humble fabrics you're supposed to wear, but the dragon? He's not exactly keeping a low profile."

"You're a group of hypocrites," she told them.

"My congregation's alleged hypocrisy will save dwarf kind from what you threaten to do," Mytrov said.

The girl did not know what to say to that. Arguing theology

with someone who simply threw out the message of half of his sermons did not seem to be an easy thing to accomplish. Surely there would be more than simply logic needed to sway a mind such as his.

But before she could make another attempt, the tunnel they traveled down widened into a larger room.

Vala had been to numerous mines—she was a dwarf, after all, and field trips from grade school often focused on their legacy of working the earth—so she recognized that this chamber had once been a kind of staging area.

It was large, maybe three meters tall and ten meters wide. Down the center was a pair of rails that vanished down a long, unlit passage, although the other direction had caved in on top of them. Another tunnel led from this large room and deeper into the earth. The corners of the room looked naturally formed as if it had originally been a small, natural cavern, although it was obvious that most of it had been cleared. For starters, the walls were perpendicular to the floor, not rounded, and lines traced across them, artifacts of the tools that had been used to scrape this space into existence.

Although its history as a center of the mining operation was long past, the room was strangely well-appointed. It looked more like a hunting lodge than a cavern. Two moose pelts hung on two of the walls, and an actual bearskin rug was spread on the floor— her mother would be aghast, she thought inconsequentially.

A couple of bunk beds had been made from hardy, rough-cut wood that looked strong enough to support even the chunky frames of the dwarves. She noticed a cooking area with a propane stove and a few extra tanks of propane, a basin to serve as a sink, and a small table. There was also a sofa which looked well used but comfortable.

Also—to her absolute shock—a small refrigerator was plugged into what appeared to be a battery that also had wires running from it to the lights mounted onto the ceiling of the cavern. Gautier was able to switch the lights on without starting any kind of generator, so she assumed there must be a solar panel hidden on the hill above somewhere to power everything.

"Nice place," Vala said, which earned her a scowl from Shaman Mytrov.

"The electrical work is—"

"Impressive?" Gautier asked, opened the fridge, and took out a case of brown bottles no doubt filled with ale.

"I intended to say extensive," their leader said. His tone was disapproving but he said nothing more.

"Where do you want her?" the dwarf who carried her asked.

"On the sofa is fine," Mytrov said, although then he regarded the fridge suspiciously. "Although maybe one of the bunks would be better. And now is not the time for ale," he snapped.

Gautier frowned but he didn't complain. He returned the ale to the fridge as the other dwarf carried Vala across the space and dropped her on a bottom bunk. She glanced at the fridge and wondered if she could use her power to animate it. Probably. Galen had shown her that she merely had to get angry. But even if she could get angry enough—that did not sound particularly difficult right now, not after being kidnapped—what would she do with one fridge against six dwarves—or eight, counting the two guards.

If something happened in there, the guards would surely come down too. The idea of making the fridge hurl bottles of ale was amusing but did not seem to be a particularly effective strategy. She had turned her attention to the cables that connected the battery to the lights mounted on the ceiling when Shaman Mytrov approached and knelt beside her bunk.

"May I pray for you, my daughter?"

"I'd prefer it if you let me go," Vala replied.

"We will. That is what we are trying to do. We will help you to let go of this…this curse that has taken residence in your heart."

"I don't think it's a curse."

"That's the magic talking, Vala."

"So you do know my name."

"Of course I do, Vala. You have been part of my congregation for years now. Despite your mother's...doubts, your father has been a dutiful follower of our beliefs. It is his faith in you that gives me hope. Even when he saw what horrors are happening to you, he kept his faith. We will fix you, Vala."

"I'm not broken."

Mytrov shook his head patronizingly like her mother would when she asked for cookies for breakfast. "The dragon wormed deep into your head, Vala. How long did you have contact with him?"

"I've never met him before. He arrived after I got magic!"

"There is much to this plot we do not understand, Vala."

"Then we should—"

"Pray, Vala. We should pray. I do not know why the dragon chose you to try to destroy the dwarf race, but I have faith that the forces of good out there are working through me. I do not think he wanted us to rescue you—"

"You kidnapped me!"

"I understand that you feel that way." The shaman patted her on the leg, which was almost enough to make her activate the fridge and order it to freeze the dwarf's hand off, but he withdrew it quickly. "But that is the dragon's influence. We have already freed you of its twisted words and now, we will work to save you from the curse he inflicted upon you. Soon, very soon, young Vala Gagnon, you will be free at last."

"Yeah, well. There's no rush, I guess."

"We will heal you, my daughter, I promise you that. We will end this curse, no matter what it takes." Mytrov's eyes were troubled. Did he truly believe all the garbage he was talking? The girl didn't know what was worse—that this was some kind of stunt or that Mytrov believed all the junk he spouted. Dwarves were created by mages using magic. That was not an opinion, nor was it conjecture. That was fact. How could he be so afraid of the force that had given existence to her people?

Her theological wonderings left her, however, when she saw what the dwarves were doing.

They had already pulled the bearskin rug aside—"Be careful with that!" Gautier cautioned them—and now stacked big slabs of rock in the middle of the room. They were large enough for a dwarf to lie on top of them.

"What are you doing?" Vala asked.

"Come, brothers, let us sing and fill this room with hope instead of the lies that the dragons will make poor young Miss Gagnon spew if we listen."

The dwarves began to sing, Mytrov first but the others joined in and harmonized as they sang in the round.

The verse was about how dwarves had driven the dragons back from their land. Being sung in rounds fit the song perfectly, for when Mytrov started in on the weapons they would use to fight the dragons, the other dwarves had reached the part about the dragons, and he punctuated their description with strikes of hammers and axes. It was a song that the young girl had always loved, if only because it was more exciting than some of the odes to dirt and rock, but it now seemed deeply ominous. Was she supposed to be the dragon in the song? And what of the weapons? Would Mytrov try to use such things against her?

Surely not, she thought, until the dwarves finished building their plinth of stacked stones and started placing the tools of ritual on it.

Mytrov finished singing first and began to arrange the tools while the other dwarves continued their staggered verses. Vala swallowed and studied the tools. She saw no axes or hammers like in the song but she was still nervous. What was that vial that the shaman had placed there so reverently?

Oh. It was merely mineral oil.

And that pile of strange, black powder?

Powdered coal, of course, to decorate themselves before the ritual.

Was that a dead animal?

No. Only a rabbit pelt. Animal skins often featured prominently in the Church of Dwarf Origins. A rabbit pelt wasn't out of place.

Shaman Mytrov then drew a long knife with a cruelly hooked blade.

Vala stared at it while her mind tried to think of a rational explanation. Unfortunately, she was certain she had never seen a knife used at the church. Not ever.

The final group of dwarves finished the song. Their deep voices echoed off the walls of the room and filled the space with a sense of peace that Vala—now that she'd seen the knife—thought was underserved.

"What are you doing?" she demanded and struggled against her bonds.

"We intend to heal you, my daughter. No matter what it takes, we will not let the curse the dragon infected you with spread. When we are through, you will have peace."

CHAPTER THIRTY-THREE

Galen had made his mind up that he had to save Vala. There was no way he would leave without knowing she was safe. He felt responsible for her but it was more than that. She had shown him kindness and seen him as something other than a failure or a reject. He liked the version of himself she thought he was. If something happened to her, he didn't know if that person could survive.

Her fight with the dwarves didn't have anything to do with him and he recognized this. And yet, what the fight was about made him feel like only he could understand. She had been captured not because of what she had done but what she could do. The dwarf shaman was no better than his spectacularly callous mother.

He also had Petrov to worry about. Even if he could sneak inside and get her out, he would need enough strength left to keep his uncle at bay long enough for her to get to safety.

It seemed far more than he could manage. His younger self would not have admitted that, but he knew he would need help. He tried his phone again but it didn't even ring. No help would come and he did not find the irony amusing at all. He was finally wise enough to ask for help when he needed it but couldn't.

With a sigh, he stood, still hidden at the edge of the forest. He had to rescue Vala and couldn't wait any longer.

Once again, the realities of the situation gnawed at his resolve

His dragon form could not fit inside the cave, period. Even if he could, it would be a difficult fight. The quarters would be tight and the dwarves would be more at home underground than he was. He would be covered in dragon scales, though, which would be an advantage. He wondered again if he could somehow lure them out.

That seemed foolish. Any attempt to do that would alert them to his presence, or at least that something was amiss. It would leave them free to escape from the tunnels via some other exit. If they did so, he might never be able to find them again.

Galen did not believe everything his mother had said about dwarves. He knew full well that they didn't live in rat tunnels beneath the earth like vermin, but he did believe that they tunneled. Most of their wealth came from minerals, after all. If they wanted to ditch a dragon in the subterranean passages, they would.

A distraction, therefore, wasn't an option. That left sneaking in using his human body. He knew this was at least possible. His dragon powers—even in his human form—would grant him speed the dwarves could not match. They were strong but so was he. He might have attempted it—numbers be damned—except for the fact that they had guns. His healing power might be able to save him from a bullet wound, but two? In his current condition, there was no way. Plus, he might be shot in the chest or the head—or a half a dozen times, for that matter. Going in with nothing but his human body seemed like suicide.

Still, he didn't seem to have another option.

"Suicide it is," Galen muttered, stepped from the woods, and moved toward the crack in the stone that hid the room he had previously explored.

He reached for his inner magic and tried to get a sense of how much power he had to draw on. The deer meat had done him good, as had most of a night of sleep and Vala's mother's stew. He had a good reserve, he decided, and could do this.

Except it still felt like there was a block, a dam in the stream as one of the professors at the Lumos School would have said. He stretched toward it and tried to untangle it and yank it free to unlock the power that had eluded him since he had transformed from his mongrel state.

Had the block been there since Tanya and her friends had helped Galen? No, he realized. His powers had been denied him ever since Boneclaw forced him into the halfway state.

The young dragon had hated being trapped between forms. It was grotesque and misshapen, with parts of both species tossed together almost randomly. He had scales and skin, and horns and hair. Although he had wings, they had not worked. He hated that form and was glad to leave it behind. But now, confronted with a fight inside a system of mining tunnels, he had to admit there were some advantages.

It was not like it had never been useful, either. He wouldn't have been able to swim to the bottom of the pool where Tiamat had been imprisoned if not for his mongrel powers. Nor would he have survived the desert if he had been stuck as a human, and he would probably have struggled to stay concealed in his full dragon form—although Petrov's tracking cast his ability to do so into serious doubt.

Now, it seemed like it was yet another opportunity where the ability to change into that state would be a boon, not a curse.

But it was gone. Right?

His inner magic seemed to increase in speed and pushed at him as if urging him to use it. He honestly had no idea how. Even if he could take that form, he was afraid he would be stuck in it again. He didn't want that at all.

But then he thought about Vala being held captive by a group of hypocritical religious nuts who swore off technology until they needed it. He would not let them have their way with her and complete their ritual any more than he would allow his uncle Petrov to hurt her. If the price of her freedom was him being trapped in that grotesque body for the rest of his life, it was a fair price to pay.

Galen stepped back in the clearing and focused on the crack in the rock that hid where the dwarves had taken his friend. "All right, magic, do your worst."

He planted his feet, spread his arms wide, and opened his hands with no response

"I'm willing to pay the price," he muttered to his belly and hoped the magic could hear.

If it could, it ignored him.

"Come on!" he grumbled. "I'll do what it takes. I'll be a monster. Please!"

He could feel the magic churning inside him, wanting to move and ready to flow, but it wouldn't.

His anger grew side by side with his blocked power and he drew a deep breath. That wouldn't help. It was his angry self who had seized the power that could summon the dead and turned those revenants against people. Again, his anger had been taken advantage of and he'd been forced into that mongrel form. It would not serve him. If he let it consume him, he would serve it.

The dragon drew a deep breath and straightened. He could still feel the magic inside him trying to flow but could not force it and would not. Instead, he exhaled and planted his feet to enable his magic to have an anchor point. He inhaled, took a step forward, and spread his legs wide before he planted his forward foot. When he exhaled, he lowered his arms and raised them on the inhalation as he brought his legs together again.

Slowly, guided by his breathing, the dragon let the same routine he had taught Vala calm him now. He moved through the various stances and let his energy flow to fill his chest, his arms, his hands, his fingers. Although he knew she was in trouble, he also knew what his anger had cost him in times past. He focused on letting it go and calming himself to allow both his magic and his sense of self flow through him.

As he continued to move, his mind became more at peace and he felt calm flow through him, along with something else. His inner magic was still blocked, however. He could feel a pool deep inside but had no idea how to reach it.

Galan thought about his intentions and what he had told himself he was willing to do. He knew he would become a monster if that was what it took, but was that what he wanted?

The answer to that question was obvious—of course not.

He wanted to help Vala—he felt compelled to help her—but that did not mean he wanted to become a monster, not if there was another option. His mongrel form was a possibility but was it the only one?

That question made him think about what he would need to face the dwarves but also about what he wanted.

First and foremost, he would need to be covered in scales. Dragon scales were not impervious to bullets or blades but barring a high-powered rifle or a big handgun fired at close range, they were close.

His hands would still need to work. Claws would be useful in a fight, but in his dragon mongrel form, they had been huge and unwieldy. He needed to be more like a mountain lion than a saber-toothed tiger. The same applied to his teeth. He didn't need dragon fangs in this form.

As for wings and a tail, he could not help but want both. He knew that he would most likely not need to fly in these tunnels but it was one of the worst things his mongrel form had been not been able to do. As for a tail, he wanted something he could use to strike with, not the thick, stubby abomination he had been stuck with before.

He tried to visualize the body he desired and continued to move through the stances that he had shown Vala. Most importantly—more important than scales even—were the proportions of his new body. It had taken an uncomfortable amount of time to learn how to use his half-breed body and he did not have that kind of time right now.

As he continued to move, he felt the air around him change. The chill that had been settling in was gone. The wind stopped blowing his hair. His movements become stronger and more precise than they had been. He felt as if he could lean farther and bend deeper as if he had a counterbalance.

But that was because he did.

The dragon paused in a pose that was supposed to reflect the power of a boulder and took stock of his body.

The first thing he noticed was his tail—a fairly long and slender appendage that whipped like that of a cat, albeit one with a barbed tip. Next, he saw that he was covered in scales. Dark-blue like bruised clouds, they covered every inch of his body. His arms and chest seemed unchanged, although his legs had added an extra joint. The ankle joint was now higher so he walked on his toes like a cat or a dog rather than on the bottom of the entire foot like a human or a bear.

He sensed that this would give him more speed and strength but proportionally, his legs were the same length they were in his human form. His toes were full-length dragon talons and wickedly sharp and his hands were still in the shape of human hands, although his fingernails were now sharp. He felt that he could use them to good effect and focused on them for a moment.

The claws extended an inch past his fingertips.

"Yes!" he said, then retracted the claws. They seemed to glow with an inner light when extended like bottled lightning.

Galen drew a deep breath and noticed that there was still a part of his anatomy he had yet to reckon with—his wings. Currently, they hung from his shoulders and folded against his back. They hung limply, more like a cape than wings. When he extended them, he realized that they were surprisingly large, although the bones were incredibly slender.

To test them, he crouched and vaulted upward, then spread his wings at the vertex of the jump and made a quick lap above the clearing. He could feel that they wouldn't carry him long distances but they would certainly keep him aloft in a fight as long as he kept moving. There were dragons who could hover in place, but he did not think he was one of them.

He landed and wondered if he would be able to change back into either his human or dragon form, but he pushed the thought from his head for now. His task was to save Vala and now, he had the body to do it.

Resolute, he picked up the claw of the Prairie King and entered the dwarf hideout to rescue his friend.

CHAPTER THIRTY-FOUR

When Galen slipped inside the crack in the rock wall, he expected to find it empty, but that proved to be too much to ask for. Two dwarves stood one on either side of a crack that led deeper into the hillside.

"Oy!" one of them yelled in surprise as he reached for an ax.

That was all the provocation the dragon needed. He lunged forward, drove into the dwarf, and hurled him against the back wall of the room in a single bound.

The other guard hacked at his shoulder with an ax. It hurt but not in a way that suggested a lethal or even serious injury. He growled and slapped him across the face with his whiplike tail.

His assailant stumbled back and clutched his eyes. His cohort had used the time to stand and swung an ax, but the dragon was quick enough to raise Claw between him and the blade. Dwarfish muscle met dragon magic as the two pushed harder against each other.

Even in this form, Galen wasn't sure that he could win but in the next moment, the handle of the weapon cracked—not completely but enough to be heard and for the handle to give slightly. That was enough to make its wielder's eyes widen with surprise. He pushed harder with Claw—it felt so right in his hands that he couldn't help but think of it as a proper weapon—but the dwarf had lost faith in his ax and withdrew it, which made Galen stumble forward.

Fortunately, he had dragon reflexes and saw an opportunity. He lunged forward using his spring-loaded leg muscles and pounded his horns against the dwarf's forehead.

A crack like thunder hurt his ears before he saw only white as he stumbled back and through a piece of furniture.

His vision returned in time to see the other dwarf towering over him. One of his eyes had a nasty welt across it and was swollen, but that still left one beady eye for his adversary to stare menacingly with while he swung an ax toward his crotch.

The dragon flicked Claw in the way at the last second and deflected the blow. The blade lodged itself into the floor and its wielder looked at him in panic.

He leaned back and kicked him with both legs. While his opponent stumbled across the room, Galen felt like the effort might have broken one of his own knees had it not been for his dragon healing powers.

As he scrambled to his feet, the two circled him warily.

"What you did to the girl was unconscionable," one of them said.

The dragon turned to face him, which unfortunately meant he could no longer see his ally.

"You dragons need to stop meddling in dwarf affairs. You and your dragon mind games."

That gave him an idea.

"No one cares about this frozen wasteland. No one wants this crappy country but you hardheaded morons."

"Hardheaded?" both dwarves roared as one, lowered their incredibly dense skulls, and charged.

The young Stormwing had no doubt that if they both collided with him, his ribs would be cracked and the organs therein smashed to a pulp, but this was exactly what he had hoped they would do.

He leapt upward and with a flap of his wings, was able to reach the ceiling. The claws extended from his fingertips, and he held on tightly as his two enemies bulldozed into each other.

Galen did not quite know how to describe the sound their skulls made when they made impact. It was not like a car crash as those came with the sounds of tinkling glass and crunching metal and plastic. Nor was it the sound of a thundercrack as those left echoes.

When pressed, he would describe the sound as that of the world's largest hammer striking the world's largest boulder. There was a single incredibly loud crack and nothing more.

He dropped on top of them. Both were unconscious, each bleeding slightly from a line of split skin on their foreheads.

Even after such a collision, they looked more like they were sleeping than like they had been in a brawl.

The young dragon swallowed. There were, by his recollection, at least another six down below. This would not be easy. He pulled his cellphone out again but there was no more signal now than there had been since he'd left town.

With a deep breath, he entered the crack dug into the rocky face at the back of the room.

Before long, he reached a fork in the path and hesitated, knowing that if he took the wrong route, he'd never find Vala. He listened intently, but despite the many powers of this new half-dragon form, he did not have ears, merely holes in the side of his head like most dragons so he heard nothing. No light came from either tunnel either and dragons did not have a particularly strong sense of smell.

Although his Uncle Petrov did.

Could he somehow call on that power? It seemed insane to think he could simply manifest new powers, but didn't this body prove that he could do exactly that?

Feeling foolish, he sniffed the two hallways with no result. Then, feeling more foolish than he had ever thought possible, he extended his long, forked tongue, and licked the air. He pulled his tongue in again and by reflex, touched it to the roof of his mouth.

To his absolute shock, he could suddenly tell that one of the paths smelled more like dwarf. Telling himself that no one was watching and that it was a normal thing for creatures all over the Earth to do, he began to sniff the air with his tongue. This untapped sense revealed their scent as clear as day.

The dragon followed and hoped he wasn't being duped by his own body.

He did the same thing at the next fork and the next. With every step, the smell of the dwarves grew stronger. Still, he was unsure that he was on the right path until he saw another scrap of paper on it, this one with an older style cellphone using its antennae as a sword. He grinned. The artwork was obviously Vala's.

As he moved deeper, he followed his sense of smell—or taste, as they seemed almost the same thing and he had never realized how inextricably linked the two senses were. Finally, he reached a tunnel where his other senses had something to do.

Light spilled into the passage, but not torchlight. It was the unflickering glare of electric lights that illuminated the way ahead. Although this came as something of a surprise, the light wasn't what unsettled Galen but the singing.

The dragon could barely make out the words due to the echo of the tunnel and the overlapping voices, but he did not like the sound of the song at all. He crept forward and moved closer to the opening at the end of the tunnel.

What he saw horrified him and made him throw what caution he had to the wind.

Vala was tied to a kind of table made of stacked stones. It looked like one that would be used to cut the still-beating heart out of a small animal to sacrifice it to some god in an attempt to appease the dragons. He knew from his family that humans had once had such barbaric customs, but seeing dwarves doing something similar—and to a person instead of an animal—was horrifying.

Galen raced into the room, Claw raised, and swung the blunt side of the blade at the back of one of the dwarf's heads. His target cried out and crumpled but did not fall unconscious.

Still, he would count his attack as successful because it disrupted whatever the hell they were trying to do to Vala.

They cried out and stumbled back as they reached for their weapons.

"Are you all right?" he asked her, although he didn't look at her but scanned the room for Shaman Mytrov. He was sure the zealous freak was dressed like some kind of chimera again. The room was filled with animal pelts, however, and he hadn't located him before she called his attention directly to her.

"Mmph!" she replied.

Galen looked down and when he saw that she was gagged, pulled the material out of her mouth.

"Galen, is that you?" she asked.

"Of course it's me. Who else do you think it would be?"

"Your face is…different," she said.

Duh, he thought. But he did not have time to even utter that as her captors rallied with their weapons in hand.

A hammer struck him in the small of his back and he careened across the room. A rib had been cracked but it healed before he struck the wall of the cave. He adjusted his position in midair and struck the wall with taloned feet. They sank into the stone and he held fast, out of the reach of his assailants.

"The dragons have sent a demon to aid their aberration!" Ah, there was Shaman Mytrov. He stood on a platform carved into one side of the cave with a bear pelt on his back, a badger on his head, and the same not-so-charming eye makeup and grit in his teeth.

"Get him!" one of the dwarves shouted before two of his fellows hoisted him up and threw him at the interloper. The dragon dropped from his perch high on the wall and landed amongst the other four dwarves.

They attacked with a synchrony that he had never seen equaled in dragon kind. He had once seen a video on the Internet of four men hammering a post into the ground at the same time and they had all timed their blows carefully to not interfere with each other.

The dwarves made them look like a cluster of clowns stumbling around a circus ring. Every time he dodged, he was struck on the opposite of his body. If he blocked, whatever part he left open was targeted.

Frustrated, he spread his wings to create some space but it barely helped. The dwarves were simply too stalwart to force them back.

Galen leapt up, dug his claws into a wall, and climbed along it like a lizard.

His adversaries gave chase and ran after him.

He dropped on the other side of the room and met the first dwarf's blows with Claw. One-on-one, he was faster than any of them. He blocked the strikes easily and even managed to lash out with a hand and slash his opponent across the chest.

But in the next moment, the others reached him. The dragon moved constantly to make sure he was never surrounded and that his magic didn't settle. He was like a tornado of claws that flowed, spun, and slashed. He kept the point of his tail, his claws, and Claw between himself and his adversaries and remained a blur as he moved as quickly as he could to avoid being surrounded.

He broke free and for a moment, all five of them stood in front of him. On instinct, he breathed in and exhaled a ball of flame. The dwarf in the lead grunted in surprise and raised his forearms to block. The flames ate through his clothes and singed his arm hair, but he simply shook his arms and patted them as his compatriots moved forward to provide him with cover.

The fireball had not even given the dwarf a blister. Worse, it had seriously pissed the others off.

They ran toward him as a group and moved in synchronization so precise that he did not think it was possible outside of army ants. He knocked the first one aside with the flat of Claw, but the next barreled into his gut, the third pushed the second back, and the fourth delivered an uppercut so hard that he catapulted away and into a wall.

Before he could recover, they swarmed him. Against the wall, he could do little more than whip Claw from side to side to try to intercept their blows. Too many got through, however, and he felt a rib bruise and one break. When one of them missed, he was able to push free.

"If you act like ants, I'll treat you like ants," Galen said. He tried to not focus on one but the five of them. The dwarves moved together and some advanced while others minded the flank. They were a unit and needed to be cracked apart.

He lunged forward and as expected, those in the front moved to block him and he whipped one of them with his tail. It worked well enough. The dwarf clutched his face and staggered back. He pressed forward and used his wings to scatter the others.

They didn't break ranks entirely as he'd hoped—they were far too heavy—but they stumbled and that was enough to break their synchronicity.

Galen was surrounded again but this time, he didn't let himself focus on any one of them. Instead, he used his superior speed and reflexes to slash at any fist, boot, or weapon that came near him.

His strategy appeared to be working.

He moved so fast that he could barely think, but he connected with his opponents, caught their fists, deflected their boots, and knocked a hammer away. They might be able to fight as a unit but he had Claw, his talons, a barbed tail, and wings. He lashed out with every appendage. If he was dueling with only one person, it would have been a foolish gambit, but it worked to prevent them from working together.

Now that they were off-balance, he looked for openings. One dwarf overextended himself and he was able to crack him across the jaw with a scaled fist. It hurt like hell but it knocked him out cold.

That unbalanced their little formation even more. He had no doubt that the four remaining fighters would compensate and work together without difficulty if he let them.

The dragon had no intention to let them do anything like that. He dropped and swept a kick at another. It almost broke his foot but he had expected it to be difficult so had kicked hard enough to crack a boulder.

That left only three.

Galen stood and spread his wings. He didn't hit any dwarves with the gesture, but he knew they hated dragons and the wings were a reminder of exactly what they were fighting.

Sure enough, all three stumbled back and looked at each other in confusion.

That left his chest completely exposed.

A thunderous boom seemed to come from his torso.

He tottered back, still on his feet. The pain was too much. It screamed at him to run from it, to black out, and to stop breathing.

The dragon looked up.

Shaman Mytrov held a gun and not simply any gun but one of the big ones. Rifles? Yeah, it was a big, high-caliber rifle and the barrel was smoking.

Galen looked at his chest. His scales were supposed to protect him from this but they had not.

He raised a hand to the wound. It came away red and sticky

with blood. His vision grew blurry but he was still standing. He could fight despite the enormous wound.

When he looked up, he realized that Shaman Mytrov also believed in his ability to fight and was determined to prevent it. The religious leader raised the rifle again but this time, he aimed the barrel at the young dragon's face.

CHAPTER THIRTY-FIVE

Time seemed to slow for Vala Gagnon. She had tugged at the ropes that bound her to no avail while she watched Galen stand against multiple dwarves. Then the sound of a gun had shattered her focus and she gasped as a mist of blood exploded from her friend's chest before it coalesced into droplets.

He staggered and looked at Shaman Mytrov. The dwarf's face was a mask of terror and anger. With the pelts and his makeup, he looked like a monster to Vala, a beast of true nightmare.

They had called the dragon a demon but she thought his new form was beautiful—although she might be biased. She hadn't expected to see him again and yet there he was.

He came for me. And he came willing to fight even though he knew he was outnumbered. But she had always known he was brave. He had seen her on the street—not only a stranger but a completely different species—and he had come to her aid. He had been angry with her, but she sensed that he had never been the kind of person who was particularly good at controlling their anger. Now, he had returned to stand up for her.

By the look of the pool of blood welling from his chest,

however, it did not look like he would remain standing much longer.

Time seemed to resume its normal speed and she used every muscle she had to strain against her bonds. She had to break free but she couldn't. Dwarves might not believe in magic or trust machines, but they knew their way around handcrafted objects like rope. She knew she couldn't break it.

Her gaze shifted to Shaman Mytrov, who aimed for a second shot at Galen. The most frightening thing about him was the look of fear in his eyes. He was terrified of the young dragon. Perhaps he truly believed he was a demon and had put a curse on her. He narrowed his eyes and tightened his finger slightly on the trigger.

Well, if he thought a demon and a cursed witch were in his presence, they had better not disappoint him.

Vala stopped trying to stay calm and control her fear, her anger, or any of the emotions she felt. Instead, she let every ounce of the fury she felt flow through her and sent it all into the weapon in Shaman Mytrov's hands.

He pulled the trigger but the gun did not fire.

It had worked. She had used her magic to deactivate his rifle.

The religious leader jumped back as if he had been bitten. Instead of looking at Galen, his gaze darted wildly around the room. And with good reason, she realized. The lights were flickering, the stove had clicked on, and the fridge had begun to open and close its door like a hungry monster from a children's story.

"Seize the witch!" he screamed and pointed at Vala.

She had to get free, which meant she had to find some way to break her bonds.

Unfortunately, she had no time to try different things. The dwarves approached her now. They had abandoned Galen to bleed out on the floor. She couldn't break the rope, no matter how hard she tried, but maybe she could do something about her captors.

One of the lights from the ceiling ripped free as she sent a surge of magic through the generator and the wire to the light itself. It fell from the ceiling and shattered. She knew enough from school to know that the light should no longer function, but she also knew that electricity was a powerful force. She forced more power through the wire and the broken bulb began to spray sparks and twitch with light.

Her would-be assailants hesitated when they saw this, so she pushed her luck. She made the broken light attached to the tentacle of copper wiring attack the closest dwarf. The broken glass did little to his tough skin but she made the wire coil around him and bind him tightly.

He should have been able to break the wire easily but he was so terrified of the magic that he did nothing but scream.

Encouraged, she made another light rip free and attack another one. He was less paralyzed by fear than his comrade. Rather than freezing up, he swung at the wire with an ax as he retreated.

Vala used that wire to try to distract another dwarf while she ripped a third light from the ceiling, crushed it on the ground, and used the broken glass of the bulb to cut the rope binding one of her wrists. It was not at all easy to make a wire tentacle put enough leverage on a broken shard of glass to cut dwarf rope, but fear and desperation were powerful motivators.

The wire finally sliced through and she had a free hand. She stretched it toward the ceremonial dagger that Mytrov had intended to use to "help" her but before she could get it, the shaman had reached her.

"Why? Why do you wish to end your species?" he asked and swung the butt of the rifle into her temple.

Immediately, the room went dark. She thought it was because she had been struck so hard but realized that it was because without her magic to animate the lights, they no longer functioned.

Only the orange glow of firelight illuminated Mytrov now.

She saw him as if frozen in time. He wore a bear pelt and a badger headdress. His eyes were like hot coals amidst the black on his face and his teeth, still blackened, looked like they could chew through bone. He lifted the rifle above his head. Every muscle in his body—his arms, his shoulders, his neck, and even his forehead—was flexed. He intended to put every ounce of energy he had into arcing the rifle toward her with enough force to crack her skull or snap her neck.

The dwarf had not expected the light of the fire to reveal his movements. His gaze flicked to the source of it and his vicious grin slid off his face as a ball of fire engulfed the rifle in his hands.

Impressively, Shaman Mytrov did not drop the flaming rifle. He recoiled, though, and in his eyes, Vala saw her friend's reflection. Except to the shaman, it was not the young dragon but a demon come to end his kind.

Galen moved around the table she was bound to and snatched the flaming rifle from his hands.

"Back, foul beast! Back to the depths from which you came!"

"Yeah, I don't think so," he said and whacked the religious leader upside the head with the flaming rifle. Wordlessly, the dwarf crumpled and fell.

CHAPTER THIRTY-SIX

Once Vala had turned the room's electrical lights into an electrified whip monster, Galen had a moment to heal.

He had collapsed against the nearest wall and tried to stop the bleeding from the hole in his chest but he was still alive. The shaman had hit him but the shot had gone upward and through his shoulder. If he were a human, he would likely be dead. If he were in his human form, he would likely have gone into shock, but he was stronger than that.

As he pressed against the wound, his muscles reknit and a layer of skin formed before finally, his scales budded and hardened.

The dragon pushed to his feet as Shaman Mytrov was about to strike Vala for a second time and blasted the moron with a ball of fire.

One would think, based on the reaction, that dwarves were super-combustible instead of not combustible at all. And that a piece of wood catching alight wouldn't be as surprising as the shaman seemed to think it was.

It had been child's play to snatch the burning weapon from Mytrov and knock him out with it.

But in the gloom of the room, the other dwarves still managed to see what he had done to their religious leader.

One lit a torch and shoved it in a sconce on the wall while the others attacked.

Galen lifted Claw and deflected their blows but he was unable to land a strike. They attacked more viciously than before, enraged at what he had done to the shaman.

"I've gone easy on you guys." The dragon grunted as he deflected another hammer blow. It was true as he had used the blunt side of Claw but he wondered if he should keep doing that. He didn't want to murder people, not if he could avoid it, but he might have to. He was worried that more blood would have to be spilled and it would be on his hands.

A hammer connected with the side of his head and bowled him across the room into the refrigerator. The door crumpled with the force of impact.

"Vala, are you free?" he asked into the gloom.

"I'm all right!"

The dragon saw a glint in the darkness and located her. She stood in the only other exit to the room and held the ceremonial dagger. She must have used it to free herself.

"Vala, can you—"

Another ax hit him and inflicted a gash on his arm. He forced himself to his feet, but a dwarf waited for him. A hammer caught him in the small of his back, followed by another in his gut. An ax chopped at his wing to deny him the ability to fly away.

The dwarves pummeled him and used their uncanny synchronization with brutal efficiency. Any hope he had harbored of defeating them was gone. Even the idea of using lethal force seemed laughable when something struck him in the leg and he fell.

They could not shoot him but that did not seem to bother them at all. They battered him with hammers and hacked at him with axes although thankfully, these didn't always cut through his scales or he'd be dead already. One of them even used a metal rod to try to shatter his bones.

Between the blows and by the flickering light of a torch, Galen saw Vala try to pull one of the dwarves off, only to be knocked back. She then tried to use her magic powers, but she had no effect on such simple weapons. Her ability seemed to only enable her to control machines—things with moving parts—but clubs and hammers were outside her ability to control.

With their constant assault, they could ultimately kill the dragon. Already, his bruises were healing slower. He felt like a rib or two had broken and it did not seem like they would heal anytime soon. If someone hit him in the head, that could be the end. He tried to force himself to his feet to make one last stand, but a hammer drove into the middle of his back and turned that into nothing but a dream.

"Stop it! You're killing him!" Vala yelled. *Cute*, Galen thought in his delirium. *She doesn't realize that is exactly what they're trying to do.*

The worst part was that there was nothing he could do about it. He was overwhelmed and his body simply could not stand against this many dwarves. It had served its purpose and freed the girl but it was too small to defeat these stalwart warriors.

That gave him an idea. It was a dumb idea, to be sure, but was also the kind of desperate, last-chance idea that was so stupid and so unexpected that it might work.

The dragon called on his inner magic and transformed into his full dragon form.

It had been impossible in the tunnels leading down there, but this room was big enough to fit his dragon body.

He wondered if it would have even occurred to him had he not been suffering brain damage from being clubbed in the head.

Mist drifted from him as it always did when he changed forms. In the dark, the dwarves did not even notice it but they did take notice when his body expanded, his limbs extended, and he pushed them all back by the sheer mass of his dragon body. He grew larger and it did not take long to realize that he had misjudged the size of this cave.

While he had correctly estimated that his body would fit there, he had also assumed there would be enough room to move.

He had been wrong.

As his dragon body materialized fully, he shoved the dwarves farther toward the edges of the room. His foot pushed through the refrigerator, his tail knocked over the table Vala had been on, and his wings pushed against what was left of the lights on the ceiling.

Galen felt himself crush the five conscious dwarves and the one unconscious shaman against the walls. Muffled cries came out from his armpit, the small of his back, and his belly. His adversaries were pinned between him and the wall, held fast by him pressing against them.

"Vala? Vala—are you all right?" he asked with barely enough room to move his mouth.

"I am!" she replied gleefully. "I dodged into the tunnel. Fortunately, your arm didn't come down here.

"Mph! Mmmmph!" The dwarves added to the conversation.

"Do you have a plan for how we can get out of here?" she asked.

"To be honest, no. My phone hasn't worked or I'd say we should call for help."

"Where's your phone?" she asked.

"It's in a pouch around my neck. But it won't work, Vala. I'm telling you."

"I'll be the judge of that," she responded and he felt a sixth source begin to tickle him. He tried not to thrash too much as the girl climbed over him. There was barely enough space for her to get through, let alone for him to wriggle. When he did twitch, he drew grunts and groans from the dwarves still pinned by his bulk.

"Got it!" Vala shouted, her voice much louder than it had been.

"But Vala, it won't work—"

"Who do you think I should call? Your friend Tanya?"

"I'm telling you it won't—"

Her magic flashed and he could hear his phone ringing, then Tanya's voice when she answered.

"Galen, are you all right?"

"I'm fine—well, not really but—"

"Amy is looking for you. Amy Williams. She says she's in your town."

"Oh, well, could you send her to our location? That is if…Vala, can you—"

"No problem," the dwarf said and did something to the phone.

"I got it, thanks. What should I tell her?" Tanya asked.

"Well, if you could tell her to get here in a hurry, that would be great. I'm stuck in a mine with a group of dwarves, and I'm worried they'll start to get smelly."

The insult was worth the knees and elbows his captives threw against the bulk that pinned them to the wall.

CHAPTER THIRTY-SEVEN

Amy did not need to speak to Tanya to understand what the pin that appeared on her cell phone meant although she did have questions about how the device could even work out there. She'd had no service for over an hour, and then—as if by magic—her phone was suddenly working and guided her to exactly where she needed to be. Still, even Trudeau could work out the answer to that question.

"Vala?" he asked and glanced at the device.

"I don't think it's Santa Claus," she replied and quickened her pace. Her power had begun to return after using her abilities to recreate the memories had drained her but she was nowhere close to where she wanted to be. There was potentially a fight ahead of her—one against beings who might be able to shrug her magic off.

But then there was what Tanya had said about hurrying so Galen's mess didn't have time to stink? What was that supposed to mean?

"That must be the place," Trudeau said. They had followed the footprints of the dwarves through the woods but to her untrained eyes, the trail seemed to vanish in a grassy field that abutted a rocky face tucked into the side of the top of this diminutive mountain.

"Where?" she asked, then did a double-take when he vanished into a crack in the wall.

The mage hurried forward and discovered that the aperture hid a chamber behind it, and behind that chamber was another crack that led into a system of tunnels. She followed the officer down the tunnel, shocked that her phone was still able to guide them beneath all this earth.

Minutes later, after a few turns down various forks along the way, they came to what appeared to be a wall made of dragon scales.

"This way is shut," Trudeau said.

"But the signal I've followed is through there," Amy said. She thought she understood what the barrier was, but it was bizarre to see a doorway completely filled with the scaled rump of a dragon.

The dwarf placed a hand tentatively against the dragon's hide, which caused a giggle to erupt from somewhere past the door.

"Hey, that tickles!"

"Galen, is that you?" the mage asked.

"Amy! Yeah, it's me. How did you know?"

"You're kind of a big deal, it seems." She chuckled.

"Are the kidnappers in there as well?" Trudeau asked.

"Galen has them trapped," replied the voice of a young female dwarf she assumed was Vala.

"Go ahead and shift, Galen. We're coming in," Amy said.

"And we expect no resistance." Trudeau retrieved a couple of pairs of handcuffs. They were made of iron links so thick that she wasn't sure her magic could damage them, or at least not in its current state.

"All right, here goes!" the young dragon said. The scales in the doorway were replaced with mist that retracted slowly to reveal a dark room ahead of them. She created a ball of light—that was easy enough to be effortless for her—and sent it in ahead of them.

Galen stood in the center of the room and held a black sword in his hand. Vala was at his back with her arms extended like a seasoned battle mage.

Five dwarves on the edges of the small room all stalked toward the two in the middle.

"That is enough. Stop right there!" Trudeau shouted. They ignored him.

"Fight on, my brothers. Fight on and push these monsters from our presence!" the shaman yelled. It was easy to tell he was the religious leader as he was the only one wearing animal pelts and face paint. He was also the only one who didn't approach the two kids in the center of the room. *Coward,* Amy thought as she made the ball of light blaze even brighter.

"All of you are under arrest," she said. "Come on over to Detective Trudeau and we'll tell your judge that you came willingly."

"What will you do to us, mage?" one of the dwarves bellowed. "Will you attack us with your powers? It won't work. You have no power here."

"Hit you with my magic?" she asked, her eyebrows raised. "Why do that when I can do this?"

She trapped the first three dwarves with the animal pelts around the room. The moose pelts wrapped around the first two and a bearskin rug enveloped the third. All three were picked up and pressed against the walls.

"How...how can you..." the shaman muttered.

The mage did not say it aloud but the answer was obvious. Just like Galen was able to press against the dwarves, so was she. She didn't pick them up with her magic but instead, picked up the objects that then trapped them. When her power reserves were full, she could pick up entire forests, so lifting two chunky dwarves using moose pelts was not all that difficult, even with her reserves as low as they were.

She lifted the couch and thrust it into the other two dwarves, although it might not have been necessary as they looked almost too scared to move.

That only left the shaman.

"You…abomination, you…you shouldn't be here. You and your dragon masters have no right…no right at all…"

The poor old fool seemed close to becoming unhinged. She briefly considered going easy on him.

"Die, witch!" The religious leader reached for a rifle.

Amy grinned. Well, that effectively reminded her that this religious leader had kidnapped a girl and intended to do God knew what to her.

She no longer felt guilty and used her telekinesis to animate the animal pelts the shaman wore.

"No, no!" he screamed as the bear pelt wound tightly around him and dragged him against a wall. "What is this? What witchcraft is this?"

He screamed until the badger pelt on his head gagged him but managed to stay conscious long enough to be lifted higher and pushed against the ceiling. At that point, his faith failed him and he fainted.

"What about the rest of you? Do you think I'm a witch?" Amy demanded of the other dwarves pinned to the walls.

They glanced at each other for a moment, then at the animal pelts and sofa that had taken them out of the fight.

"Is that you, Detective Trudeau?" one of them asked.

"It is, Roy," the officer responded.

"I was thinking about how I would be more than willing to go with a dwarf officer who could sort out this…uh, mess."

A few minutes later, the dwarves were down and Trudeau had them all cuffed, even the shaman who was still unconscious.

Finally, after days of searching, Amy could talk to the young mage.

"Vala Gagnon, I presume?" she asked. "Amy Williams at your service."

"You're magic," the girl said bluntly.

She chuckled. "I'm a mage, yeah. So are you from what I hear."

"I guess so, thanks to Galen."

The mage darted a look at Galen and wondered what nonsense he had put in the poor dwarf's head.

"That's not true, Mage Williams. Vala has a gift. I only wanted to help her."

"You did help me. I'd be dead without you."

"We wouldn't have gone that far."

"Quiet!" Trudeau snapped at the dwarf who had spoken.

"Get them out of here," Amy said to him.

"Gladly." He directed one of the dwarves to lift the shaman on their shoulders and they started up the tunnels.

She turned to the kids again.

"How exactly did Galen help you, Vala?" she asked. While she had seen him training her, she could not shake her history with the young dragon. The Galen she knew was a power-hungry, inconsiderate jerk. He played with things he did not understand and recklessly endangered others for a chance at fame. She had expected to face him in battle, even after what she had seen in the mist.

"He rescued me from these dwarves three times."

"Four, but who's counting?" the young dragon mumbled.

"He showed me how to use my powers and came to rescue me even when he was angry."

That made Amy smile because it was the Galen she knew. But that also made her trust Vala's account of what happened more. If the girl thought he was some perfect, shining knight, she would know better than to trust what she said. The fact that she'd seen his temper told her that he was not trying to hide who he was from her and she respected that.

"Is this true, Galen?" she asked and turned to the skinny, perpetually scowling kid.

He nodded. "I saw her in trouble and wanted to help. Things kind of escalated from there."

"You're not giving yourself enough credit," Vala said. "Seriously, Mage Williams, Galen is a hero."

"I only wanted to help," he insisted. "That's what Tanya or Kylara would have done."

"I suppose it is, isn't it? Headaches be damned, those girls do like getting into mischief." The mage smiled.

"It wasn't mischief. He truly did save my life." Vala stamped her foot and some of the lights in the room flickered. Amy made a note of that. This one had an interesting power.

"I believe you," she said. "And, for what it's worth, I think it's cool to see you starting to grow up, Galen."

"Grow up?" He snorted, which was classic Galen.

"Maybe that's giving you too much credit," she corrected herself. "Maybe it's simply that you've finally found some good friends and they're rubbing off on you."

"That seems more likely, I guess," he said and smiled at Vala.

"Well, whatever it is, I'm glad to see it. I have to ask, though, what's next?"

The dwarf and dragon shared a long look. She said nothing and seemed to be waiting for him to speak. Amy waited too until finally, he realized the question was being asked of him.

"Well," he said hesitantly, "I'm not too sure now. I thought that maybe Vala could go to the Lumos School. Maybe you could take her to the US and help her get enrolled and set up so she can train properly. From what I can tell, there's nothing like a mage school up here."

"There's definitely nothing like the Lumos School," the mage agreed and rubbed her chin in thought. "I think that makes sense.

The school semester has already started but I'm sure Professor Sharra could catch her up in the basics quickly enough. Does that sound good to you, Vala? I can promise you that the staff there will treat you with respect and do everything in their power to help you master your new abilities. But the choice is yours, of course."

"That's very generous of you..." She trailed off.

"But?" Amy prodded.

"Well, I don't want to simply leave. My parents...I have to make sure they're safe, plus Galen has been teaching me and I've already learned so much."

"What about the dwarf cult of anti-magic?" he asked her.

"What about them?" Vala asked Amy. "Will they go to jail?"

"Oh yes. Trudeau will charge them with everything he can. They won't walk free for a while, especially not their leader."

The girl nodded as if this reassured her of her path forward. "Then I know what I want to do."

"Great!" Amy responded.

"I want to stay here and have Galen teach me," she said as if it were the simplest thing in the world.

The mage had no words to answer such a request. She stood in silence for a long moment and looked from one to the other in utter astonishment.

Galen summed up what she was thinking surprisingly well. "You want me to what?"

"An otter can't learn to swim from a squirrel," Vala said with a quirky little shrug. "It needs a beaver."

"Wait, am I the squirrel in this?" he asked, although he grinned like a fool. It seemed he was both surprised and flattered.

The mage currently felt only one of those emotions.

"You're the beaver," Vala said.

"Vala, it's great that Galen has made such an impression on you, but I'm certain that mages could better teach you how to use your skills."

"I'm not," the girl replied. "I'm not a mage, am I? Or maybe I am but not a human one. Are you sure a human could teach me better than he could?"

Amy thought back to how she had barely been able to sense Vala's power. She thought about what she had seen her powers do. "I'll admit, I haven't seen powers like yours before. I suppose we could work something out. But let's check with your parents first. All right?"

"Yes, we should," Vala agreed and three of them headed up the tunnel toward the surface.

They talked a little more about potential plans. The mage suggested that maybe Vala could do some remote learning with either the Lumos School or some of the mages in Detroit, which the young dwarf liked and Galen seemed amenable to. She was starting to believe the boy had turned over a new leaf. It seemed like he had finally put his troubles behind him and was trying to help others instead of helping himself.

Although it seemed his troubles were not done with him yet.

A roar from outside the hidden chamber in the rock wall was followed by the sound of a massive dragon landing.

"Galen Stormwing! I can smell the stench of your fear from here. Get your dragon ass out of that warren of dwarves and face your fate right now!"

CHAPTER THIRTY-EIGHT

The blood drained from Galen's face and his knees buckled. "What time is it?" he asked.

"Uh...it looks like mid-morning by my estimate. Do you know who that is out there, Galen?" Amy asked.

He nodded. "It's my Uncle Petrov. I...I thought I had more time. I thought I had all day still!"

"You thought you had more time for what?" she asked.

"Now, Galen! You have wasted enough time," the dragon bellowed from outside.

"My family was less than excited for me to come home. They...might have given me three days to live," he explained in a rush.

"More like two and a half now," Vala protested.

"It doesn't matter," he said and tried to convince himself that his words were true. "My uncle was supposed to give me more time but it wasn't like I had any ideas about how to get away from him. I can't stay here, Vala. I could never have stayed, not with my family after me."

"Three days to live?" The mage was furious. "Do you have proof of this? Because if you do, I'll gladly lock this joker away."

"I grow impatient!" Petrov roared. "Come now, Galen. We both know your time is not worth so much."

"I don't have any proof, no, but it doesn't matter," he said. "This isn't about Vala or you, Amy—I mean, Mage Williams. This is about me and my family. I'll go out there and face him. That should give you enough time to get Vala to safety."

"Galen—" she started to say but the dwarf cut her off.

"No way!" Vala stamped her foot to emphasize her point. "You have risked your life for me again and again. I won't simply walk away." She marched closer and took him firmly by the hand.

"I appreciate that, Vala, honestly I do, but maybe you didn't see the entrance to this place. There's nowhere for me to run. If there was a power station or...I don't know, a razorblade factory around here, I'm sure you could help, but we're in the middle of nowhere. Your powers can't help me here."

"And mine?" Amy asked.

"I—" That stopped Galen in mid-sentence. "Wait...you want to help me? Even after all the trouble I caused?"

She grinned. "You may have been a little turd but you seem to be maturing into something better."

"Thanks?" He had been called many things by his family but that was a new one.

"The thing is, dragons committing murder is definitely in the purview of the Steel Guard."

"We're in Canada," Vala pointed out. "We never agreed to be policed by the Steel Guard."

"True, but I very much doubt Galen's uncle had his passport stamped when he came here either. I'll drag him south of the border and bust him there if I have to."

"I grow impatient, you rat!" Petrov roared and blasted the entrance of the cave with fire.

Amy acted quickly and created a barrier of magic. It completely blocked not only the fire but the heat itself.

"Your nose," Vala said and pointed at her.

"Crap." The mage wiped a line of blood that had dribbled out of her nose. "I used more energy than I realized. It's fine, though, Galen. I have your back. I'm sure we can take him." She clenched her teeth but she did not seem fine to him.

Still, he was honored that both these strong women were willing to help him. He had fought so hard against Amy in the past, yet she was willing to fight for him. If that was not a lesson in forgiveness, he did not know what was.

And Vala, when he had met her, had been a terrified wreck and practically useless. But now, she had not only stood against the dwarves who had captured her but was willing to fight a dragon on his behalf. She might be useful and would be resilient against his uncle's fire, after all. But to use her as a shield? He couldn't have that.

Not when he had a better idea.

"I'm grateful, I truly am. And...well, I might still need your help, but I want to face my uncle alone," he said.

"Galen, no offense, but going out there is not smart at all. You're still a vanilla dragon and he has decades of combat experience on you," Amy said.

He smirked. "Oh, I won't go out there. I'll invite him in here."

"I don't see how that will change any—"

"I tire, boy!" Petrov yelled.

"I don't have time to explain. Trust me, all right? Give me a chance. If he beats me senseless...well, I still think you should run," Galen said hurriedly before he yelled at his uncle. "If you're so tired, why don't you come in and take a nap?"

A disgruntled snort from outside was followed by the sound of the wind ripping at the hillside, and a moment later, his Uncle Petrov entered the chamber with fury in his eyes.

CHAPTER THIRTY-NINE

Galen wished that his uncle was less intimidating in his human form but sadly, this was not the case. He looked like the kind of human who would hunt predators for sport—grizzled and scarred—and at the moment, he appeared to be pissed off.

"Is this what you've reduced yourself to?" He snorted. "You won't face me in combat so you hope to use these two beasts to help you in this fight?"

"Who are you calling beasts?" Amy demanded.

The older dragon did not deign to give her a response. "We've played this game of cat and mouse long enough. Now come outside and face me like the dragon you're supposed to be."

"You're early. I was given seventy-two hours."

"You've had two and a half days and what do you have to show for it?" Petrov demanded. "You cling to that weapon but what else? A dwarf? Why would we want a dwarf to serve us? We tried that in the seventeenth century and they proved to be horrible workers. Obstinate, lazy creatures who didn't wish to contribute to the vision we had for them."

"What you mean is that you made my ancestors slaves," Vala all but snarled.

Petrov acknowledged that at least. He laughed out loud. "Slaves are useful, you foolish creature. Your kind never was."

"I don't know if I can sit this one out," the girl grumbled.

He laughed louder. "Did you honestly lure me in here so your little minions could watch? Galen, even for you, this is especially pathetic."

"I had more time," he replied. "If you go back to the family with me early, my mother will be furious."

"My sister doesn't care an iota about you. But let's say, for the sake of argument, that you're correct. How about I bring you back dead once your time limit has expired?"

"Is that a threat?" Amy asked.

"Do you wish to take it as one, mage? I know who you are. Sometimes, it is worth learning the names of animals. But I also know you're tired. I can feel it in your aura. What will you do to me?"

"Nothing. Your fight's with me," Galen said.

"Finally. A challenge. And I was getting so bored," Petrov said.

He raced forward in a blinding blur of dragon speed and threw his shoulder into his nephew's chest. The young dragon had expected the attack, of course, but that was not the same as being prepared for it. The force of impact catapulted him into a wall.

"Galen!" Vala screamed and ran to his side. He tried to push to his feet but was disoriented and she had to help him to stand.

"I'm fine," he said and dusted himself off.

"Are you sure?" she asked.

The boy nodded. "But now, it's my turn."

His expression set and hard, he called on his inner magic to make himself transform. His skin hardened and he grew claws, horns, wings, and a tail.

"Oh, the mongrel has returned," Petrov mocked.

Galen leapt at him and smacked his uncle across the face with the blunt side of Claw, so hard that he roared in pain and stumbled back. He had hoped for a little more than that but he'd take it.

The older dragon might have taken a solid blow but he was not defeated. He ran toward his opponent and lowered his shoulders so he could throw his whole weight into his gut. But the boy had wings and launched upward so Petrov careened underneath.

He pounded into the back wall, dislodged a few stones, and widened the crack that led to the tunnels beneath the hill.

His nephew landed behind him and attacked with Claw.

Petrov screamed as he raised his forearms to block the blade. Galen knew he should turn the cutting edge of the weapon on his uncle but he could not. He was still his family, after all. Even after everything they had done, he could not simply decapitate his uncle although part of him told him that would be the easiest way out of this mess. Except it wouldn't be. If his uncle was killed and he failed to return home—he had no plans to return to Stormsiege—his mother would send more dragons after him. He had to beat his uncle but he didn't want to kill him.

Although it was the more difficult choice, he used the flat side of Claw and rained blows on his adversary's forearms.

"You're strong, boy." Petrov spat, rolled out of the way, and somehow landed on the back of Galen's blade. He screamed when the sharpened side cut into him but he did not slow. He had knocked the weapon free and before his nephew could retrieve it, he kicked it down the tunnel into the gloom.

Galen hesitated. He could not lose that weapon. While he was certain that he would need it in times to come, he couldn't simply turn his back on his attacker either.

"What's this?" Petrov looked at the blood on his hands. "You... you showed me mercy?" He seemed genuinely shocked to learn that he could have sliced his hands off already.

"There are other ways besides cruelty," he said. "My mother only knows fear. But if we show mercy, we can be strong."

"Wrong!" The older dragon lunged forward and collided with

him, and they tumbled across the room. He threw vicious punches into Galen's ribs but he was not used to punching dragon scale. His blows did not crack any bones as they might have had he not been in this more armored form.

He tried to punch his uncle and force him back but he faced a skilled fighter. Throughout the exchange of blows, the older dragon held his arms in tightly and blocked each attack.

Finally, the boy drew his claws.

When Petrov tried to block again, he sliced gashes into his forearms.

His adversary screamed in pain. "What weapon do you possess now?" He managed to thrust both his feet into the young dragon's gut to knock him off and hurl him across the room.

"Nothing but my own body, Uncle," Galen said, breathing hard with his claws extended.

"You cheat!"

"No more than you do when you track me using your powers," he countered.

Petrov snorted, and then—to the boy's complete shock—he turned tail and fled down the tunnel.

"He'll make a run for it," Amy said when he had gone.

"I don't think so," Galen said and walked toward the tunnel.

"Galen, it's a trap," Vala said.

He shrugged. "I can't keep running from him. I won't. This has to end today."

"You haven't killed him yet because that's not who you are anymore," the mage said. "Will that change if you go down there?"

"I don't know."

"Then don't go," the girl pleaded.

"I have to." He entered the tunnel and paused in the darkness to sniff for his uncle's scent. "Amy, get outside. If he tries to make a run for it, stop him."

She nodded. "With pleasure."

Galen hoped she wasn't bluffing but at the same time, he did not want his uncle to make her show her power. He had to stop him.

For the second time that day, he ventured into the dwarf tunnels, knowing full well that what waited for him in the darkness wanted nothing more than to kill him.

But unlike the dwarves, his uncle had no other agenda and nothing else to occupy his thoughts. That meant he did not have to walk far before Petrov attacked.

Galen raised his claws to block but pain erupted in his palm.

"Only a child doesn't take care of their toys," his uncle said before he vanished into the darkness.

It was almost impossible to see in the dark but he still knew what had sliced into his hand—Claw. His uncle had fled down there to arm himself.

Galen moved forward and this time, barely managed to get his claws up when Petrov attacked from the blackness.

"Your powers won't save you, boy. I'll cut you and keep at it until your time is up. I'm a tracker. The darkness is my friend. What are you?"

"A dragon." He inhaled deeply and blasted fire down the tunnel. His adversary's eyes widened before the fire caught him in the chest and hurled him off his feet. He struggled for a moment where he had sprawled before he ripped his coat and shirt off and left them burning on the ground.

The older dragon grinned wickedly in the dark. "Let us end this."

Galen knew the muscles of a dragon's form were not what made them strong. He was not particularly muscular, yet he possessed more strength than humans who were twice as well-built as he was. But still, seeing his opponent's barrel of a chest, massive pectorals, and bulging arms with pulsing veins powering them was intimidating. The effect was heightened by the scars that slashed through the hair on his chest.

Petrov picked Claw up, ran into the attack like a cornered wildcat, and made no attempt to use the blunt side of the weapon. He tried to eviscerate the boy, to bleed him out, or to cut his eyes out.

With every strike, the young dragon raised his claws defensively—they were the only part of him that could block Claw—but the weapon chipped away at them each time it struck.

Even armed with Claw, his uncle did not limit himself to only the weapon. He pressed in close and when he had the opportunity, planted a boot in the center of his opponent's chest.

The force of the kick would have hurled him off his feet but he was able to use his tail and wings to avoid a sprawled landing. He tried to extend his wings to launch himself into an attack but he could not fly in the narrow confines.

That moment of trying something impossible cost him, though. Petrov barreled forward and tried to drive Claw through his chest.

Galen was able to deflect the strike before it turned lethal, but only by moving his wings in the way and letting the weapon slice through the membrane that gave him flight.

It hurt like hell, but flexing his wings knocked Claw from his adversary's hands and it skittered away into the darkness.

"Fool!" the older dragon snarled as he turned and ran after the weapon.

His nephew let him run. He doubled back and took a turn, then another. He tried to catch his breath as he clutched his wing and willed it to reknit itself while he reminded himself repeatedly that he could win. It wasn't a mantra so much as a necessity —he had to beat him but how? If they went to the surface and Petrov took his dragon form, he would obliterate him. This was not dire thinking but a simple fact.

But to stay in this tunnel was no better. It was too tight and he couldn't use his wings or his tail the way he'd like to.

With that in mind, he set off to where he knew he could fight in this body.

His uncle followed him through the tunnel and tracked him easily while he yelled threats that echoed off the stone walls around them and made it sound like he was all around him.

"We always knew it would come to this, eh, boy? You trying to stand and ultimately running like a rat. Honestly, I should thank you. I haven't had a hunt like this in decades. I forget how delicious it can be to root out particularly well-entrenched vermin."

"Is that all you are? A rat killer for my mother?" he shouted in return, unable to resist the urge to taunt him.

Petrov's laughter—loud and piercing—made him regret it, though. It hammered into his skull and he wished he would simply go away.

"Are you so ashamed of your family that you think of us like that? Do you think your mother is a corrupt master and we're dogs at her feet? Have you no respect for power? Have you no idea what survival of the fittest means? She gave you a chance at a place at our table and you squandered it."

"A place at the table begging for scraps!" he roared as he entered the chamber where he had fought the dwarves. "I'd rather fight for my life than beg for the one my mother wishes to throw away."

Galen, furious with the truth of these words and at how little his family thought of them, exhaled a massive ball of flame that filled the room and set the animal skins and sofa on fire.

His uncle entered a moment later. "So this is where you choose to make your last stand?" he demanded with a wide and vicious grin. "In a place the humans you so resemble would call hell?"

"Only for you, Uncle." He pumped his wings and bulldozed into his adversary with enough force to dislodge Claw from his hand. They both paused as it clattered across the room.

His opponent's eyes widened. He knew how this fight would

go without that weapon. Unfortunately for him, so did his nephew.

The young dragon pressed his attack and slashed at his uncle with claws that cut red gashes on his chest and forearms. When his more experienced foe attacked, he blocked with his wings and when Petrov blocked, Galen swept his legs with his tail.

His uncle fell heavily as the flames all around him began to burn lower.

"You're...you're cheating!" he rasped, pushed to his feet, and yelped as the nearby bear rug—still burning—scorched his fingers. That meant his healing powers were beginning to fail him as fire should not have affected a dragon much at all.

Still, the fight wasn't over. Petrov managed to stand. "If we were in our dragon forms, I would have killed you, boy. I'll kill you yet."

By now, he had heard quite enough of these threats. He struck with speed and precision and used the four claws at the tips of his fingers to stab his adversary's right thigh, then the left. His uncle collapsed and his healing power was unable to work fast enough to keep the stubborn old bastard on his feet.

"You're right, Uncle. I don't think I can beat you in my human form either. You're more experienced, bigger, and stronger than me. But only a fool fights where they lack advantage. I'm no fool."

"I'll kill you!" Petrov snarled but he could do little more than stumble forward.

"It's over, Uncle," Galen said and kicked him on the shoulder with a taloned foot. When his opponent fell, he stepped on him and dug his claws into the wound. The older dragon writhed in pain.

"It's not over until I say it is."

"Or until I do." Amy Williams stood in the doorway to the room beneath a glowing orb of light. "Attempted murder is not taken lightly by the Steel Guard. You're under arrest. I heard you confess to trying to kill your nephew."

Petrov looked at Amy in terror. "You...you have no power here."

"True. I suppose I can always turn you over to the dwarf prisons. Have you read about the facilities they built during the second war to hold the dragons who invaded their land?"

He struggled under his opponent's talon, which confirmed that he had indeed heard about the dwarf prisons. "Release me!"

"They say they dug them so deep that they're no longer cold, even in the dead of winter. From what I've heard, there are still dragons down there—or their remains, anyway, left when one of the walls broke and magma flooded their chambers. It seems the dwarves dug out enough so you can see their bones and rebuilt cells in the same location."

Petrov looked wildly about the room but he ceased his struggles. "Do you swear you'll take me to the States if I go willingly?"

"I swear it," the mage said. "But only if you swear that you will tell the Stormwing clan that Galen goes free."

"He did nothing to impress me!" The older dragon snarled disdainfully.

"You're not impressed that I kicked your butt?"

His uncle sneered so fiercely that Galen thought he might be able to shift into a half-dragon form of his own, but he was fortunately still trapped by a talon through his shoulder.

"Fine. You have a deal. Take me to the States and get me out of this frigid wasteland and I'll tell the clan that Galen's oath has been fulfilled."

Amy nodded.

The boy removed his talon and his uncle stood slowly. He stumbled and fell forward into the wreckage of what had been the fridge but pushed himself up.

"There's no guarantee they'll believe me," he mumbled to his nephew.

"What was that?" Amy asked pointedly.

"Nothing!" he snapped and shut up with a grimace locked on

his face. The mage approached him cautiously, retrieved a pair of slender silver handcuffs, and closed them around his wrists. Immediately, he wilted.

Every dragon knew what those cuffs were and what they were capable of. They had been used for centuries to block mages from accessing their full powers. The times when such a punishment was reserved only for the beings who made them, however, were long gone. Now, the Steel Guard used them on dragons, mages, or anyone else who broke the peace. Galen wondered if they would do anything to a dwarf, though, but decided it was a question for another day.

The young dragon retrieved Claw and the three of them moved through the tunnels and to the surface.

"Galen, you're all right!" Vala said when they emerged from the room hidden by the rockface and stepped out into the field. She ran forward and hugged him, even though he was still in his half-dragon form. He returned the gesture, relieved that she was all right, and even allowed himself to feel a little pride at a job well done.

Thus distracted, he was not able to react quickly enough when his uncle shoved Amy to the ground.

"Stupid move, Stormwing," the mage snapped, settled into a crouch, and ripped a huge piece of flat stone off the wall behind them.

Without his dragon abilities, the rock would crush Petrov. There was no way a human could withstand such a thing, and without access to his dragon powers, he had no more power than a human.

But before the rock crushed him, the cuffs were off and the older dragon landed on his back and stopped the boulder from crushing him with what must be the most impressive leg press ever performed.

"Get him!" Amy yelled and wiped a fresh stream of blood that trickled from her nose.

"In your dreams." Petrov transformed into a dragon and took to the air.

Galen lifted Claw and stood in front of Vala as his uncle blasted them with fire. It did nothing to them, thankfully. Claw absorbed some of the flame, he deflected some of it with his wings, and the dwarf simply shrugged off the fire that reached her skin.

"This isn't over, Galen! I'll tell the clan that you proved yourself in battle. I'll give you that much. But if you ever leave this frigid wasteland and the protection of these fat, hairy beasts, you're dead. Do you understand?"

"Ten seconds! That's how long you have to get out of my sight!" Amy yelled at him, undeterred by her freely bleeding nose.

"Keep your eyes on the clouds, mage. Every time it rains, it might be a Stormwing. I hope you enjoy the sunshine while you can," he crowed as he flew south and increased his speed until he was gone over the horizon.

The young dragon was finally safe—for now, anyway.

CHAPTER FORTY

Galen hadn't believed that his uncle's promise to not return to Canada would hold, but a month later, he had yet to come under attack. And it wasn't like he exactly kept a low profile.

Only this morning, he and Vala had finished recording an actual television commercial. It was set to air for the first time any second now.

"There it is. There it is—Galen, turn it up!"

He pointed the remote control at the television in their little storefront. Their shop was in the same strip mall as Trevor Miller's store. Another immigrant business—a Palestinian restaurant—stood between them and had been the boy's lunch venue every day that they had spent here while setting their new business up.

"Has your enchanted broom refused to stop sweeping?" Vala asked from the TV screen. She looked adorable. Her parents had —wisely, in Galen's opinion—forsaken their religion and in doing so, freed the girl to wear whatever she wished. She now dressed in the brightly colored knitted clothes that most dwarves wore and she'd let her frizzy hair hang loose. It was like the poof of a halo all around her head.

Galen, by contrast, thought he looked like a fool. His smile was plastered on but twitched at the edges as he stood back-to-back with her. "Is this a ghost or has an appliance found a life of its own?" he asked from the screen.

He couldn't help but laugh because he sounded so enthusiastic.

"Shut up. You sound fine," she scolded him. He must have told her a hundred times that he did not want to be in the promo.

"Are you cursing a curse?" she asked.

Thankfully, the camera cut from the two of them to a shot of Vala standing in front of the shop.

"Then come on down to Magic Managed!"

The next shot was of Vala standing behind their counter. "The world is changing faster than it ever has before, but that doesn't mean that you need to be left behind."

Galen grimaced when she pointed at the camera when she said "you." It was way too cheesy.

She seemed to think so too and laughed uproariously.

"Why not come down and let us troubleshoot your magical problems?" he said with about as much enthusiasm as one might muster to scrub a toilet.

"And remember, even if the power's out or your battery is dead, we're only a magical phone call away," the dwarf said from the screen. The phone on their counter rang in the commercial and she picked it up. She pantomimed talking to a customer over the phone while the name of the store, *MAGIC MANAGED*, flashed on the screen in bright yellow capital letters, as well as a phone number and the address.

The commercial ended and something else came on about how delicious nine-layer burritos could be.

"That was great!" Vala gushed and grinned from ear to ear.

"If you say so." He snorted.

"I do, for your information," she said and seemed unflappably optimistic. "You didn't like it?"

"I liked it if you did. But come on, it was a little cheesy."

Vala shrugged. "Maybe. But I'm sick of hiding who I truly am. I'd rather people think I care too much than too little."

"That's why you don't wear beige anymore?" he asked.

The dwarf nodded. "Precisely. Hey, I'll go next door and get some falafel. Will you mind the phone?"

"No problem. Get me some lamb?"

She patted him on the shoulder and left.

He drew a deep, contented sigh as he surveyed their shop. It wasn't even that, though. They had nothing to sell, nor did they need to store any equipment there. In all honesty, they could have worked out of her parents' house, except Viktor would not let them even consider such an option.

When Vala had first told Galen that, he had thought the dwarf did not want anything to do with magic, but he now understood that her dad had given up on his beliefs about magic. He loved his daughter too much to let the doctrine of a kidnapping shaman get in the way of their relationship. It also didn't hurt that Amy had called Timeflash in to fix their house. Magic had a way of earning its keep in people's minds when it restored their damaged belongings.

The reason he did not want their business to operate out of their home was because he thought they would do better and look more professional if they had a storefront. Then, he'd helped fund their startup.

"Dwarves hardly understand telephones, let alone this Internetting of yours. You need a shop where people can talk to you dwarf to dwarf. Or, dragon, I suppose," he had explained, which was as close as he had come to saying he was all right with Galen.

The young dragon decided he would take it, though. Vala's mom more than made up for it in her enthusiasm for him staying to help teach Vala about magic and work with her at Magic Managed. She had almost been offended when he had told her that he did not want to live with them and would be more than comfortable living above the shop in a little apartment.

Marma might not have accepted it but her daughter had told a little white lie and said he sometimes breathed embers in his sleep. That had been enough to keep the dragon from sleeping in their handcrafted and freshly restored wooden house.

When the girl arrived for magical practice every morning, she always brought a hot breakfast, courtesy of her mother, for him to eat.

All in all, Galen was happier than he had ever been. He had a purpose in life with helping both Vala and the community at large. They had yet to get any actual clients but their commercial had only now aired so hopefully, that would come.

She was confident that their business would be successful. Over the years, magic had not stayed completely out of Canada, despite many dwarves wishing that it would. She had told him enough stories to make him believe that they would serve a real purpose there.

The young dragon did not know if he would ever feel like he could do enough to outdo all the harm he had caused when he had gained the ability to raise the dead. He had brought a monster back, and even though Boneclaw had led the worst attacks, he would always feel responsible. If not for his naïveté, he could have prevented so much pain.

In his darkest moments, he also blamed himself for the rise of Tiamat. She had come because he had messed around in the pond she had been imprisoned in. If he had not been so arrogant and self-entitled, she might never have come and taken Kylara's body over. It was a small solace that Marma had said his shame about his past actions proved that he was growing as a person.

Galen knew he would feel much better when they had a client and he was able to help more people.

When the phone rang, he was therefore quick to answer it.

"Magic Managed, Galen speaking," he said and tried to sound

peppy like Vala had instructed.

"Oh, my God. This is real?"

"Tanya?" Galen asked. He'd recognize her voice anywhere.

"Hi, Galen," she said demurely.

"Uh. Hi? How can I help you solve your problems?" he asked and thoroughly fumbled the line he was supposed to ask.

"I'm still at the Lumos School, so we have dozens of mages here. But I saw what you're doing there, Galen. It's awesome!"

"Wait, you did?" He realized that he was twisting the phone cord around his finger like a teenage girl from a movie.

"Yes! That commercial you and Vala cut? It's hilarious."

"It's not supposed to be—"

"You are so droll, Galen. And then Vala is so perky—it's the best! How many takes did it take for you two to get it so perfect?"

"I…only a few?"

"Well, I like it, Galen. And it's so awesome that you've decided to stay there and help Vala."

"You're not mad?"

"No, Galen, why would I be mad?"

"You haven't called me."

A moment of silence followed during which he wondered if she had hung up. Finally, she cleared her throat. "You haven't called either, not since Vala called me to get Amy for you. I assumed you were getting settled in but when I saw the commercial online, I had to talk to you."

The young dragon felt like he should be angry. She should have called. After all, he was the one forced to make a life in a new country. He was tasked with helping a dwarf learn powers that no other dwarf had ever possessed. Rather than voice this reaction, he drew a deep breath and told himself that was the old Galen speaking.

"Well, I'm glad you did. It's been hectic here but I should have made time to call you. I'm sorry about that."

"Oh, wow! Galen Stormwing, apologizing? What next?"

"I don't know. I might even start telling people how I feel about them."

"Is that right?" she asked, her voice like candy to his ears.

"Yeah. Tanya—"

Vala pushed the door open and hurried in to place their plates of food on the table. They ate at the restaurant so much that they didn't take to-go containers. They merely took plates, washed them, and returned them each day. "Who's that?" she mouthed.

"Uh…" he said into the phone.

"It sounds like you have a customer," Tanya said cheerfully.

"Something like that, yeah," he muttered. "But hey, maybe I can come visit sometime?"

"I don't think that would be smart, Galen. My parents say your family has been seen all over the States. They haven't forgotten about you. If you come here…"

"Yeah, I get it," he said and tried to keep the disappointment out of his voice. He was thankful that Vala could not read his aura and that Tanya was so far away that she could not either.

"I planned to say that maybe I can come visit sometime," Tanya said.

Galen grinned like a fool.

Vala, not one to even pretend to not eavesdrop, gave him a huge thumbs-up.

"Yeah. That would be great. Let's …uh, talk more later this week?"

"I'd like that, Galen. I'd like that a lot."

He waited for her to hang up and thought he heard her start to sing before the phone clicked. Honestly, he felt like he wanted to sing too but he had too much self-respect for that, of course. Instead, he allowed himself a small smile, thanked Vala for dinner, and settled into his new life with his new friends, and—luckily—some of his old ones as well.

Vala could not believe how well everything had turned out. She sat next to Galen in her own shop and they shared a delicious dinner. While she would not go so far as to say it was good that she was kidnapped, but if she could go back in time—something dragon magic could do, at least to buildings— and avoid being kidnapped, she was not sure if she would. She had this shop now, her dad had forsaken his stupid religion, and she had a friend—a real friend.

"Who was that?" she asked Galen.

"Tanya."

She wiggled her eyebrows suggestively. "Is she still mad?"

"I guess she hasn't been."

"Lucky ducky!" The girl smirked. "Do you think she could bring more books next time she visits? I only managed to keep one of those she brought last time, and the exercises you showed me are getting old."

"Old? You've barely scratched the surface of what physical exercises can do for manifesting power," Galen replied.

"We'll have to practice more tomorrow, then." Vala grinned. She wasn't bored with their training sessions at all. She merely continued to be surprised that he wanted to stick around and help her. While she knew he couldn't go home, that did not mean he had to stay there. He could have gone to the wilderness and hunted for everything he needed. With his new powers, he could have gone to a foreign country to make a name for himself. Instead, he seemed more than content to live there and even seemed to be actively trying to live in her shadow.

Which, oddly, was growing quite large.

The young dwarf had thought their commercial was great. She thought it was energetic, informative, and perfect, but it seemed the Internet liked it. On one site, it had already had over thirty thousand upvotes and it had only been online for an hour.

It wasn't only the commercial, though. Local news crews—both human and dwarf—had come to interview Vala once word had spread that she was a dwarf who could do magic. Those stories had been picked up and gone national, then international. A dozen other reports about her existed too, although they used the same clips from the crews that had talked to her so they were essentially regurgitated.

But it was enough to make her famous. She had signed up for social media accounts and was already flooded with people asking her for interviews, book deals, and to endorse products as "the first dwarf mage."

She declined them all politely. It wasn't that she didn't want to be famous—she was a little surprised by how much she liked being known—but she wanted to focus on making this business work.

If she could be a mage in her hometown, still have breakfast with her parents, and give back to her community...well, she could not think of a better life than that. She would take the fame —why not? But she would rather be known as the dwarf mage who helped other dwarves than merely the dwarf mage who did interviews.

That meant they needed clients. She knew that if anyone tried to call them, their power would reach the red phone on their desk because she had enchanted it to accept any call from any phone that tried to reach her. Whether the device was connected to a landline or a cell phone tower wouldn't matter. Her enchanted phone could tell if anyone was trying to reach her and would make the connection happen. It had demanded a tricky use of magic to accomplish, but Trevor Miller had been able to offer a few tips and she found that she seemed to have quite a knack for devices. There was something wonderful about giving life to these objects that needed electricity to power them if not for her.

But she could not make anyone call. Hence, the commercial.

"Do you think we're crazy for doing this?" Vala asked after a few bites of falafel.

"You mean painting a giant target on our faces as the first dwarf mage and the only dragon working with a dwarf?" Galen asked sardonically.

She giggled and honestly found his sense of humor to be hilarious. "When you put it like that, maybe we should have simply dug a hole and lived down there for the rest of our lives."

"Let's not go that far," he replied. "If we can make this work, it'll change the world. It's a big if but if it works, it'll be worth it."

"You act so pessimistic but you're an optimist at heart, huh?" the girl asked him.

"Yeah, but...don't tell anyone that, all right? I have a reputation to maintain," he said.

"I don't know. Maybe our next commercial could feature you talking about hope or something—"

Vala stopped teasing him when the phone rang long and loud. The little bell inside jiggled from side to side to alert her to a potential client but she was frozen. Was this truly happening? Was someone calling her for help?

"Will you simply let it ring?" Galen asked.

She jerked out of her stupor and answered. "Magic Managed. Vala Gagnon, the magic dwarf speaking. How may we manage your magic today?"

The person on the other end of the phone line spoke in a blur and rambled on about how they had found dead mice, scratches on the front of their couch, and how they would hear hissing in the depth of the night.

"Do you have a cat?" she asked.

"I did..." After a somewhat disjointed explanation, he broke down in tears.

"Not to worry, sir. Magic Managed can help." She managed to pry the address out of the man and told him they would arrive soon before she hung up.

"You have that look on your face," the dragon said. "What happened?"

"We have our first client."

"Yeah, I assumed that much. What's the deal, though? I heard you ask them about a cat. We aren't veterinarians."

"It seems they had a cat. It died—he wasn't sure how—and he now thinks they are being haunted by its spirit."

Galen laughed. "Wait, our first job is to get a cat spirit out of a house?"

Vala nodded. "Are you worried you can't handle it?"

He snorted. "Are you serious? After everything we went through to get here, I'm sure we can handle a mountain lion haunting. A house cat should be no problem."

"That's the spirit!" she said and winked at her partner, who groaned at the pun.

The two of them loaded their supplies. She had not had much to focus on with enchanting objects but with a little help from Trevor, she had managed to create a wristwatch with a minute hand that would point to a source of magic and an hour hand that showed how relatively powerful the magic source was. A handheld vacuum cleaner was supposed to be able to handle most lesser spirits but...well, this was their first client. Trevor said he thought it would work but time would tell. She packed all these things in a bag and put it on the counter.

The dwarf pulled a trench coat on over her brightly colored knit sweater and Galen wore one to match. They had decided that he wouldn't take his half-dragon form unless absolutely necessary. Still, with the coat and using Claw as a walking cane, she thought he made quite an imposing figure.

She glanced at herself in the reflection of the storefront as she packed her bag. Finally, she looked like herself. After years of not knowing how to fit in her hometown, she felt like she had a place there and knew she had Galen to thank for that.

Together, Vala Gagnon and Galen Stormwing set off to help their community, one magical problem at a time.

We've followed a dragon who didn't know she was a dragon in the Steel Dragon series, and then we explored the story of a mage who *thought* she was a dragon in The Dragon's Daughter, and there was a lot of pixie action in those stories too! When Michael and I brainstormed "what's next?", it was pretty clear where we had to go next: we hadn't done much with the dwarfs yet!

That's how Vala and Galen's story was born; we wanted to look into the parts of this world we hadn't pierced yet, so having a dwarf on board was key. Working Galen into the story was easy enough, and we really wanted to do something to complete his story arc, as he's grown from a mean, self-sabotaging kid into something more.

It looks like we're going to have six books for this series as well, so you should have *tons* of great reading material coming up! In fact, I'm working on the outline for the sixth book right now, and it's going to be absolutely epic. We're talking a true cast of thousands, bringing most of our old heroes back together against an existential threat!

But that's not how this story begins. Galen and Vala's tale instead focuses on small things to start. We look at one young woman coming into her own, and a young man (well, young dragon) firming up his move from being a fairly gray character to one who's firmly on the side of the 'good guys.' It's a small story, not a world-shaking epic, and in some ways I like those stories even more than the other kind.

This story of tale lets us really explore the natures of the characters involved, which makes it an ideal place to start the Dragonclaw Sword series.

In other news... I'm moving to Iceland for a bit! Don't worry, this won't impact your reading *at all*, as Michael and I have every intention of continuing our work together. My wife will has been invited to attend a program next year at the University of Iceland, so we'll be hanging out in the land of ice and fire for a little bit, starting late summer.

I've been to Iceland a few times, and I have to say I've never had a *bad* visit. We love the place, and it's going to be a fun and exciting adventure while we're hanging out in Reykjavik (the capitol).

If you start seeing some snow, glacier, or volcano themes leaking into my writing, though, you'll know why!

I'm expecting to be able to get quite a lot of writing done while I am over there. Winters have *really* long nights in Iceland, with daylight showing for as little as a couple of hours near midwinter. That's going to feel *weird*, I know, but I figure it ought to also buy me plenty of time this winter for writing more words.

I wanted to offer a special thanks to Rachel Beckford, my beta-reader extraordinaire. Her help on these books has been instrumental in making the tales as enjoyable as they've been. She spots the little snags and problems so I can go in and fix them, and I am enormously grateful for all her help in turning these stories into the tales you know and love.

That's it for this time, but I'll be back next month with yet another segment of Galen and Vala's adventures!

MICHAEL'S AUTHOR NOTES
JUNE 10, 2021

Thank you for not only reading this story, but these author notes as well!

So, Kevin is moving to the land of Ice and Fire, hmmmm?

I think we should do something with a devious Ice Dragon. Wait...wait.

We've maybe done that before? But, you know what, I'm not telling you how we will do anything next, that would spoil the reading experience (which has nothing to do with the fact I don't know, so you can't make me spill the beans.)

BUT...

What if we had a red dragon (associated with fire) and it was scared of flame? So much so that it decided to move... to Iceland?

Of course, I'm just throwing stuff up against a wall to see what sticks. I haven't actually mentioned any of this to Kevin and suspect this won't go anywhere. Tune in to the next series to find out whether this idea got anywhere (did I even speak to Kevin about it at all?)

DRAGONS LOOK BADASS LARGE OR SMALL

Well, small they look cute. Even the meanest-looking dragon, when you scale it down to about three inches across, has a hard time looking too mean.

I have this opinion because at the last convention I was at in Scotland, I purchased a handful of dragons that were made of metal… and they were small.

Even the toughest, meanest-looking dragon couldn't be more than… cute.

I would purchase more dragons if I had the room to display them. Also, I have been outvoted down one to one (wink) regarding putting up a big 12' fabric wall hanging with a dragon on the stairwell.

Apparently, that type of picture clashes with our Italian décor.

Damn.

Until next time!

Ad Aeternitatem,

Michael Anderle

BOOKS BY KEVIN MCLAUGHLIN

Steel Dragon Series

(with Michael Anderle)

Steel Dragon 1

Steel Dragon 2

Steel Dragon 3

Steel Dragon 4

Steel Dragon 5

Dragon's Daughter

(with Michael Anderle)

Never A Dragon (Book 1)

Dead Dragon New tricks (Book 2)

Thicker Than Blood (Book 3)

Dragon Fire and Pixie Dust (Book 4)

The Cult of Tiamat (Book 5)

The Sum of All Magic (Book 6)

Adventures of the Starship Satori (Space Opera blended with military SF)

Finding Satori - prequel short story, available only to email list fans!

Book 1 - Ad Astra: Book 2 - Stellar Legacy

Book 3 - Deep Waters

Book 4 - No Plan Survives Contact

Book 5 - Liberty

Book 6 - Satori's Destiny

Book 7 - Ashes of War

Book 8 - Embers of War

Book 9 - Dust and Iron

Book 10 - Clad in Steel

Book 11 - Brave New Worlds (2019)

Book 12 - Warrior's Marque (2020)

The Ragnarok Saga (Military SF)

Accord of Fire - Free prequel short story, available only to email list fans!

Book 1 - Accord of Honor

Book 2 - Accord of Mars

Book 3 - Accord of Valor

Book 4 - Ghost Wing

Book 5 - Ghost Squadron

Book 6 - Ghost Fleet (2019)

Valhalla Online Series (A Ragnarok Saga Story)

Book 1 - Valhalla Online

Book 2 - Raiding Jotunheim

Book 3 - Vengeance Over Vanaheim

Book 4 - Hel Hath No Fury

Blackwell Magic Series (Urban Fantasy)

Book 1 - By Darkness Revealed

Book 2 - Ashes Ascendant

Book 3 - Dead In Winter

Book 4 - Claws That Catch

Book 5 - Darkness Awakes

Book 6 - Spellbinding Entanglements

By A Whisker (short story)

The Raven and the Rose - Free novelette for email list fans!

Dead Brittania Series:

Dead Brittania (short prequel story)

Book 1 - King of the Dead

Book 2 - Queen of Demons

Raven's Heart Series (Urban Fantasy)

Book 1 - Stolen Light

Book 2 - Webs in the Dark

Book 3 - Shades of Moonlight

Other Titles:

Over the Moon (SF romance)

Midnight Visitors (Steampunk Cat short story)

Demon Ex Machina (Steampunk Cat short story)

The Coffee Break Novelist (help for writers!)

You Must Write (Heinlein's rules for writers)

CONNECT WITH THE AUTHORS

Connect with Kevin McLaughlin

Website: http://kevinomclaughlin.com/

Facebook: https://www.facebook.com/kevins.studio

Twitter: https://twitter.com/KOMcLaughlin

Instagram: https://www.instagram.com/kevins.studio/

Connect with Michael Anderle

Website: http://lmbpn.com

Email List: http://lmbpn.com/email/

https://www.facebook.com/LMBPNPublishing

https://twitter.com/MichaelAnderle

https://www.instagram.com/lmbpn_publishing/

https://www.bookbub.com/authors/michael-anderle